Someday
MAYBE

A DEFINITELY MAYBE NOVEL

Ophelia London

Entangled Publishing, LLC
2614 South Timberline Road
Suite 109
Fort Collins, CO 80525
Visit our website at www.entangledpublishing.com.

Embrace is an imprint of Entangled Publishing, LLC.

Edited by Stacy Abrams
Cover design by Jessica Cantor

ISBN 978-1-50277-302-9

Manufactured in the United States of America

First Edition October 2014

embrace

To Jane Austen. Again. Girl, you have me excessively diverted.

Part I

"All the privilege I claim for my own sex…is that of loving longest, when existence or when hope is gone."
~Jane Austen's PERSUASION

Chapter One

I blew a bubble and leaned on the doorjamb of Roger's office. Although you could hardly call it an office. It was smaller than an IKEA closet and didn't have a door that shut or a light switch.

"Hey, Trouble," Rog said, grinning at me over his laptop.

"Hey, Double." I returned my brother's grin. "They're finally gone."

"Yeah? How bad did Dad cry?"

I laughed. "More than when the Dodgers lost but less than when he watches *Rudy*. And Mom was doing that hovering thing. It got so bad, I had to kick them out of my dorm room." I collapsed into a folding chair on the other side of his desk.

Rog chuckled, clicked his mouse, shut his computer, then set his full attention on me. School hadn't started yet, and I knew he was already crazy busy, but my *very* important big brother was making time for me.

"She's always been great at the hovering thing," Rog said. "But I'm thinking you should be grateful they drove you all the way up here; they didn't do that for me freshman year."

"I guess," I said, propping my red Chuck Taylors on the stack of posters from last year's University of San Francisco student body president elections.

"And of course they got weepy," Rog said. "They might be gone a long time."

"Hallelujah. No more hovering."

"Rachel." He shot me his serious brotherly expression. "Mom's worried." His words held his serious, brotherly tone. "She doesn't like leaving you alone."

"Alone." I snorted. "I'm with ten thousand other students."

"I'm worried about you, too. Are you still dead set on carrying eighteen credits? That's a really heavy load for a freshman. I've been there."

I nodded and picked at a nail. I'd just gone over this with Dad. Why did no one think I could handle it?

"If your GPA drops below a three-five, you'll lose the scholarship, right?"

"I know, I know." I rolled my eyes. "Dad just gave me his final lecture. It was a doozy."

Rog grinned and rubbed his chin. "Did it include the pie chart?"

"How did you know?"

"I told you, I've been there." Roger's cell beeped, but he silenced it and slid it in a desk drawer. "Look, Rach, they put me in charge of you, and I'm sorry but I'm taking that seriously. I even warned my roommates not to mess with you." He walked around to the front of his desk and sat. "Remember all those Jackie Chan movies I used to watch?" Rog formed his hands into a kung-fu position. "If I catch any lameass, starry-eyed jocks hanging around you, I'll unleash the big guns." He karate-chopped the air along with the appropriate *hiya!* ninja call.

I couldn't help laughing. "Scary, Rog." It was easy to mock the sternness of my brother; he was the most easygoing guy I knew. "I shall do my best to be a model student while under your stewardship."

He sighed at my smartassness and rubbed the back of his neck, taking on the familiar gestures of our dad more and more every day.

Yes, I was being a pain, but I knew the deal. Just because our parents would be overseas for months at a time didn't give me carte blanche to screw off. I understood the gravity of being at USF on scholarship more than anyone. And anyway, eighteen credits was nothing if you had an implacable plan like mine. You might say I was kind of a control freak when it came to school. Okay, I was a *huge* control freak about school. But there was no other choice.

In the years before I'd started junior high, our family didn't worry about my college fund. Mom and Dad were both lecturing professors, we had vacation homes, and Dad had lots of investments. But like fifty percent of the country, he wasn't prepared for the bottom of the economy to drop out.

"And it just so happens, I'm taking my education seriously without your help," I said. "But I *am* going to spend one last day as a teenager in college before classes start tomorrow."

He blew out an exaggerated breath and gave me his indulgent grin. "I guess that sounds okay."

"I marvel at your generosity."

He laughed, and when I stood to leave, he added, "Hey, don't forget Sunday brunch at my place. You can give me a full rundown of your first week."

Dude, I was so over the hovering. Wasn't one mother enough?

"Come on, it'll be our tradition. If we Skype with the 'rents every week, they'll be less prone to worry. And if you play your cards right, I bet the dean will score me tickets to a Giants game. You've never been to AT&T Park."

Ooh. My brother was playing dirty. Bay Area professional sports made me want to relinquish my SoCal birthright and pledge my devotion to the 49ers.

"Sound like a plan, Trouble?"

I groaned, trying to sound all blasé and teenagerly. "Sounds like a plan, Double."

It took me ten minutes to walk back to Phelan Hall. Within that short time, Rog sent me five texts. In the abstract, it was cool that he worried about me, but in reality, he had nothing to worry about. My ten-year plan was already in motion.

To enjoy my last evening of teenaged freedom, I met my new dormmate and a group of other girls at a campus cafeteria. After that, we'd be hitting Greek Row. At dinner, we were just getting into the "Justin Bieber: old-hair-or-new-hair" debate when a figure standing at my right pulled my attention. I glanced up.

It was a guy. Dark hair. Cute. "Hi," I said.

"Hey." He blinked and tilted his head. "Don't I know you?"

He was tall and kind of lanky, broad shoulders under a yellow T-shirt with the Partridge Family logo on the front. Nice face, though I didn't recognize him in the slightest. "I don't think so," I said. A second later, whoever was next to me kicked my leg under the table.

"Hmm, that's funny." He shrugged those broad shoulders. "My mistake." Then he pulled back a slow, adorable boy smile.

I instantly regretted my standoffishness, because, wow… he was more than cute. Although he'd made the tragic mistake of wearing a backward baseball cap, I could see his hair was curly and dark, a richer brown than mine. He had big, lightish-gray eyes, long lashes, and that smile…it made my stomach go melty.

"Maybe it wasn't a mistake." I straightened my posture and pushed my hair over one shoulder. "You probably recognize me from all those TV ads when I was running for Congress."

Really, Rachel? If I had one of those sci-fi machines that rolled back time to retract stupid jokes, I would've used it right then.

He stared at me for a moment, then burst into laughter—cute laugh, too. Deep like a man, but…silly. I'd never heard anything so carefree. "Wasn't it the Senate?" He slid his hands into his back pockets, taking on a posture of ease.

Damn, he was self-confident, too. Major turn-on.

"It was both," I replied, enjoying his flirty game. "But I don't like to brag."

When he laughed again, I noticed a dimple in his cheek. *Oh, my.* He took ahold of the end of the table and crouched down so we were the same eye level, giving me a lovely whiff of his delicious boy smell. "So look," he said, his voice lower because we were so close now, his pretty gray eyes looking right into me. "I know how exhausting the campaign trail must be. I was just about to grab a bite. Want to join me," he tipped his head to the side, "over there?"

The control freak in me was about to reply that I already had plans for dinner—obviously, since I was currently eating—and that I had other plans with my friends the rest of the evening. But when he graced me with another smile, this one touched with the slightest hint of vulnerability, it wasn't even a choice.

We rose to stand at the same time. He picked up my tray with the half-eaten burger and untouched green salad.

"I'm Oliver," he said as we walked toward a corner table.

"Rachel."

"I know who you are, Rachel." He glanced at me out of the corners of those silvery eyes and cocked a sexy half grin. "I've seen you around." A botanical garden's worth of butterflies flew loose in my stomach.

We sat, neither of us touching the food on the table between us. He told me about his three roommates who were all cousins from New Jersey, then I told him about my first night in the dorms. His story was better. Sometimes, he rubbed a knuckle under his chin when he spoke. And when he wasn't looking straight at me, he looked down. It was cute, catching those moments of vulnerability.

His fingers brushed against mine when he passed me his phone to show me a picture of his dog back home. The tiny touch shot a tingle up my arm, making my heart stutter. When our eyes met, I could've sworn he'd felt the same thing.

Before I knew it, the janitors were mopping the floor around us and the lights were switching off.

"What do you think they're trying to tell us?" Oliver asked. He had this nervous habit of pushing up his sleeves. He was doing it now. *I* was making a hot guy nervous. Unprecedented.

"That time flies when you're having fun?" I replied, feeling its truthfulness through the cliché. I'd been having more fun talking to him in the cafeteria than I'd had at my senior prom.

We stood to leave, ignoring the glares of the janitorial staff as our sneakers squeaked across the wet floors.

"This was only *fun* for you?" He held open the exit. "Damn. I was going for mind-blowing. I have my pride."

The golden sun floated at the horizon as he walked me home. My stomach actually ached from laughing, while my brain was massively preoccupied by how much I wanted him to kiss me. I'd been subtly staring at his mouth for the past three hours, could almost taste the sweetness on this boy's happy-go-lucky lips.

We stopped in front of the glass doors of Phelan Hall. My most recent "first kiss" had been so uneventful that I could hardly remember it. As I gazed up at Oliver, at the bluey twilight sky behind him, I wondered if ours would be a gentle kiss or if he would grab me in a rush of passion like I'd always daydreamed. I was so caught up in my anticipation that I almost missed his words.

"Well, it was nice to meet you, Rachel. Good luck with classes tomorrow." And without so much as a friendly hug, or a stupid fist bump, he turned and walked away.

My mouth fell open. He seemed so...unaffected, so completely oblivious.

Baffled, I remained statue-still and watched him leave, regretting it more and more when I noted his long legs and confident stride...the way his butt in his jeans was the most perfect boy butt I'd ever seen.

The moment he was out of sight, I blew through the glass double doors, stomped up the stairs, and slammed my door, declining any and all end-of-summer parties. Instead, I sat on the end of my bed and dissected every word Oliver and I had exchanged. What the hell had I done wrong?

It took me ages to fall asleep, and the few winks I did manage to catch were filled with dreams of the grinning face of a cheerful, sexy boy with metallic gray eyes who hadn't asked for my number. In my dream, though, he didn't need my number, because the moment of our good-night had gone much differently with my creative subconscious in charge.

Unable to get that fantasy out of my mind, I rolled out of bed the next morning—three hours before my first class—pulled on my running clothes, and walked down the stairs, in desperate need to clear my head before officially starting my college career, Day One of the ten-year plan.

Apparently, I'd had my last-day-of-freedom fling, after all. Though now it seemed rather anticlimactic after the super-sexy make-out session I'd dreamed about last night. Probably for the best that nothing really happened—I'd never been particularly coordinated at balancing school and boys. And now was not the time to screw up.

The second I stepped out the front door, I spotted Oliver on a bench, monitoring the entrance. Seeing him made my heart beat fast, like I'd just finished running wind sprints. He'd been writing in a notebook, which he slid into his backpack when he saw me.

"Good morning, Rachel." He strolled over, hands in his back pockets. His entire frame screamed totally relaxed and confident.

"Hey. What are you doing here?" I asked, self-consciously playing with the end of my ponytail. He looked hot, while *I'd* only managed to make sure I'd brushed my teeth before I'd left.

"Waiting for you," he said. That same smile that had kick-started my heart yesterday stretched across his face. He ran a hand through his dark, baseball cap-free hair. It was chestnut with glints of auburn under the early morning sun.

"It's six a.m." I was queen of pointing out the obvious when confused.

"I know, but I forgot to do something last night."

"What's that?"

He cocked an eyebrow. "Blow your mind."

With no fear, no thought of rejection, Oliver stepped up to me, slid a hand around the back of my neck, and pulled me in, that perfect mouth crashing over mine. My head buzzed with the dizzying sensation of wonder mixed with relief and raging bliss—wiping out everything else.

The kiss was better than I imagined, better than I'd dreamed last night. His arms were suddenly around me. Had they always been there, holding me up? As the kiss deepened, he tasted sweet like berries and something rich like dark chocolate. I never wanted that taste to leave my mouth.

"Whoa." I swayed back, grateful for the support of his arms. "Oliver, you—"

"Still able to speak, huh?" He shut his eyes and kissed me again, tilting me into an almost-dip. I was panting for breath when we finally broke apart.

"Whaa...," I wheezed, my entire respiratory system working overtime just to pump oxygen to my brain.

After a long moment with only the sound of our mutually heavy, labored breathing, he grinned and whispered, "Finally." His eyes closed as he rested his forehead against mine. "Now that your mind is sufficiently blown, how about breakfast before school?"

School? a tiny corner of my mind repeated as I stood on my toes to kiss him back. *I have no idea what that is.*

Chapter Two

Six years later

If staying fastened in place by my safety belt while clinging to the seat in front of me with both arms was an option, I might have taken it. Instead, I pulled on my metaphorical big-girl panties, hefted my overstuffed carry-on, and stumbled into the aisle.

Time to face the future. And the past.

As I exited the revolving doors to baggage claim, I spotted Meghan and Giovanna. They were scanning the crowd and Megs held a huge-ass sign that read: "Welcome Home Rachel."

A combination of joy and dread hit me.

Home.

I had to stand still and just breathe while other passengers rushed past to hug their waiting friends and families. San Francisco hadn't been my *home* for two years. And even then, I'd only attended college here. Could returning to a place I'd lived for a mere four years really be considered a "homecoming?"

"Rach!" Meghan flung her sign skyward like it was Mary Tyler Moore's knitted cap, broke into a run, then crashed into me at full speed. After we stumbled and my bags went flying, she grabbed the tops of my shoulders and shook me like I was being punished. "I can't believe you're finally *here*, *Rachel*!" We'd been best friends since third grade, so she was allowed to yell at me and shake me to show she was happy.

"Yee-haw!" Giovanna called. Instead of a southern twang, it was laced with her French-Canadian accent.

My two closest friends in the world had no idea that, behind my huge smile, I was majorly freaked at being back in San Fran. But why should they suspect anything? I'd never told a soul about what happened six years ago. The fruity smell of Meghan's hairspray and Gio's cackling laugh…being with them again made me almost giddy with relief. The fist of dread that had been clenching my insides since touchdown started to loosen.

We loaded the car and by the time we made it up the Bayshore Freeway, across Sixteenth Street and into the Haight-Ashbury neighborhood, I had tears in my eyes from laughing. The more we squealed and caught up, the more I felt a nervous/happy flutter in my stomach at the adventure lying ahead.

So what if San Francisco harbored unhappy memories? The *real* reason I was back was for my fabulous new job. I'd actually been *headhunted*, for damn's sake! NRG Interactive saw a special talent in me — or whatever that email had said — and I'd be embarking on a career I had no idea I could do a year ago, something I…I didn't have a ton of professional training at.

Suddenly, the nervous flutter overtook the happy one.

Meghan double-parked on the hilly street and the girls helped me haul my bags up the stairs to my brother's second-story apartment.

"Wanna grab some takeout?" Meghan asked.

"No thanks," I said. "I have four morbidly obese suit-cases, five boxes, one tiny closet, no idea where I packed my favorite yoga pants, and I should attempt to look present-able for work Monday morning before they discover I have no talent at copywriting."

"We'll leave you then." Megs hovered at the front door. "So…" She rushed forward, pulling me into a surprisingly tight hug. "Welcome home, bestie. I'm so happy you're here."

I hugged her back just as tightly, feeling hot tears at the back of my throat. "So am I." I so wanted to mean it.

The apartment felt empty and quiet after I bolted the door, except for the sounds of foot traffic, gridlock, and the surprisingly comforting *clang-clang* of cable cars. It would feel empty pretty often with Roger out of town so much. I'd have to get used to that with all the time he'd be overseas for work.

That was one of the reasons he suggested I take up residence in his second bedroom. Another reason was to be stepmother to Sydney, his black-and-white beagle who'd stumbled bleary-eyed out of Rog's bedroom when we'd ar-rived. She was now nudging my leg, a red ball between her teeth.

"Hey, Syd." I knelt down, scratching her behind the ears. She yapped happily then rolled over so I could get to her tummy.

I jumped when Roger's landline rang. I let it roll to voicemail, though it could have been my sister, Kristine. We'd only talked six times today, but after my long flight, I wasn't in the proper mood to hear about Krikit's latest domestic catastrophe, or to have her ask me again why I'd bothered moving all the way to California but not back home to Santa Barbara, and how soon was I coming for an extra-long visit?

The phone continued to ring. It might've been someone from my new office. They had Rog's home number but I'd returned my work Blackberry a few days ago, so now I was going old school with a pay-as-you-go disposable.

Currently, I did not have an official home address, phone number, or residential state driver's license. That fist clenched in my stomach again.

The phone call was a telemarketer. I picked up the handset and erased the message. Good little sister, am I. Another voicemail immediately started to play. Even through the crackling of the bad connection, I knew it was Rog leaving a message for me. Though I could only catch every third word. I was about to delete that message, too, when something he said made my finger freeze, hovering over the *delete* button.

"Rach, we need to talk."

In and of itself, the comment was benign, but my insides instantly turned heavy and cold, a block of ice. The last time Roger had said that exact phrase to me—six years ago—was the day he'd found out about Oliver.

I stared at the face of the phone, listening to the automated voice ask if I wanted to save the message, delete, or replay. My hand remained frozen in place while my mind whirred like a top.

I flinched when the robot voice asked the question again. "I don't *know*," I hissed at the phone. "Give me two damn seconds."

I debated replaying the message, but instead made a tight fist and extended my index finger. The tip of said finger turned white as I pressed hard on the proper key, deleting the cryptic message forever. I dropped the phone on the kitchen counter, determined to forget the whole thing.

To clear my head, I grabbed Sydney's leash and the two of us padded downstairs. The square of grass a few streets from the more popular Golden Gate Park was bathed in light from street lamps. We played a few games of fetch, then Syd did what doggies do and we trudged back up the hill.

I entered my dark bedroom, weaving around boxes and suitcases. Rog left a blanket on the foot of the bed. I spread it out and crawled on top, inhaling faint fumes from the pipe store across the street. I rolled over and smiled sleepily, thinking about Meghan and that over-the-top "WELCOME HOME RACHEL" sign that was now leaning against my closet door. My best friend was one of the reasons I could return to San Fran.

Chapter Three

The moment Oliver spotted me from across the diner, his face lit up and he waved me over. It was startling how his simple acknowledgement caused my heart to thump up my throat, and my stupid, giddy grin was right on cue.

"Hey, you," he said, closing his black notebook. "You look pretty."

"Aw." I grinned all dopily, my heart gooing at the compliment as I slid into the booth, bumping his side. "You're early."

"Seeing you is the best part of my day. I couldn't wait." When he leaned over to kiss me, my heart did an excited little jump. But then I froze out of habit and peered past his shoulder.

He exhaled and removed his arm from around my shoulders. "What's the problem?"

"Nothing, nothing." I patted his leg and scooted away a few inches. "Everything's cool. How are you? How was English Lit?"

He frowned and pressed a fist over his mouth. "Rach, I haven't said anything before, but now…whenever we're out in public, I don't know, I feel like you're hiding."

"What?" I squeaked.

His gaze slid from mine and down to the Formica table, where he played with the saltshaker, not speaking for a moment. "Are you seeing another guy? We never said we were exclusive — officially, but I need to know."

"Oliver." I couldn't remember when it happened, but we'd been exclusive in my head for a while. "I swear, there's no one else."

"Okay." He nodded, his gaze finally lifting to mine. "But you're hiding from someone, aren't you?"

Hmm. You mean, *other* than my lab partner who I was ditching to have lunch with the hottest boy on the peninsula?

I rubbed my nose. That wasn't the answer he was looking for.

"Or, are you hiding *me* from someone?"

"No! No, no, I…" I grabbed his water and took a drink, my throat dry and scratchy. His gray eyes watched, a little notch forming between them. Seeing his concern made me like him even more.

It wasn't supposed to happen. I wasn't supposed to meet someone like him. Then he'd planted that kiss on me outside my dorm, turning my bones, brains, and resolve into a puddle of love goo. I'd never recovered.

"Who are you dodging?" he asked, looking straight into my eyes. "You can tell me."

"My brother." I blew out a breath, part of me relieved to finally get the subject out in the open. "He's kind of a big deal around here." Deep down, I knew if my family found out my grades were slipping because of a boy, their knee-jerk reaction would be to blame Oliver, when it was my own damn fault that I couldn't manage to say no to him—even if all he wanted was to meet for lunch when I should've been at lab.

"Rach." Oliver chuckled, pushing a hand through his dark hair. "I know who your brother is. His picture's on the home page of the school's website."

"I know."

When the door of the café opened, I jumped and hid my face behind a menu. "This is bullshit," Oliver muttered, then scooted out of the booth. "Let's go."

"Where?"

"A study room in the library?" he suggested, dropping a few bills on the table, even though we hadn't ordered. "Or my place. Pretty much anywhere but here, right?"

My face felt hot, a blush of shame at being caught. I hung my head and nodded as I followed him out the door. He didn't seem angry, though I was sure the scene hadn't thrilled him. We walked in silence for a while, then he turned a corner and we were in an alley behind two restaurants. He stopped and looked at me, waiting for me to explain.

This was our first relationship snag—that *he* knew of. Even so, I'd been waiting for it, the sign that it was time for me to get back on track, back to the plan that I had control over: classes, tests, graduation, career. Complete stability. Maybe we should end this thing before I failed one more pop quiz.

Was that what I wanted? A sharp pain stabbed at the back of my throat.

"Oliver." I wrung my hands, not knowing how to continue. I was temporarily reprieved when he bent forward and kissed me, both hands cupping my face. Within seconds, my body and my worries melted, all cares dissolved, like they always did. I never freaked out about quizzes or essays or whatever when I was kissing Oliver. My fingers splayed across his chest, his muscles flexing as he held me close. Our hearts beating together.

"Feel better?" he whispered over my mouth.

"You always make me feel better." My whole body was lighter than air, held to earth by his arms around me. "Can we just go to your apartment for a while before class?"

"Sure." He laced his fingers between mine as we continued to walk. "By the way, that was meant to distract *me*"—he nodded back at where we'd been making out—"not you. You need to tell me what's going on."

"It's pretty simple: Rog can't know I'm spending my free time with you." There, that was easy to say, too.

"Why does your brother care who you date? Do you have an arranged marriage?"

"No." I laughed and leaned into his side, forming what I'd say next. But then I hesitated.

I'd seen the looks people gave me when I'd lay out my ten-year plan for them. The kinder ones said I was maybe a little too detail-oriented about the future, while others called me a rabid perfectionist.

If Oliver saw that side of me, would he stop liking me?

"No, no." I added, "It's nothing like that. I just promised him and my parents, everyone, I guess, that I'd ace my classes this year." Well, that was one way of putting it.

"Why?"

I opened my mouth, but then closed it.

Why was it so hard for me to tell him about my family? How my father had lost all our savings because he'd gambled with our future by not planning for it. I loved my dad like crazy. He was my first example of what it meant to have a strong work ethic, but even I knew he'd made bad, risky financial choices. When we finally did get back on our feet, those years of struggling and fear stayed with me, changed me into someone who needed a fail-proof plan. I needed steps of progress to control in order to feel safe, because I never wanted to be that scared again.

If I told Oliver about that, would he think I was too difficult? If I didn't tell him, would it affect our relationship right now? Oliver was the furthest thing from a control freak. He was more like Roger than me, in fact. Rog didn't understand why I had to carry eighteen credits this semester, and nineteen next semester, and double up on the general ed. Oliver wouldn't understand, either, so why tell him anything about it? But he was looking at me, patiently. I needed to tell him something.

We waited for two cable cars and a double-decker tourist bus to pass before we crossed the street toward his apartment. "Did you know I'm here on a scholarship?"

"That's not uncommon," he said.

I pressed a fist to my head, massaging my left temple. "I guess not, but…"

"Do you have a headache?"

"A little one."

He reached for my purse. "Where's your peppermint oil? That always helps."

"At home." I sighed, loving that he did know so many

other things about me, like how I used essential oils to feel better and alter my mood, and that I hated country music and was allergic to sesame seeds. He carried extra Benadryl and an EpiPen in his backpack, just in case I ever forgot mine.

"So, because you're on a scholarship," he said, "your family doesn't approve of you having a boyfriend?"

Boyfriend. I tipped my chin to meet his gaze. As our eyes met, tingling warmth spread up the back of my neck.

This was meant to be a casual thing, a last-minute amendment to the plan, a fling to start my school year in true college fashion. That was something I could wrap my brain around. It fit in the plan. At least, that was how I'd rationalized it at first. But words like "boyfriend" and "exclusive" did *not* fit.

"Sort of," I said. "But there's more to it."

"I'm listening." We climbed the stairs to his apartment. He let me in first and I knew immediately that it was empty; a rarity with four guys living under one roof.

I shut the door behind us, wanting nothing more than to feel his arms around me. After thinking back on those years of worry and helplessness, I needed to feel taken care of. "Can't we keep 'us' on the down-low for a while? Just you and me?"

Oliver exhaled and looked at his shoes. He wasn't happy by the notion—probably a bruise to the ego—so I stood on my toes, slid my arms around his neck, and kissed him.

He didn't respond to my satisfaction, and that worried me. We'd only been together a few weeks, but suddenly, I couldn't stand the idea of it being over. Despite the bother of hiding our relationship and the guilt of skipping a class here and there, I was happier with him than I'd ever been.

I moved closer and held the tops of his shoulders. Oliver's hands clamped around my hips—it was our usual stance, but the usual wasn't going to cut it, not with how I was feeling: panic mixed with longing, curiosity, and the need to control something about the situation.

When I parted my lips against his, his fingers dug into my hips. He shifted his body weight like he was about to pull away, so I held a hand at the back of his neck and ran my other down his chest between us. When I got to the hem of his T-shirt, I drew it up a few inches. His stomach muscles tightened at my touch.

"Rach," he whispered, a hint of confusion behind his silvery eyes, but there was also an intensity I'd never seen before. "What are you doing?"

"If you can't figure it out, maybe I'm doing it wrong."

His fingers hooked around my belt loops, pulling my hips against his. "I need to know you're sure," he whispered. "Because *I'm* sure. I'm sure about you."

Going off instinct, I pressed the rest of my body against him and reached up to his mouth, answering his question the only way I knew how. With my next inhale, it was like each of my nerve endings multiplied and I sensed everything: the pressure of his lips, the taste and smell of him, the touch of his fingers as they moved under my shirt, my heart pounding in my chest the higher his fingers crept.

I didn't know that day was about to be our first time together. I hadn't gone through the steps yet, hadn't weighed the pros and cons, couldn't even remember if I was wearing pretty underwear. But when Oliver's fingers slid into my hair and he whispered my name in a tone so sweet, so devoted, then backed me up until I hit his bedroom door, I couldn't think of a single con worth worrying about.

Chapter Four

"Rachel. Rochel. Rachel Bachel...Ray-Ray."

"Still funny," I sing-songed, tapping a pen on the side of my desk, forcing a polite smile.

Bruce, my new work colleague, was the genius behind my string of office nicknames. He was the first person I met Monday morning. Or rather, he was the loudest. His official title was Assistant Creative Director, meaning he was my immediate supervisor under Claire, the scary Creative Director.

Bruce gave me a tour of the office and introduced me around. He was a really jokey guy, though I didn't find his particular brand of humor funny, especially when he made an extremely unfunny joke about me coming from Dallas, even though I'd told him numerous times that I was from Southern California.

"Hey, you hear why the baby Jesus couldn't be born in Texas? No? No? It's 'cause they couldn't find three wise men and a virgin. Ha ha ha! Get it?"

After that, he was your garden-variety jackwad, cussing out coworkers for no apparent reason, sporting those not-so-ironic logo T-shirts, and most importantly, when it was just the two of us in the ad department's war room, it wasn't long before I sensed that I knew more about advertising than he did. And most of my game came from Wikipedia and *Mad Men*.

"You can call me *Rachel*," I said as Bruce was leaving my cubical.

He chuckled over his shoulder. "Sure, Ray-Ray."

Hmm. I had a pretty good nickname for him, too. Bruce the Moron.

I slumped back in my chair. My new cubical was nice—as far as cubical living went. Our building sat just north of the Financial District, and NRG Interactive took up the thirty-eighth and thirty-ninth floors. Huge windows faced east, showing the picturesque Embarcadero and San Francisco Bay. From my desk, if I leaned forward and craned my neck just right, I had a lovely view of one corner of the Oakland Bay Bridge.

I still had a lot to learn at my new job, but I was also kicking some serious ass at it. I loved the excitement, and even the long hours made me feel needed. Most everyone left me alone while I worked, probably because I knew what I was doing. After the first few brainstorming sessions, I realized I *did* have a flair for sitting in a room with five other copywriters and spit-balling until we came up with the exact words to go on the front of a pack of mechanical pencils. Bruce and his gang of high intellects' suggestions always included subtly phallic images, leaving me to roll my eyes and think up something last minute that wouldn't get us sued.

I'd studied creative writing in college, but it wasn't until my senior year that I'd tweaked my ten-year plan and tagged on a marketing minor. Writing was where my heart was, and maybe I'd get back to it. Penning fun short stories to add to my "someday I'll be a writer" file was one thing, but in the real world, that career path was way too risky.

"*Rachel*"—my intercom buzzed Claire's voice—"*in my office.*"

Yeah, Claire was still plenty scary, but after two weeks, I could tell she'd noticed my hard work and dedications, and she knew I was paying my dues. We'd warm to each other, eventually.

She was my scary boss, though, and my stomach did lurch as I grabbed my tablet, scraped back my chair, and rounded the corner toward her office. We hadn't spoken face-to-face since I'd given her my proposal, the first one I'd attempted on my own—pretty ambitious, I know. She must have read it by now and was ready to give me another assignment—maybe something cool and important.

"*This*," Claire said before I'd taken a full step into her office. "Unacceptable." She stabbed her pencil at my proposal that sat on her desk, then slid it toward me like it was contagious.

I blinked and glanced behind me. Did she think I was someone else? Bruce the Moron stood at her side like a sentinel, arms folded, nodding like a moron.

When it was obvious Claire knew exactly who I was, I said, "Umm, sorry, I thought—"

"It's like you have absolutely no training in copywriting," Claire added through tight lips.

I didn't speak. Claire was the one who'd interviewed

me. *Twice*. She *knew* I'd come from print journalism. Now, however, was not the time to remind her of that.

"S-sorry." I picked up my proposal that had several coffee cup rings graffiti-ing the top page. And was that a lipstick blot?

"Ask for help next time." Bruce exchanged a look with Claire. Just as I was about to peg him as a cruel ass and not a moron, he shot me a look and mouthed, "Ray-Ray."

Moron.

"Okay." I pulled at the side of my skirt so I had something to do with my free hand. "I will."

It was a rude awakening. I wasn't supposed to fail. Well, my personal life was a big fat failure, but—except for a tiny hiccup freshman year—school and work I'd always nailed. I kept my chin tucked and blinked rapidly as I headed to my cubical, really wishing I had an office with a door I could close in case I decided to burst out crying.

Instead, I forced myself to swallow the lump in my throat and work on the weekly newspaper ads about the Vondome, a luxury high-rise being constructed and leased. It was one of my bigger clients, though the work wasn't that difficult. If I had to regurgitate the same basic copy for the next sixteen weeks, I was going to do it with flair. Claire wanted the first month's worth by the end of the day, but I prepared double.

My copy wasn't Shakespeare, but it would be sufficient to get me on Claire's good side.

I held my breath for a second before clicking send. Not three minutes later, I got a reply message. I stared at the screen, needing to read the email twice. If I couldn't get this right, she was going to give the Vondome project to someone else. That was the entire message.

What was happening today?

My heart thudded when my desk phone rang, with Claire's extension flashing in big red numbers. Sweat pooled in my palm as I reached for the receiver.

"This—" my throat felt like it was shriveling around my vocal chords. "This is Rachel."

"Do you need me to explain?" Claire asked in her scariest voice. "I'll explain again, if you need me to."

I opened my mouth. Explain what? "Um, yes, please."

Claire sighed. "Well, I don't have time now. But remember, I told you to ask for help if you need it. Remember that. I don't know why this is so hard for you."

I clutched the phone. Hadn't I just asked for help? She was right, I didn't understand. I didn't understand anything today. "Okay," I said, feeling like I might puke. "Um, whenever you have time—" But the line was dead.

How had my day gone from awesomely bright to steaming crap on a platter?

I did my best to hide from Claire the rest of the day, knowing I really would have a meltdown if she confronted me again. Though I didn't want to be unavailable if she did need me. So I worked through lunch, in case she happened to walk by and I was taking my government-allotted food break.

I'd never been a quitter, and I was totally prepared to do what it took to be a stellar employee, but I wasn't a mind reader.

"Hey."

A shadow over my shoulder blocked the overhead florescent lights. I looked up to see Bruce the Moron pointing at my rejected, coffee-stained proposal on the corner of my desk. Okay, so it wasn't up to Claire's standards, but I didn't want him anywhere near it; I didn't want him to breathe on it.

"There were three misspelled words on the first page," he said with a smirk. "Ask me to proof it next time, Ray-Ray." He chuckled and walked off.

The boiling, about-to-be-released scream that had been building inside my stomach for hours started creeping up my throat. I had to get out of there, so I shut my laptop, grabbed my purse, and took the long way to the elevator so I wouldn't have to pass Claire's office. If nothing else, I was going to do a first-class job at sneaking out of work early.

Not until I shut my car door with me inside did I feel all the tension in my shoulders, neck, and head. Was work supposed to be this grueling? I fired up the ignition, flipped to a hard rock station, and sang/shouted along.

As I started for home, road construction put me on Golden Gate Avenue and multiple detours. It was a déjà vu moment when I found myself idling beside the familiar green-and-gold signpost and meticulous landscaping of the University of San Francisco entrance. The one place in town I'd been avoiding like the plague.

Instead of continuing home like I should have, I made a U-turn and pulled over. Just through those trees were the aquamarine windows of the S.J. science building and the land-mark spires of Saint Ignatius Church. Up the next hill were the University Center and law buildings. I used to cross the green-belt of the Gleeson Library every night on my way home.

On impulse, I climbed out of my car and peered up the steep stairs past the USF sign. It was plenty warm for four o'clock in the afternoon, so why did I shiver like it was winter? I slid on my silky-lined suit jacket, crossed my arms, and began to walk up the hill toward the center of campus.

The way my high heels clicked on the walkway sounded strange, way too grown-up and mature for a place where I'd worn sneakers or ballet flats nearly every day. When I'd first moved to San Francisco, my most prized possession were my vintage Chuck Taylors that I'd found at a thrift store. I'd been wearing those the day I'd met Oliver.

My cell rang, and I smiled when I checked the caller ID. My sister, Krikit.

"Rach!" She started in before I could finish saying hello. "You won't *believe* my day!"

We chatted for a while about her daughter's new soccer team and how Krikit offered to be the "snack mom" but was outvoted because the other parents knew she would forget. By the time we hung up, I had a stitch in my side from trying not to laugh, and I looked up to find myself standing at the mouth of the freshmen dorm café. Students rushed past, eager to get in line before the next class got out. My feet wouldn't stop until they took me the rest of the way to the entrance of my old dorm.

I placed a hand over my lips, unable to halt the inevitable memory of our first kiss from rushing back. The taste flooded my mouth, fruity and rich. I later learned that he'd been sucking on multi-flavored Tic Tacs while he'd waited for me to come outside. Tic Tacs, and Oliver.

I peeled off my suit jacket, still cold on the top layer of my skin, while my insides were sweltering, uncomfortably, unwelcomingly.

"Stupid, *stupid* Rachel," I muttered as I turned to march back down the hill toward where I'd parked, purposefully taking the hilly loop so I wouldn't have to walk past the path that led to *his* apartment. By the time I got to the car, my

Someday
MAYBE

hands ached from clenching tight fists. I grabbed my purse and dug through its contents. No luck. I opened the glove compartment but the only thing inside was the still-unread owner's manual.

"Crap." I touched the screen of my phone, opened a search engine, and let my fingers do the walking until I found what I was looking for. "Palo Alto?" I said aloud. How annoying! With all the new-agey stores in San Francisco, the only place in the Bay Area that sold my preferred brand of essential oil was across the bridge, forty miles away.

I slid on my sunglasses and headed south, taking advantage of having skipped out of work. An hour later, I parallel parked between a Subaru Outback and a black convertible Jeep across the street from *Another Time & Place*. Plucky, sitar-y music was playing when I entered the store. Multi-colored crystals and various orange salt rocks lined one whole side of the room. It took me a minute, but I spied the display of essential oils near the front. I was exhausted and weary thanks to getting chewed out by Claire and Moron Bruce, and a bit emotionally unstable from that literal walk down memory lane at USF, so I wanted to grab a few bottles of oil and be on my way, maybe even soak in a lavender bath and hit the sack before midnight for a change. But I noticed my brand—which ran a little more pricy—was on the employees-only side of the counter.

A girl with blond hair stood a few feet away from it behind the register. I'd thought she was alone at first, but then she started laughing and leaned a hand on the glass counter while her other hand pressed against her throat.

"Um, hi. Sorry," I said, feeling like I was interrupting.

She jumped, her other hand flying to her throat.

"Sorry," I repeated, wondering if she did actually work here. She was behind the counter, so I assumed so, and she wore a nametag with the word "SPRING" in block letters.

"Hi." She tucked some hair behind an ear. She sported a few tiny braids along her part, barely noticeable. She looked a couple years younger than me, so I figured she went to Stanford or one of the other colleges nearby.

"Um." She smoothed down the front of her shirt. "Can I help—*ahh*." She bit her lip and backed up. It took me by complete surprise when a guy appeared from out of nowhere. He must have been on the floor behind the counter, doing *what* to make her gasp that way? I did *not* need to know.

Her eyes locked on his and when he turned to the side, I could see he was smirking. "He was just…uh…t-tying my shoe," she said, glancing at me. The guy started laughing, and her cheeks turned bright red. I felt my cheeks turning a similar color in sisterly empathy.

"Springer," the guy said. "You know I live to tie your laces."

I felt like those weren't words I was meant to understand.

"Henry Knightly…" she murmured softly, censuring him. Though her breathy voice told a different story.

Dressed in a white T-shirt with an argyle sweater vest over the top, he had dark hair and was pretty damn cute. But I figured it was useless to lust after a guy who was obviously very much already into someone.

Besides that, my lusting days were over.

"Meet me in the study room tonight," he said, then leaned in and kissed her on the cheek. "You know which one." As he was backing away, she fisted the front of his sweater and kissed him on the mouth. It was a quick one but when I saw the way they locked eyes for an intense second afterward, even my toes curled.

"Bye, Knightly," she whispered, then swatted him on the ass. I couldn't help watching her as she watched him walk through the store and out the door.

Yeah, they were in "the zone"…that perfect relationship-y sweet spot when you know you're in love and everything is new and exciting and easy and feels like forever is within reach.

I'd been in the zone. Once.

Speaking of a big fat failure of a personal life…

"Anyway," she said, her cheeks slowly losing their embarrassed blush. "Sorry, again. He likes to drop in and… Anyway. Can I help you find something?"

"Oils," I said.

"What kind?"

"Naturally Pure." I pointed at the display. "I need lavender, Citrus Joy, and the biggest bottle of peppermint you've got."

She lifted her eyebrows. "You know your oils."

"It's kind of my thing."

"Really?" She glanced at my perfectly pressed pencil skirt and silk blouse. Apparently I didn't seem like the holistic type.

"I'm allergic to perfume," I explained. "I found out when I coated myself in my mother's Obsession when I was twelve."

She laughed. "Classic."

"I can't even use scented candles." I scanned the rest of the display. They had oil mixes I'd never heard of. "Plus, the peppermint zaps my headaches, and I pretty much can't get going in the mornings without diffusing LifeLong blend."

"Have you tried Xing-Sing?" She pulled a small black

bottle off the shelf. "It's brand new and I'm totally obsessed with it."

For the next half hour, Spring and I—yes, *Spring* was indeed her given name—talked oils, supplements, and other homeopathic wonders. She'd been working at *Another Time & Place* for a few weeks and had just started her senior year at Stanford.

I felt calmer and more myself with each whiff of oil. The last one she had me sample was spicy and heavy on the cloves. "It's not for everyone," Spring said when I told her I was passing on that one. She held it under her nose and inhaled deeply. "It's my boyfriend's favorite on me because he says it reminds him of Thanksgiving."

"The holidays bring out the little boy in him?"

"Henry? No." She laughed softly and her cheeks started pinking. "He's got a...a *thing* for cranberries."

"Ahh." I handed her a card to pay for my new stash of goodies. "Enough said."

"Come back and see us again." She passed my bag across the counter. "It was nice to meet you, Rachel."

"You, too. And thanks for all your help. You're a life-saver." I held up the bag, the oil bottles clinking within. "This place is definitely on my list."

As I was about to walk out the door, I turned back and Spring had that same bottle under her nose again. Seemed as though her boyfriend's "thing for cranberries" was a thing for her, as well.

I smiled as I crossed the street toward my car. What I wouldn't give to be in "the zone" again. But I had a feeling one chance at the zone was all I was going to get. And that had come and gone.

Chapter Five

Oliver's hair smelled like his shampoo with just a hint of the wild orange and vanilla I'd dabbed on that morning. We tended to mix scents in moments like these. I hugged his head against my chest as we sat on the foot of his bed, me on his lap.

"I love you," he said against my neck.

"I know." I held in the laugh for as long as I could, then cracked up.

"Why do you feel the need to quote *Star Wars* when I say that?"

To tighten my grip around him, I hooked my ankles together behind his back. Yes, I was aware of the famous Han Solo/Princess Leia cinematic interchange, but that wasn't why "I know" was almost always my gut reply. I said it because Oliver's words were superfluous—he showed it.

"Because I know it drives you crazy," I said, scooching closer. "And driving you crazy makes me so *very* happy."

He rested his mouth on the hollow of my throat, sending fresh tingles down my spine. Then he slowly reclined so that I rested on his chest. "I'll show you crazy." He moved his lips to my shoulder, trailing kisses up my neck, zeroing in on the spot behind my ear. My blood zinged and I giggled whenever he nuzzled me there. "Mmm, you're wearing the one that smells like Fruity Pebbles."

I cradled his head, taking in my own intoxicating breath of him. "I thought you said it reminds you of Dreamsicles in the summer."

"Either way, it's my favorite."

"Yeah?"

He lifted his chin to give me a look. "Have you ever heard the expression, 'I want to eat you alive?'"

"I think you mentioned that this morning." I slid down and adjusted one leg between his. His mouth was at my neck again, nibbling contently, breath hot on my skin. In a few seconds, my mind would drift to that empty space of bliss with no worries…

"I ran into Roger today."

My body tensed above his. Hold that bliss. "Not funny." I propped myself up by the wrists.

"Not a joke." He reached up to hold my hair back from my face. "We literally bumped into each other on campus."

I stared down at him, my arm muscles flexed and shaky as I held myself up. "What did you say to him? What?"

He stared back in silence, like he was considering his answer, or maybe he was dissecting the shrill tone in my question. Finally, he exhaled and smoothed my hair behind my ears. "I didn't say anything, Rach. I mean, I said 'excuse me' or something, but I didn't tell him I knew you, or that we're—"

"Good." I rolled off, even though the front of my body still hummed from our contact. Oliver's questions were coming more frequently. Of course my boyfriend had every right to meet my brother and my friends—just…not now.

"Where are my shoes? I have class in twenty minutes and can't be tardy again."

Oliver chuckled, lying back on the bed.

"What?"

One long arm was thrown over his eyes, blocking out the overhead light. "If you're planning on going outside this room, it's probably not your *shoes* you should be worried about." He sat up, head tilted, examining me with admiration in his gray eyes. "But I wish you always looked this way."

I looked down, realizing I was more or less topless. When he burst into laughter again, I couldn't help joining in. Not that I'd grown so comfortable in his presence that I constantly strolled around in the buff, but I never felt more like myself than when we were together, never so comfortable in my skin, free from stress and all the crap I didn't want to think about.

"Oops," I said. His pull on me was like gravity, and I crawled back onto his lap—my favorite place. He moved my bra strap an inch to kiss my shoulder. "I can't stay," I whispered, though my actions were not backing up my words as I pulled his T-shirt over his head.

"Rach, you can always stay with me…" We locked eyes for one intense moment, then tumbled onto the bed in a tangle of limbs.

It didn't take much for me to justify being late to class, then missing it all together. When Oliver and I were alone, the problems of the world dissolved like he had me under a love spell. It was a bit more complicated when those "problems of the world" included my skipped chemistry lab, and the pop quiz I'd missed the week before, and how Professor Elliott had cornered me after class and informed me that my grade had slipped from an A to a C-plus.

But with Oliver's hands in my hair, his mouth on me, I couldn't make myself care; I couldn't fight his gravitational pull.

Five months into my ten-year plan, I was already five months behind. The control freak side of me hated the girlfriend side. She was weak and reckless. We had to find a balance. If I could just go to the library more. Study more. Maybe if Oliver studied more, too. But when we tried to study together, I always ended up tearing off his shirt.

It wasn't until the afternoon sun arched to the west that we came up for air. "Should we order pizza?" I asked, buttoning my shirt as I heard one of his roommates come home. I glanced at Oliver sitting on the edge of the bed. His dark hair was messed up and his eyes still held a hint of the familiar intensity that hung on even hours after we were together. It made heat pool in the pit of my stomach…never quite finished.

"Or we could go out," he suggested.

I stopped buttoning. "Uh, no. Let's stay in. If we bother to leave, I might as well go to the library."

"Rachel." The frustration in his tone gave me pause. That was becoming familiar, too. He raked both hands through his hair then bent forward, resting his elbows on his knees, staring at the floor. "I know the reason you don't want to go out, but it's going to happen sooner or later."

The thought of Oliver and Roger finally meeting, together in the same room, made that lovely heat in my stomach turn to cold liquid. It couldn't happen, not until I came up with a solid game plan.

Besides, Roger wouldn't get it. Just the other day, during our traditional Sunday brunch, he'd mentioned that no one ever saw me around anymore. What was keeping me so occupied? Rog would take one look at my boyfriend and assume I was only infatuated by his looks, when there was so much more to Oliver than his ripped six-pack and perfect face. We talked for hours about nothing, and I loved his sweetness, his carefree, totally content nature, even when it scared me.

We were so in "the zone."

But why wasn't he letting the subject go?

"If it's such a big deal for me to meet your family… Oh. I get it. " His gaze dropped to the floor. "You don't think I'm good enough."

The sadness of his words pierced my heart like an arrow tipped with poison. I'd never meant for him to feel that way. I took full responsibility for being the fraidycat in this relationship.

"You?" The single syllable squeaked out of my throat. I crawled over, placing myself between his knees, and framed his face with my hands while gazing into those silvery eyes. "You're perfect," I whispered. "And I love you."

"Rach." He touched his forehead to mine. "I love you."

Even though we'd been saying it for a month, it filled my insides with warmth and peace whenever I spoke it. Before

Oliver, they'd just been words. I never knew they could coat my soul, push back the fear, and help me feel like I could let go of some of my control, if only temporarily.

Aside from dodging the subject of Roger, moments like this were as perfect as they came. The only thing that mattered was finding a way to make the perfection last.

"Look," I said. "Sneaking around sucks, but it's just for a little while longer."

"You said that a month ago."

"Roger has spies. I can't even trust my very best friends. They know about you, I mean, they suspect I'm dating someone, but they don't *know*."

He ran a hand up my arm, cupping my elbow. "Meghan would like me. So would Gio."

"It's not that." I touched his face, my thumb sliding across his cheek. "You'll meet everyone soon. I swear." After a kiss, I reached for my bag and jacket, guilty about having to keep deflecting his questions. I didn't know when my answers started to feel like lies.

"I think I'll head to the library. Want to come?"

"Naw." He flipped on his Xbox and grabbed the hand control. I heard the theme music to *Halo*. *That* was becoming more than familiar.

"So, uh, have you declared your major yet?" He shook his head, staring at the TV. "Isn't the deadline coming up?"

"I think so. I'll get around to it."

"Oliver," I said, watching him from the doorway.

"Yeah?"

A lecturing nag sat on the tip of my tongue. But then I gazed at him, practically seeing the golden aura I sensed surrounding his being. He was the best person I knew. It did needle me that he wasn't taking his classes seriously. But if I loved him, I should love him exactly the way he was.

"Rach?" He lowered the hand control. "What else is wrong?"

I wanted to tell him. I even started to. "To understand me, you have to understand my family." I bit my lip and stared out the window toward the brick wall covered with graffiti across the street. "My mom and dad are professors. They travel all over the world as guest lecturers."

"I know what your parents do for a living."

But did he know they lost their entire life savings in a matter of days? No one grasped how much that still affected me. It was never about money, it was the stress of watching my parents struggle, Dad's guilt, Mom's sadness, all because they hadn't planned for the future. I would not let that happen to me.

The future wasn't what Oliver was concerned about. He didn't even have a major, and that really did scare me, because I was obsessed with the future...which was easy for me to remember when we were a room apart from each other. I didn't know how to say that to him, though. Most normal freshmen didn't have a major yet, or if they did, they changed it ten times.

He stood and walked over to me. "This is upsetting you more than I thought." He hooked his index finger under the strap of my backpack over my shoulder.

"Yes," I said, my bottom lip trembling. Though I wasn't sure which "this" he was referring to.

He rested a hand on my cheek, then drew me into a warm hug. I could feel the steady beat of his heart as he whispered my name and assured me that everything was going to be okay. The instant he touched his nose to my cheek, I let out the breath I'd been holding and released my clenched fists. His hands ran circles across my back, breath warm against my skin. Oliver calmed me more effectively than any oil blend.

"If you don't want me to bring up your brother again, I won't," he said. "I know you'll introduce us when you're ready."

I exhaled until my body slumped against his, hugging him back, so tight. The amount of relief that coursed through my heart and mind was startling. I hadn't realized until that moment that I'd never planned on letting them meet. And Oliver had just let me off the hook.

What did that say about me?

Blinking back tears I wouldn't be able to explain, I kissed him slowly, trying to convey my feelings, as muddled as they were. "Thank you." I pressed my forehead to his. "It'll happen when the time is right."

I wasn't sure if I was lying to him or to myself.

Chapter Six

Taking advantage of one of the blue sky Saturdays, Meghan and I put on shorts and headed to the wharf. After loading up on clam chowder and sourdough, we veered toward the marina at Pier 39 to check out the pack of sea lions lounging on floating planks. We found a spot at the railing and just stood and watched. It was like staring at a campfire or a lava lamp—there wasn't a ton going on, but it sure was hypnotic.

"So, finish telling me about your dream," Meghan requested, after she'd glared at her cell phone for the hundredth time in an hour. "You had webbed fingers, and…"

"That was it," I said. "But that's not the one I want you to analyze."

The late afternoon was sunny, not much fog or wind for a change, in the mid-sixties, and just a salty hint of San Francisco Bay in the air. Damn near perfect weather.

"Webbed fingers." Meghan rubbed her chin and leaned against the railing, her strawberry blond spiral curls blowing in the breeze. "There's something in your life you can't grab onto. Something you're dying to scoop up and reclaim, and yet you're trying to paddle away from it at the same time."

Megs had always been something of a mystic. I humored her most of the time when she offered to read my palm or the bumps on my head. As for me, I'd always been a dreamer; not in the romantic sense of the word, but the literal sense. My dreams were quite detailed and vivid, and—according to Meghan—they absolutely intertwined with my wakeful self.

"Okay, now let me tell you about the other one. The only thing I clearly remember is this rusty cup lying in the middle of the hiking trail. I didn't want to touch it, but someone kept whispering for me to pick it up."

Meghan didn't reply, but frowned down at her phone, flicked its face, and sighed. "You're on a journey," she finally said. "Or you'll be going on a journey soon. Dunno. Dreams are funny sometimes, there's no science, you never can tell."

I stared at her, opened-mouthed. *This* was not Meg's typical analysis. But I didn't call her on it right then or pick a play fight, because I didn't have the energy. First, the weird dreams waking me up at all hours, then the fact that I'd been at work until almost one a.m. the night before, proofreading ads for cell phone apps. Both Bruce and Claire cut out hours earlier. I'd worked over twelve hours a day for the past week and still felt like everyone looked at me like a flunky. Yep, word about the Vondome and my botched proposal were the hottest water cooler topics. As the days progressed, I felt like I was on the chopping block.

Work sucked, but I was over halfway into my ten-year plan, well on my way to where I wanted to be at the end. A lot rested on my job at NRG Interactive. There, I could finally start adding to my savings account, and I'd just opened a 401(k). But career and finance weren't the only facets of my life requiring stability. I wanted marriage and a family some-day. But I also needed balance between work and relation-ship—and that was something I'd failed at in the past.

Meghan and I moved to a bench outside a bakery—the glorious, pungent scent of sourdough in the air—with a view of the tour boats headed to Alcatraz. She had a gluten-free green tea ice cream cone in one hand and a Diet Coke in the other. I doubted either was within the limits of her most recent cleanse.

Even after I added a few more details about my dream, it was obvious Megs hadn't heard a word. "Earth to Meghan," I said. "Why do you keep checking your cell and snubbing me? I will not be snubbed."

"He hasn't called."

Ah. There was a "he." Now we were getting somewhere. "Who's the guy?"

She sighed and finally looked at me. "We met a few weeks ago at Tim's party—"

"Wait." I sat up straight. "This is the guy you picked up? You programmed your number into his cell?"

She gazed off like she was remembering something bliss-ful. Confirmation confirmed. "He's from Iowa, or Indiana. One of those corn-husker states. He works down in SoMa."

"He's a techie?" I asked, knowing many of the major dot-commer software companies had offices in the South of Market district.

"I think so. He works in that big building across from the Jewish Museum."

"Is he cute?"

"*Hot*," she tweaked. "And he's, like, a grown-up." She set down her soda and ran a hand over her grinning mouth. "I can't think of the last time I was interested in someone who wasn't still in school or working at Chuck E. Cheese."

"What's his name?"

She grinned. "Rad."

"Rad?" I echoed, not bothering to hide my mocking. "Like, short for Radcliff? What—is he from a regency novel?" When Megs didn't catch on to my teasing, I added, "Why am I just now hearing about this guy? How long have you been dating?"

She cut a quick glance at me, her ecstatic expression faltering a hair. "We've only been out once—technically. He and Tim live in the same neighborhood now. They knew each other in college, or maybe it was one of the other guys who live up there in North Beach."

"Ahh, North Beach. So he's a techie *and* a beatnik." I laughed. "That's quite a mash-up. I do love that neighborhood, all those cool restaurants and Victorian houses. Wait." I grabbed her arm. "Is that why you wanted to eat at Mama's the other morning? Does he live by Washington Square Park and do sunrise tai chi with the other Chinese seniors?"

"Rad doing sunrise tai chi." She bit her lip and grinned. "How smokin' hot would that be."

Despite my teasing, I was proud of Meghan. It was like she said: she never dated *men*, genuine emotionally available men. Perhaps this guy was the one to drag her into an adult relationship.

"What about you?" She nudged my shoulder. "Got your eye on anyone super-sexy-special?"

"Right." I snorted. Currently, the only males on my

mind were my brother, Moron Bruce, and—thanks to that unplanned detour around USF campus—Oliver Wentworth. *Le sigh.* "If you hadn't noticed," I continued, "I've been busting my ass trying to not get fired. Please say I don't normally have such massive bags under my eyes. I'd trade a man for a good nap any day. I think I'll have that put on business cards."

Meghan wadded up a napkin in her hand. "You're too cynical, so afraid of taking chances or getting hurt. You'll never get a boyfriend with that attitude." She froze and stared at me, looking startled at what she'd just said. "Oh. Sorry."

As I stared back at my best friend, each beat of my heart hurt. Meghan looked away. Not only did my heart hurt, but now my head hurt. "That was bitchy," I said in a flat voice. "Tell me how you really feel."

"I'm sorry, Rach." She stared down at the ground. "I didn't mean that. I'm sure you have your reasons."

"Reasons for what?"

She lifted a quick smile and jumped to her feet. "Nothing, nothing. Maybe I'm PMS-ing. I mean, I obviously need more chocolate, right? It's getting late. Let's hit the bricks, chick."

I knew when someone was dodging a question. I was queen of that. And Megs was definitely dodging. I followed her to a trash can to dump our wrappers, and we washed our sticky fingers in an open fountain behind the carousel. Afterward, she busied herself by digging through her purse, probably trying to blow off the way I was glaring at her profile. Though I was glad she'd cut herself off when she'd started in about how I wouldn't take risks with my heart. I so didn't want to go there.

Aside from my new job and moving to San Francisco,

Rachel Daughtry *not* taking risks was the norm. Megs knew my ten-year plan almost as well as I did. Freshman year, she didn't know Oliver. She thought I'd been sneaking around with some random guy behind Roger's back, but she didn't know the truth. In the six years since, I'd never filled her in.

The sun was just starting to set as we walked in silence toward the trolleybus stop. Well, I was silent while Meghan chatted about something I couldn't be bothered to care about. On the bus, she was playing on her phone while singing the new American Idol song—which gave me time to stare out the window and remember a time when I wasn't afraid of getting hurt, or hurting someone else the way I'd hurt the one person I'd never meant to hurt, the one person I loved more than anything, trusted explicitly, could stand completely naked before and know he saw nothing in me but perfection and love, and how he would touch my—

"And don't forget to watch Monday night. Rach?"

I gasped and twitched, returning my attention to Meghan one seat over. "What?" My whole body felt hot and glowy as I flushed at a memory that felt way too recent. I made the motion of scrubbing my cheeks with my hands so Meghan wouldn't notice my burning face. What would I tell her anyway? That I'd been ignoring her while fantasizing about someone I'd known during a part of my life she knew nothing about?

"They're replaying it at eleven o'clock," she added. "Channel sixty-five. I don't come on until nine minutes in."

Megs went on to talk about her newest pulled-from-the-pages-of-history movie project, while I exhaled, long and quiet. Off the hook.

We hopped off the trolley across the street from Golden

Gate Park. To the left was the café we'd talked about eating at, and to the right was the street toward home. Before I could come up with an excuse for skipping on dinner, we both headed right.

"Okay," Meghan said, "I can tell you're totally wiped out. Get some sleep, bestie. We're all going out tomorrow night, no?" When I gave her a doubtful look, she got right in my face. "You promised, Rach. You totally bailed last weekend."

"Okay, okay." I laughed, as we stopped on the corner between our two apartments. "I'll be there."

She stepped in front of me, her head tilted to the side. "Take care, you." She kissed me on both cheeks, something she'd been doing for years, attempting to appear more Hollywood. "Mmm, you smell dreamy." She stuck her nose to my neck and sniffed. "What *is* that? Lemon zest?"

"Tangerine and chamomile oils. It's supposed to be grounding." I took a whiff of the inside of my elbow. "You like it?"

"Totally yumsville." Megs grinned and did a little twirl on the corner, waiting for the light to turn green. "Have a good night, Rach." She stopped in the middle of the crossway and turned back to me. "Hey. Just think, maybe you'll meet Mr. Right tomorrow night. I've got hot friends."

"Works for me!" I waved good-bye, catching sight of her again as she crossed the next street. Her apartment was two streets over from Roger's. I could actually see her porch light if I squinted just right.

After I made it up the steps, I leaned my elbows on the ledge and gazed up at the sky. It was wide and bursting in a colorful sunset. The kind of sky a Californian could be proud of. I sighed, feeling a bit more grounded and at peace at being here.

Right on the heel of that peace came a pang of the old regret. I hadn't expected Oliver to invade my thoughts so much.

Face it, Rach. You'll never be ready to meet a Mr. Right, a Mr. Almost-Right, or even Mr. Maybe-For-A-Few-Hours until you banish all memories of Oliver Wentworth.

After I zeroed in on one silvery star, I wrapped my arms around myself, moved inside, and bolted the front door, hoping I wouldn't dream about Oliver again.

Chapter Seven

Roger was uncharacteristically quiet as we moved around his kitchen, preparing our traditional Sunday morning sibling brunch. After eight months, we were like a well-oiled machine at it. Though it was odd not to be making even small talk. Graduation was looming and Rog had been accepted to both Stanford and NYU for grad school, though he hadn't yet decided if he was ready to give up being a West Coaster.

I figured that was what occupied his mind, until he said, "How serious is it, Rachel?" He was cramming two pieces of bread in the toaster. "With you and Oliver Wentworth."

Hearing that name come out of Roger's mouth made me drop the egg-covered spatula I'd been holding. I stared at my brother across his kitchen, my mind going a million miles an hour in a million directions. He stared back, his expression giving nothing away. Was he pissed? Shocked? Disappointed?

I glanced at the front door, wondering if he could catch me if I tried to flee the scene without answering.

"Um, serious," I finally replied, moving the pan of scrambled eggs off the heat before I burned them any worse.

"When can I meet him?"

"Ha!" I couldn't help snorting. "You guys are so *anxious* to meet each other, why don't I set up a date for just the two of you?"

Roger's eyebrows shot up. "He's been wanting to meet me?"

My stomach dropped. This wasn't a joke. I brushed past him to dish out the eggs. "How did you find out?"

He folded his arms and leaned against the counter. "So it *was* a secret."

I scoffed and rolled my eyes, doing my best to play the role of surly little sister.

"Let's go out tonight," he said, both of us dodging each other's questions. "We'll do dinner—my treat, no pressure." He smiled, though there was a dare behind his eyes. "Unless you have something to hide."

Of course I had a choice; my brother wasn't lord and master over me. But he was a master at hitting where it hurt. "I'm not *hiding* him, we've been busy," I said, bending the truth to the point of almost snapping. Because the glaring truth was, Roger would be pissed to high heaven if he found out about my sucky grades. Though, knowing my big brother, he'd be more pissed at Oliver. "Why do you always suspect I'm up to something?"

"Because you always are." His calmness while being

logical made me crazy.

"Fine, Roger, fine. You wanna meet him? No problem whatsoever." I gave him a tight smile, holding my eyes wide and steady, taking his dare. "Just say when and where."

"Excellent."

"Sure is."

It hadn't registered—what I'd just agreed to in my ir-rational haste—until smirking Roger was programming the address of the restaurant where we'd be meeting into my phone. Dammit. I braced myself against the sink, feel-ing queasy and feverish, sweat breaking out under my hair. Maybe if I said I was coming down with West Nile Virus, Rog would cancel.

But Oliver would learn I'd weaseled out of the meeting, and that would crush him.

Oliver held open the door to let me enter first, but I wasn't ready. "You'll do great," he said, touching the small of my back.

"Yeah, you too."

He laughed and gazed past me into the restaurant. "You're the one who's worried, Rach. I've been looking for-ward to this for months." He was grinning when he looked down at me, but it dissolved, maybe sensing that I was stress-sweating under my clothes and that my stomach was tied in a very complicated sailor's knot. "Hey, hey, it'll be fine, seriously." He pressed his lips to my temple. "Don't worry, sweet pea."

It shouldn't have surprised me that the guys got along,

had typical guy things in common. They were only three years apart, though Roger always seemed like a "grown-up" rather than a peer. I wanted them to get along—I did. Two of the most important men in my life. But the stress-sweating kept up all through dinner.

Right as we agreed to order dessert, Roger scooted his plate and glass away, folded his arms on the table, and leaned forward. "So, tell me, Oliver." There was a slight clench to his jaw, the first hint of aggression all night. "What are your plans for the future?"

"Rog," I said, squirming in my seat. "What happened to your promise of no pressure?" Though, secretly, I'd been wondering this same question for months.

My brother didn't move his eyes from Oliver. "Can't he answer for himself?"

"*Roger.*"

"Rach." Oliver touched my knee under the table. "It's cool. He's in big brother mode now." He moved his eyes from me to Roger. "I respect that." Then he cleared his throat and spoke of his plan to lifeguard back home over the summer, and of a job his uncle had waiting for him with his construction company.

Evidently, Roger had been holding back during dinner, because he went on to question Oliver about everything, from his still-undeclared major to his student loans. I couldn't pretend those issues didn't irk me, too, but I wouldn't voice that in front of Roger. I'd never really voiced it to Oliver, either.

My brother wasn't letting it go, though, and the tension of not being able to help was unbearable. I had to do something to get him off Oliver's back.

"You should probably know, Roger," I interrupted when I couldn't take it anymore. "We're moving in together next year."

Oliver did a double take at me. "We are?"

"Yes." I nodded, glancing at him first, then glaring at my brother. There was no way he would call my bluff.

Roger actually chuckled and leaned back in his chair. "Did you tell Dad?"

I huffed. "It's no one else's business."

"So, that's a no."

I was ready to bare my teeth and go for his throat, protection instinct kicking in, and more than a little sibling annoyance.

"Rach," Oliver said, slipping a tiny bottle of lavender oil into my hand. "Why don't you take a walk?"

"I'm not leaving you with him."

He laughed under his breath and glanced across the table. "I swear not to throw the first punch if he promises the same."

The first smile in a half hour crossed my brother's face. "Deal." He nodded toward the courtyard. "Give us a minute, Rach."

I glanced back and forth at them; both of their expressions were eerily blank, so I gave up. "Okay." After coating my pressure points in lavender, I made exactly one loop around the parking lot then returned to the dining room. Neither guy was smiling anymore, but I didn't notice any blood, either. I took that as a good sign. Oliver was on his feet by the time I got back to the table.

"If I don't hear from you this week," Roger said to me, "I'll see you next Sunday at breakfast." He nodded at Oliver.

"Wentworth."

"See ya," Oliver said. "Thanks for dinner."

"You're welcome." Rog leaned back in his chair and had his phone out, paying no further attention to us.

"Um, bye," I said.

Oliver clasped my hand and had to pull me away from the table. "I only wish we could do that every night," he said the second we were outside the restaurant.

"What happened in there?"

"The president of the student body grilling me, you mean?" He dropped my hand and put an arm around my shoulders as we set off to walk the six blocks to my dorm.

"Was it bad?"

He chuckled. "Not even a little, Rach."

I scrubbed at one eyelid. "Wow. You're braver than me."

He pulled me into his side. My limbs were shaking from leftover adrenaline, but I wasn't as relieved as I thought I should be. In fact, the whole thing was kind of...disappointing. Had I *wanted* there to be blood? Had I wanted Oliver to throw a punch or demand my hand in marriage? Or had I expected Roger to *order* me to break up with him?

"What a relief," I said, smiling at him, while gnawing the inside of my cheek. "I was afraid you might cut your losses and head for the nearest sorority house in search of a less complicated girlfriend."

"Sweet pea, I crave your kind of complication." He twirled me under his arm then into a hug. He was so damn happy. After he planted a kiss on top of my head, he said, "So, we're moving in together, huh?"

My heart thudded inside my ribs. I still wasn't sure why I'd thrown that into the conversation. "Um, if you want to."

"Hell, yeah. Are you kidding?" He took both my hands and laced his fingers between mine. "This"—he tugged me forward to kiss my forehead—"all day, every day."

"Yeah," I said, trying my best to sound as jazzed as him. But a brick sat in my stomach, and a heavy, antsy feeling I couldn't explain made it hard to breathe.

He draped an arm across my shoulders as we walked. "You're constantly surprising me, Rach." In silence, I played with his fingers until we reached my dorm. "Thank you for setting up tonight. It meant a lot to me."

He sounded really happy, which made me happy that I could do that. The moment we kissed, that brick of dread in my stomach got blasted to bits by an eruption of heat and love, making my knees buckle, making me want to do more than kiss him. *This*…this was what I wanted. *This* was all that mattered. Why couldn't my head and my heart ever communicate properly when it came to Oliver?

"You're so sexy when you're my superhero." I squeezed him tight. "Wanna sneak up to my room so you can show me who's boss?"

He exhaled a playful groan into my hair. "I'm dying to, but we can't get caught again."

"What about your place?"

"The guys are having a party; there'll be fifty people over."

"Okay, then. I'll drag you into the bushes. It'll only take six minutes." I knotted my fingers in the back of his hair and kissed his neck. "Maybe less."

His body shook with laughter. "You're so sexy when you're trying to be hilarious. I love that about you." He dipped his chin to kiss the spot behind my ear. "Wait until the party's over at my place and spend the night. I want to watch you sleep."

"Oliver," I said, giggling into his warm neck. "You don't really do that."

He cupped my face, lightly running his fingertips over my eyelids. "All the time," he said. "I can tell when you're dreaming about me."

I giggled again, a little self-consciously, like he truly did know how often he frequented my REM cycles.

He kissed my eyelids. "When you're just waking up, too. That might be my favorite moment. It's what I picture when you're not right here." He touched his forehead to mine. "Every night I'm not with you, I can still see you waking up beside me."

The fluttering in my heart was almost painful, but I felt warmth, followed by an acute sting behind my eyes that wasn't at all unpleasant. He pressed me against the glass doors that were about to lock me out for the night, kissing me one last time. When we were done, he waved good-bye through the window and turned toward home, leaving me to drift upstairs to my room.

Despite the surprising success of the evening, my sub-conscious would not allow me to rest. I tossed and turned all night with intense, stormy dreams. There was thunder and rain, earthquakes, and I woke up sweating bullets, my covers kicked to the floor.

The sun had barely risen when a knock sounded at my door. I scrambled out of bed, expecting to see Oliver. But it was Roger, holding two cups from Starbucks.

"Rach." He extended a cup. "We need to talk."

Chapter Eight

Hearing Roger's chipper voice through my cell made me smile.

"Hi, Double."

"Hey, Trouble." I leaned back in my office chair, also happy for his crystal-clear voice after only emails and fuzzy phone connections. "When's your flight home?"

"Tonight. I'm so tired of traveling. How's my dog?"

Rog would be a great daddy someday. He'd been out of town for less than two weeks, but Sydney's well-being was always one of the first things he asked about.

"After a run through the mud last night, I let her roll around in your bed, then we had a marathon petting session. You missed all the fun." My brother laughed as I gave him a blow-by-blow account of Sydney's actions, while I stared at my blank computer screen, needing to come up with a brilliant idea to sell some odd-tasting table crackers from Romania before Claire came at me with a hatchet.

Roger and I caught up, chatted next about the Golden State Warriors basketball game we'd both watched an ocean apart a few days ago. I also told him I'd gone to the wharf with Meghan and stocked up on sourdough bread bowls.

"She invited us to some party on Friday." I toyed with a mini bottle of peppermint oil, the one I carried around with me like old-fashioned smelling salt. "Not this Friday but next."

"Is it at Tim's house?"

"Yep. If I go, I'll probably stay here at the office then meet you guys since I'm already halfway to his place." I ran my hand across my desk, temporarily relieved that I didn't have any overdue project cluttering the smooth surface. "But can I tell you, I'm getting pretty sick of going up to North Beach. I work close by, we do dinner up there, the best theaters are up there, and so far every happening social gathering worth attending has been in North Beach."

"Was there a party up there last weekend?"

"Yes."

"Did you go?"

"No, and Meghan almost stroked out, but is it not my right as an American to boycott North Beach for one weekend?"

Roger didn't reply. Had our overseas signal died out? I was ready to start in with the old "can you hear me now?" back-and-forth when he spoke again.

"That's good, Rach, because it's actually the reason I called. You should definitely stay away from those parties at North Beach, okay?" His voice sounded weird, overly-protective, reminding me of that first year at USF.

"What are you talking about?"

"Nothing, nothing," he said after another silent moment.

"I guess you don't know—or you *do* know." He sighed, and I could picture him pinching the bridge of his nose in concentration. Right as I was about to worry about his level of stress, he broke the tension by chuckling. "You know what, it's not a big deal. I just wanted to tell you—"

"Rog, hold on a sec." I hated cutting him off, but Bruce was barking at me from around the corner about how I needed to edit the copy on the Shreveport Slow Boat poster *STAT!*

STAT? Really? Who talked like that outside an ER?

"Sorry, Rog. The world's about to come crashing down if I don't save it with my mad editing skills. See you tomorrow?"

"Yeah, okay. See you tomorrow."

After I cut our call short, I reached for my computer tablet. Some days, the only notion that kept me going was that if I got my act together and hung on, I would probably have Bruce's job in a few years, then the career possibilities were endless. My plan was on track. That was all that mattered.

"Move it, Ray-Ray."

I scooted out my chair, and with a roll of my eyes rounded the corner toward his gym-socks-smelling office. An hour later, emotionally drained, I returned to my desk and slumped into my chair.

Roger had phoned again and left a voicemail. I clipped on my Bluetooth to listen to the message while I packed up to go home. Through heavy static, it was tough to make out what he was saying—he was doing the stammering thing he'd done during our earlier conversation. When his voice was clear and stable for two seconds together, however, I could've sworn he said…

I dropped my bag on the floor and stared blankly out

into the hall, twisting my computer cord around one finger.

I am actually going crazy now. Certifiably. I closed my eyes, trying to convince myself that I'd misunderstood Roger's message. When that didn't work, I played it again.

Yep, I'd heard right.

Okay. Obviously, I was losing my mind and hearing things that weren't really said. First that whole "Rach, we need to talk" voicemail last month. Now this? Being back in San Francisco was giving me daytime nightmares about the subject, that's all.

I collapsed into my chair, fumbling for the king-sized lavender oil I kept beside my pencil holder. I rubbed a drop into my palm, dabbed my index fingertip into the pool, and massaged the sweet-smelling oil into both temples. Then I rubbed my palms together, cupped my hands, and breathed in. My nostrils burned and tingled, making my eyes water.

But Roger's phone message still played in my head.

Looks like you need something stronger, Rach.

When my phone bleeped with a text, I jumped a mile. I could *not* talk to Roger. I just couldn't. I peeked at my cell. Shew. It was Meghan wanting to meet for dinner. I stared at my phone, wondering when I should tell her about Oliver. I mean, if I was hallucinating that Roger was talking about him, why not come clean to her? Maybe then, all my nightmares could go ahead and come true.

Chapter Nine

Roger brushed past me, waved at my dormmate who'd poked her head out of her bedroom when she heard voices, then he sat in the middle of my couch like he owned the place.

"Come on." He patted the spot next to him. "Let's talk."

"It's early, Rog." I took a sip from the to-go cup he'd handed me. "Can't this wait?"

"I don't think so." His tone sounded remorseful. He set down his cup, rested his elbows on his knees, and laced his fingers. "You know it can't."

He didn't have to explain what he meant. It could only be one thing. My latest gulp of latte tasted bitter in my mouth. I struggled to swallow it down.

"Oliver and I aren't your business," I said, cutting to the chase. "You wanted to meet him, to *check him out*, and you did last night. It's done."

"Rachel, sit down, please." He was trying to be calm—which always pissed me off. "I'm not happy about this, that you've been lying to me all year." He looked pointedly at me but I only stared back. "I was thinking about you, about *this,* all night. I want to make sure you know what you're doing."

"You don't approve of Oliver because he's not just like you. How can he be? He's nineteen."

"Exactly." He wiped a hand over his mouth and blew out a loud exhale. "He has no idea what he wants."

"He wants *me*."

Roger's face drained of color and he shifted on the couch. "That's not what I meant. Just calm the hell down." He glanced toward my roommate's door. "You're worked up over nothing."

Was I? I crossed my arms and tried to control my breathing. What had Roger said so far that wasn't true? Actually, I hadn't given him a chance to say much of *anything* yet. But I knew what was coming, the churning in my gut knew, too, because I'd dreamed about it all night.

He pushed both hands through his hair. "Look, Rachel. I know you dropped a class."

My stomach fell. "And how exactly did you acquire that personal information?" I said, going for insulted, but even I heard my voice shake.

"I know a lot of people at this school. I hear things."

I threw my hands in the air and huffed, ready to go on the defensive. But it wasn't Roger's fault that he found out I'd been slacking off, worse than slacking off.

Right after midterms, I'd had to drop chemistry because I was failing. Oliver never pressured me to hang at his place instead of going to class. But once I was there and we were together, sometimes the thought of leaving him for one hour was unbearable. It was *my* responsibility to control my hormones and be mature enough to put school before sex, yet I'd let our relationship knock everything in my life off balance.

If I didn't get my act together pronto, my ten-year plan would go straight down the crapper. Was I really willing to trade the future I'd been planning for years to be with the boy I loved right now?

The glaring, final answer terrified the hell out of me, though it had been there all along. Once I was still and calm enough to think for two seconds, it wasn't even a matter of talking myself into it—it was going to happen. I clutched the kitchen counter, feeling like I was about to be sick.

"Rachel?"

My eyes were shut tight, but I felt Roger come to my side. "You don't...." I held out my hand to push him back. "You don't have to say anything else."

"I knew something wasn't right with you," he said. "I've seen it coming, but I didn't know it was because of *him*."

"It's not his fault, it's mine." I opened my gummy eyes. "I screwed up my grades because I want to be with him... all the time, Rog." My lungs shook when I inhaled. "What if they kick me out of school?"

My brother put a hand on my shoulder. "They won't. We'll go talk to your counselor tomorrow."

"You'll go with me?"

He nodded. "But first, you know what you have to do."

It took one text to get him to meet me an hour later, at the bench outside my dorm. The scene of our first kiss. I'd been crying while waiting for him, but when he appeared, I was determined to keep every tear at bay.

"I can't come over anymore and you can't call me." It was like my words were coming from someone else's mouth. "It's over. This has to be over." I moved my index finger an inch to point at him. "Us."

Oliver's head flinched back, and he stared at me in silence, for a long time. It made my stomach twist with pain to know I'd blindsided the boy I claimed to love.

"I'm not an idiot, Rach," he finally said. "I know it's been bothering you for a while, and you're freaked out that I haven't decided on a major. I'll get around to it; it's not a big deal."

But it was a big deal—to me. A huge deal. If he couldn't see that, what did that mean about his future? *Our* future? If I couldn't get myself back on track, I had no chance of helping him. There were some things in life worth taking a risk over, but right now, my future wasn't one of them.

"If this is about school, I can't believe it," he said.

"It is, but it isn't."

"Meaning?"

My eyelids felt dry and tacky as I stared down at my empty hands. "It's a symptom."

"Of what?" He reached for my hand but I pulled away. If he touched me, kissed me, I would lose all my resolve and be back at square one: completely unbalanced and completely petrified, maybe even resenting him. The thought made me sick.

I turned into the wind, smelling salt and sea in the air—

or maybe it was the salty tears I was trying so hard to hold in.

"I know how important your family's opinion is to you," he said in a quieter voice. "Tell me the truth, did Roger say something?"

I stared at him, about to say no. Though Roger had put the bug in my ear, *this* was my decision. Oliver was looking at me with those big, beautiful gray eyes, worry and doubt but still hope swimming in their depths. My mouth could not admit the cowardly words…that because I was with him, I couldn't keep my priorities straight, I couldn't do what my parents expected me to do, what *I* expected me to do. I couldn't admit that if we stayed together, I had no faith that I would get the kind of future I wanted—healthy and positive and balanced.

I lowered my head. "Um…yeah." Making Roger my scapegoat was complete chicken shit, but maybe that was what I was turning into. Spineless. Pain from holding in another sob radiated behind my eyes. "My parents are overseas, so he's basically my legal guardian. He told me we can't see each other anymore. He made me swear."

Wow. So I'm a liar now? I turned my face away, not wanting him to see what his girlfriend had become.

"It'll be fine." He shifted to stand. "I'll talk to him."

"No!" I grabbed his arm. "That'll make it worse. Trust me."

Trust me.

His metallic eyes searched my face for the answers I was too gutless to give. "You're saying it's because of Roger." His voice was slow and toneless. "And you have no choice."

I nodded.

"But you don't want me to talk to him about it."

I shook my head.

He sat back and exhaled in frustration, raking a hand through his hair. "Rachel, I…that doesn't make any sense, unless…" He blinked and stared at me like he was seeing a person he didn't know. His jaw muscles clenched and un-clenched as his gaze slid from mine to the space over my shoulder. "Then I guess it really is over."

Oliver—who knew me so well he could finish my sen-tences—did not try to talk me out of it. He didn't beg or yell or remind me about the thousands of midnight kisses we'd shared. He simply picked up his black notebook and walked away without a backward glance.

If the breakup truly upset him, I didn't see it, though debilitating grief choked me breathless the second he was out of sight.

I saw him one other time before the end of the school year. He was sitting on a bench at a BART stop, wearing a purple Colorado Rockies baseball cap, the one he always wore when he felt self-conscious about his hair. A bus came, stopped, waited, then departed, all without Oliver lifting his eyes from the ground.

A month later, I flew to Santa Barbara to a parentless house and a summer internship that I couldn't remember signing up for. Ashamed by my actions, I swore I would nev-er broach the subject with a living soul.

Chapter Ten

Meghan's cell sat on the edge of her bed between a stack of glossy magazines we were flipping through and the plate of leftover pizza crusts from dinner. Since I was the closest when it started to ring, I grabbed it.

"Hello, Meghan's phone."

"Hello?" a voice replied. Male. Oops.

"So sorry. One moment, please." I lowered the phone and cringed with my bottom teeth. "I think it's for you."

Meghan tossed her last piece of crust onto the plate and grabbed her phone from me. "Hello? Hey, Rad." She was beaming now, even I could hear it in her voice. "Oh, did I?" She snapped the air in front of my face and grinned, wanting me to hear this next part. "I can't *believe* I left my sweater in your car last night." She listened for a moment then winked, and I gave her the thumbs-up. "That's so sweet. You'll be at Tim's on Friday? Perfect."

She leaned against the wall beside her framed print of

La Belle Dame Sans Merci, looking much like that angelic, belle strawberry blonde in the painting. "Oh, nothing much right now," she continued into the phone. "Making room on the bookshelf for all my awards. Emmy season's right around the corner. Right? Ha ha!" She slid to the floor and laughed hard at whatever he'd just said. "No, no, Rachel's here." She winked at me again. "Rachel Daughtry, my best friend in all the world. You met her brother the other—" Meg's eyebrows came together, like she was struggling to make out what he'd said. "Are you still…?" She listened intently. "Oh, okay. Yeah, see you later."

After she hung up, I flopped down on her bed. "That was Mr. Totally Awesome, I presume?"

"Yep. Can't believe he called about my sweater. That almost *never* works." She chewed her thumbnail, a wistful smile on her mouth.

I perched my head on an elbow. "Meghan, you should be more careful. What if by some unforeseen and tragic occurrence, I couldn't find you when he called and we talked for hours and fell in love like *Sleepless in Seattle*?"

"You're thinking of the wrong movie."

I bit my lip. "*Pretty Woman*?"

"Errr…no." She grimaced then laughed. "I would *kill* you, by the way. Rad is mine. Good thing he isn't your type or I wouldn't let you or your perfect little face near him."

"Perfect face," I repeated with a snort.

"You *act* all supportive, Rach, but you might be a man-stealer in disguise. If you pilfer Rad…" She pointed her index finger at me then ran it across her throat.

"Oy. Duly noted." I slid to the floor with a magazine. "So, why isn't this guy my type?"

"He just isn't. I don't know, maybe you don't have a type." She frowned, looking thoughtful. "Or maybe you do but I forget because I haven't seen you on an actual date in a hundred years."

"We double-dated all the time in high school," I said, not quite meeting her eyes.

"That doesn't count. You hardly dated in college. All you did was study and work on that damn ten-year plan. Unless…" She cackled and twirled some hair around a finger. "Unless you had a secret boy toy you met every night behind the stacks—like freshman year."

While she went on chortling, I fixed my expression into a breezy smile. Shit.

"What were you laughing at?" Giovanna asked, poking her head into the room.

"Remember how Rach was always hiding out freshman year?" Meghan said, jerking her thumb in my direction. "She had an undercover lover."

"When did I admit to that?"

"Scandalous." Gio sat on the bed and bounced. "'Cause we never actually saw her date, right?"

I stood and walked to Meghan's bookshelf, annoyed at the direction the conversation had turned. *Not* my favorite subject. Plus, I might start blushing and be forced to tell them both everything about Oliver right here and now.

"Whatever happened to that Jason guy in Dallas?" Meghan asked me. "I thought things were going well with him last year."

"He just wasn't"—I paused to shrug—"the guy."

Meghan shook her head. "You're too hard on men. You need to rein in your intimidating chi."

"Sure, Megs." I snorted. "I'm as intimidating as a lost puppy in the rain."

"Nice try, babe." She circled me slowly, tapping her chin. "You're tall, you walk fast, and you always act like your mind is made up. Like no one can persuade you into anything, or out of it."

"Is that why Roger can still talk me into doing his laundry and how Krikit manages to make me feel guilty for not living in the house next door to her? *Intimidating*," I muttered. "Damn straight, I am."

"I'm telling you, if you'd be a little more forgiving of human frailties, you'll have better luck with guys. I've set you up on three lunch dates since you've been back and you blew all three off."

"I did not. We went to lunch, but I didn't connect with any of them. It just wasn't…they weren't…"

"See." Gio pointed at me. "You're not investing. You're not even trying."

Before I could open my mouth to argue, I bit my tongue. Maybe they were right. Maybe I wasn't doing everything I could to invest in someone new. The thing was, I didn't think I wanted to. My heart was still broken from a million years ago.

Meghan leaned a hip against her dresser. "You're a tricky one, Rachel. I can't imagine you with any kind of guy in the long run."

"Great." I moaned, toying with a piece of pizza crust. "I hope you're not using your mystical powers to foresee my future. Please tell me you don't see me in a rundown shack with twenty cats."

"*You're* the one having the mystical dreams lately."

I tried to laugh while rubbing the back of my neck. I didn't want to relive *those* memories, either. I still couldn't get the image of that rusty can out of my mind. Just the thought of my recent dreams made my stomach roll, wondering what kind of dream I would have tonight.

"Don't worry, Rach." Megs gave me a wink. "I won't rest until I figure out the perfect man for you."

Chapter Eleven

I turned to a fresh page in my notebook and tapped my pen. Evidently, I was being too loud because Claire gave me the stink-eye. I hadn't had a run-in with her for ten whole days. My longest stretch to date. Time to reset the clock, Rach.

"Does anyone else have a thought?" Claire asked, making it a point to hold scary eye contact with each of us gathered around the conference table. I tried to inconspicuously slink down in my chair. "Rachel? Input?"

Damn. I consulted my clean, blank page. "Not yet, um." I hadn't written it down, but I did have an idea—a pretty good one, in fact. But Claire and Moron Bruce were about to leave for another meeting, and I'd much rather wait and bounce the idea off the smaller group of copywriters. While Claire talked for a few minutes about the direction the project should go, I scribbled down a few lines, crossed out three, circled one. I even sketched what I thought the photo art might look like. Yeah, this could be really cool.

Moron Bruce and Claire finally stood to leave. "Prepare to stay late tonight," Claire said. "I'll take any and all ideas for this one, so get creative."

I inwardly groaned at the prospect of working late, but if I could be part of the creative leadership this time, it would be worth it. "Want me to order in dinner later?" I asked as they were leaving. Claire had an assistant to do this kind of thing, but I was trying to be a team player, drink the Kool-Aid and all that. "You guys like the takeout from Pakwan, right?"

"Actually, Rachel." Claire dabbed a fingertip at the lip gloss on the corner of her mouth. "You won't be staying tonight."

Oh, shit. Please don't say I'm fired.

"You're a USF alum, correct?"

I cleared my throat. "Yes."

Claire leaned toward Bruce and whispered. Bruce glanced at me and smirked. "Somewhere on my desk," Claire said to him. "Rachel, you'll meet her for dinner—it's purely routine since she's already hired, but there's no way I can make it."

"Meet who?"

"The intern." Claire actually rolled her eyes. "The address is on my calendar, you'll have to look it up yourself."

"Tonight?"

"Yes, tonight." She sighed impatiently. "In two hours." She glanced at the red client folder beside my notebook. "Turn that into Bruce, you won't be needing it."

"I'm off the project?"

She sighed again. Girlfriend was a master at the impatient sighs. "Naturally. Since you won't be here tonight—we won't need you. There are plenty of other assignments to keep you occupied, aren't there? Are we not keeping you busy enough?"

"No—I mean, yes, of course."

"Get her the employee file," Claire said to Bruce as she exited the conference room. Bruce shot me a look that said for me to come with. So I stumbled to my feet, grabbed my things, and followed them down the hall.

Maybe it was an honor to take Claire's place at this meeting. Maybe she'd chosen me specifically because she knew I had what it took and I was a trustworthy face for NRG Interactive.

Claire veered to the right toward her office, and Bruce stopped in his tracks and turned around to me. "Looks like little Ray-Ray's on babysitting duty." He chuckled under his breath.

That sounded anything but important. "What?"

"Wait here." He returned a few minutes later and handed me a skinny manila folder. "The appointment is on Claire's calendar. Don't be late."

"Um, Bruce?" I swallowed and clutched my notebook containing the clever sketch and the perfect one-liner. "I have an idea for the project, if you want to see—"

He held up a hand. "No, no. You heard Claire. Not your concern anymore." He quirked a smirk and strolled away.

After weeks of lying low, I finally had something cool to share, and it would never see the light of day because I'd be *babysitting*. What the hell? I stomped toward my cubicle and dumped everything on my desk, desperately needing a cocktail or a mainline of lavender oil or a Moron Bruce-shaped punching bag.

Someday
MAYBE

The Tipsy Pig was all the way across town, and I was ten minutes late to the dinner meeting. Well, if Claire couldn't be arsed enough to show up herself, why should I break the speed limit?

As I crossed the parking lot, I spotted a girl waiting in front of the restaurant as planned.

"Ms. Reynolds?" she asked me, looking smiley and eager. Good little intern.

"No, I'm Rachel." I extended my hand to shake. "Claire is very sorry but she was called away at the last minute." Lie. "But I'm more than happy to meet with you tonight." Lie.

"Hi." She shook my hand. "Sarah. Nice to meet you. Is that your black Bug?" She nodded toward the parking lot. "What a cool car."

"Oh, thanks. I love it." I returned her enthusiastic smile as we entered the restaurant. "But sometimes convertibles are more trouble than they're worth."

"Not to mention the manual transmission in a city with a bunch of hills."

I laughed, remembering that I'd had the same conversation with my father a month ago when I'd told him I was buying a car in San Francisco. My Bug was used and a great deal, so Dad agreed with my logic in the end.

Sarah was twenty. She looked twenty, but that was only the first impression. After a few minutes of conversation, I discovered she was very together, despite the earlier conversation about my car. Her maturity was refreshing after being around Meghan, the habitual teenager.

"I'm in the art program," she explained as we sat across from each other, eating our gourmet bread and salads. "My focus is oil painting but I throw pottery, too."

"What made you apply for an internship at an advertising agency if you're an artist?"

"Art is my passion, but I don't know how sensible it is to hang my future on what paintings may or may not sell at the whim of some Upper East Side art gallery." She took a bite of spiral noodles salad. "So I'm taking business classes, too."

That seemed smart. And familiar. I'd pretty much done the same thing in college, though this girl was a year ahead of me. Huh. I wondered if she had a ten-year plan, too.

"Tell me some of your upcoming objectives," I asked, trying to sound like I knew what the hell I was doing. Neither Claire nor Bruce bothered to give me any instructions, and Sarah's employee file sat unopened on the passenger seat of my car.

"I've been accepted to study for a semester in Rome." She took a drink. "USF won't pay for it, but they're holding my spot, so I've been saving."

"For how long?"

"Two years."

Her passion for studying art in Italy was evident, which made me wonder why she hadn't already gone. I knew a few people who would've simply charged a trip like that on a credit card or two. But as I looked into her wise eyes, I reconsidered. Maybe it was a different sub-generation of shopaholic girls who did such things.

Sarah had earned her AA degree from a community college in the Midwest I'd never heard of. "I also got accepted to the Art Institute in New York. I was all set to go, but a few months ago I changed my plans."

"You changed your mind to *not* go to New York?" I asked, picking the currants out of my chicken salad. "I thought that was the mecca to study art, all the galleries and museums."

"San Francisco has amazing museums." She sounded a little defensive, like she'd had this same argument with someone before. "One semester in Rome is more important to me than four years in New York."

I saw her point, and was even more impressed. I was starting to look forward to reporting my assessment tomorrow.

Sarah pushed her dark brown hair behind one shoulder. "I love living here so far, but it's been kind of hard to meet people I really connect with. The kids in my dorm are pretty immature."

To be labeled immature by a twenty-year-old? Had things changed that much since I was in college? As I took a bite of salad, I felt a bit sorry for her. San Fran was a big city, and being all alone in a new place could be terrifying, despite how grown-up you may appear. Maybe she didn't make friends easily. Maybe *she* was intimidating.

Ahh! A kindred spirit.

"You can hang out with me," I blurted. "A bunch of us are headed to a party next weekend, not too far from campus. I can pick you up or we can go together from the office."

Sarah's mouth fell open, and for the first time all evening, she looked young and impressionable. "Seriously?" Her eyes lit up as she smiled. "That's extremely cool of you."

I sat a little taller. It felt nice to be considered cool. "Here's my number." I passed her a business card. "It has my cell and you'll memorize my office number in day or two.

Call anytime, seriously. I know what it's like to not, ya know, fit in all the time."

"Thanks." She was kind of beaming now. "Just this morning I set a goal to make friends outside of school."

"You made a goal to make friends?"

Her cheeks turned red at my question and she glanced down, stirring her straw around in her drink. "I know. My whole family's kind of embarrassing that way. We're a bunch of nerdy goal-setters."

"Oh, yeah? What kinds of goals?"

"I don't know, we read a lot." She took a sip of water. "It started the summer I was fourteen. Mom wanted to read the complete works of Shakespeare and Dad read something like ten books on finance and took a bunch of online courses. A year later, he started his own business. It's always been his dream."

She paused to lick mayo off the back of her fork, casually, like this kind of information was commonplace.

"I decided to read the *Little House on the Prairie* series, then I moved on to Jane Austen." She set down her fork. "My brothers and I had these major debates about it, but I preferred Austen to the Brontes, didn't you?"

"When you were fourteen?"

She nodded, wide-eyed.

I slouched in my seat, feeling about as intimidating as a de-winged butterfly. "Wow, your family sounds amazing." Oh, please don't ask me if I've read the complete works of anyone besides Dr. Seuss. "You said you have brothers. Are they as ambitious as you?"

Her whole face brightened, but a second later she chuckled under her breath and bowed her head. "Sorry. I can't help being braggy sometimes. I hear myself, but I can't stop."

"You don't sound braggy." I leaned my elbows on the table. "It's interesting. Go on."

She bit her lip. "My oldest brother kind of started it all—the family goal thing—that summer before I started high school. I'm not sure why my parents encouraged it at first, but it completely changed our family. He went to Creighton for his MBA, finished in a year and a half." She was absolutely beaming now. "It was awesome having him close to home. He was our inspiration."

For a moment, I thought about Roger, Krikit, and my parents. We were close-knit but I wouldn't have called any one of them my inspiration. Maybe we should work on that.

"He writes software now, like these amazing graphic artistry programs, and he travels all over the world to train…" She broke off. "Shoot. I'm doing it again. Sorry."

"Sarah, it doesn't bother me in the least. I have an older brother, too. I can tell you're a very proud sister—there's nothing wrong with that." I felt another wave of simpatico toward her: a big part of me understood this girl.

"Anyway, thanks for letting me gush."

"Anytime." I reached for my purse, pulled out my iPad, and opened the NRG Interactive calendar. "Okay, I suppose we should talk about work for a bit, so I can claim this dinner as a business expense. When is your first day? You'll have a phone and computer, but I don't know if IT has set up your…" I trailed off when I looked up to find Sarah staring across the table at me. "Something wrong?"

"No, I was thinking that…you two would hit it off."

"Who?"

"My brother. My friends say he's a hottie and *you're*

completely *gorgeous*."

I snorted. "Oh. Well, thanks, but I don't do blind dates anymore. Never, ever again."

A flash of light from the window just past Sarah's shoulder pulled my attention. I caught a glimpse of another bolt of lightning over the marina. My heart leapt with excitement. Autumn rain storms: another thing I loved about living close to the bay.

"Okay," Sarah said. "But after I describe you to him, you'll probably be getting a phone call from a stranger." She flashed my business card then tucked it into her purse.

"Very funny." I chuckled, still gazing out the window at the incoming storm. "What's his name?"

"Oliver Wentworth."

A loud clap of thunder shook the ground, rattling the windows. Sarah squealed in alarm, but I'm sure my shriek drowned hers out.

Chapter Twelve

On the way home from the Tipsy Pig, I had to pull over twice. It wasn't crying or screaming or throwing myself off the Presidio wall that I needed to do, nor was it projectile vomiting the chicken salad from dinner.

Like the over-analyzer I was, I had to process.

The only thing that got me and the Beetle back to my neighborhood in one piece was knowing the Bay Area is massive, *millions* of people. Five million, maybe. Six? Twenty? Meaning, there was a more than massive chance I would never run into Oliver.

Run. Into. Oliver.

Yes, the Bay Area was huge, so it wasn't like I'd bump into him on the street. And yeah, Sarah was an intern, but she'd be gone soon, so there'd be no chance of her brother coming to visit the office.

Oliver. At. My. Office.

And sure, I'd invited Sarah to Tim Olson's stupid-ass

party next weekend, but she'd probably make friends her own age by then and forget about it and we'd never run in the same circles. So yeah, it was totally fine. The whole thing was just a crazy coincidence.

The more I processed, the better I felt. It was stupid to get all freaked over nothing.

My cell had been on silent since dinner, and when I grabbed it and my bag off the passenger seat, ready to go inside, I noticed it flashing with an incoming call.

Number unknown.

It might've been someone from work, so I was forced to answer. "Hello?"

"Rachel? Hi, it's Sarah Wentworth."

My tongue, mouth, and throat went dry, and I stared through the windshield. "Oh. Um, hey, Sarah. H-hi."

"I wanted to thank you again for dinner. It was amazingly cool to meet you and I'm even more psyched to start work Monday."

Huh? I narrowed my eyes and waited. But that was it.

"Um, great," I finally said, unable to form anything above monosyllabic words. "I'm sure you'll learn a lot. It's a…a fun office." If you like torturechambers.

"Well, if you're there, I'm sure it'll be awesome-sauce."

I couldn't help smiling. The girl was laying it on thick, though she didn't seem like a suck-up. Maybe she was one of those genuine people.

"Anyway, I guess I'll see you—sorry, hold on." There was a rustling like she was covering her phone. "Ollie, I heard you the first three times. Stop being bossy. Sorry, Rachel. My brother was telling me something."

Sand filled my mouth, coated my tongue so I couldn't

speak at all now. Desert air dried out my eyes as I stared unblinkingly up the street for about a thousand years.

Oliver was with her, probably standing beside her.

"Rachel?

"Yeah." I coughed inside my throat and swallowed, tucking some hair behind my ears, trying to, I don't know, look presentable? "I'm right here."

"Sorry, I stopped at my brother's on the way home. He wanted to hear every detail about our meeting so I gave him a full four-one-one, right down to what we both had to eat."

Sweat pooled on my upper lip and my head felt too light. "Ha ha, brothers are like that."

She laughed. "Right? He asked me a million questions, but I think he's finally satisfied now. Are you *satisfied*, Ollie?" I heard a low voice say something I couldn't understand. Whatever it was made her laugh.

This was eerie.

Did he know it was me? Did he know his sister had met Rachel *Daughtry* tonight? She said she'd given him a full report, but it didn't seem like Oliver had disclosed anything to her about our history, because Sarah hadn't said, "Oh, by the way, he mentioned you were desperately in love six years ago, almost moved in together, until you dumped him flat."

"Anyway, Rachel, I'll let you go."

"Okay." My voice sounded way too high. "Thanks for, um, calling and—"

"Oh!" She cut me off. "I almost forgot the entire reason I called. You said we're going to a party on Friday at some guy's house named Tim. It's Tim Olson, right?"

I blinked. "How did you…?"

"I swear this is such a small world. Ollie totally knows

him. He'll be there, too."

It took all of two seconds for my cell to slip from my hand, hit the steering wheel, ricochet off my leg, and fly to the passenger side floor, yet I saw the whole thing in slow motion.

"Rachel? Are you okay?"

Sarah was on speaker now. It must've activated as it fell. A tiny, primal whimper started quivering in my throat. I sucked in a breath and slapped a hand over my mouth, flinching back from the phone.

"Rachel? I don't know, I think I heard a crash."

I didn't want her to think I'd had an accident on the road and call the cops, but how could I speak when I was in the middle of hyperventilating?

"D-dropped my cell in the car," I croaked through my fingers, staring down at my phone, trying to blink away the black spots.

"Oh, sorry," Sarah said, "I didn't know you were driving. I'll let you go. Thanks again, Rachel. See you Monday morning!"

"Yeah." I swallowed, my heartbeats pounding behind my ears. *Unthinkable. Unbelievable. No, unreal.* "B-bright and early."

A hard knocking rattled my bedroom door. I hoped it was the grim reaper with his long, gnarly death staff coming to take me away. My room echoed with the sound. I couldn't tell how long it'd been going on, because my head had been making the same noise all night. It must've been past eight, which meant I needed to either haul myself out of bed and haul ass to work, or call in sick.

Of course I'm sick… This whole thing is sick.

"Rachel? Something wrong? Rach?"

I rolled over and groaned, not having the strength to even laugh at the irony of the question.

Roger tapped at my door again and I pulled the duvet over my head. "Are you going to work?"

I moaned something about taking the day off. While ensconced under the covers, I heard my door creak open. I peeked out to see my brother's face. "I'm all right," I said, rolling over again to bury my face in the pillows. "Couldn't sleep last night."

Even with two sisters, Roger never knew how to deal with crying or moodiness or any other unmentionable female problems. "You're okay, though? I mean, do you want me to call someone or…do you need castor oil?"

I pulled back the covers and glared at him. "Castor oil? What do you think is wrong with me?"

He held up both hands. "I have no clue."

My head pounded when I laughed. "I'm taking a personal day."

"Okay. Well, call if you need anything, or if you want me to pick up some…some chocolate syrup or whatever, I don't know."

When I didn't comment, he shut the door and left the apartment a few minutes later.

"Sarah Wentworth." I said the name aloud, staring up at the ceiling. "Oliver Wentworth." I listened to how the name came out of my mouth. It sounded like a language I used to know.

Why hadn't I taken two seconds to read her file yesterday? I would've seen her last name: Wentworth. I would've looked to see where she was from: Nebraska. I would've put two and two together and then I would've moved to the Yap Islands.

Rach pick up — Rach pick up — Rach pick up…

Unable to ignore the annoying outgoing ringtone Meghan had recorded for her incoming calls to me, I glanced at my cell way over there on the floor. If I didn't answer now, she'd keep calling until I did. So I leaned over the edge of my bed, stretching until I could reach my phone.

"You're not checking your email."

I flopped back on the bed and threw an arm over my eyes. I should've buried my phone and gone back to bed, or caught the cable car to one of those all-you-can-eat sushi places, or had a lovely sob day in front of the Lifetime Movie Network.

Instead, I allowed Meghan's voice to fill the space between my ears. She was still on cloud nine over her new dude. I activated the speakerphone and let her drone on as I massaged about a gallon of clary sage oil onto my temples, all while trying to figure out how I was going to dodge my sweet new intern.

Wentworth.

As I sat on the phone with her, chewing off my gel nail polish, I knew it was high time to unload the whole Oliver saga. Meghan was my best friend, she could help. Well, maybe not *help*, but she was a great listener.

"He smells so sexy, Rach, like a millionaire lumberjack. I could easily turn into his love slave, if he'd let me."

Well, she was usually a great listener. On second thought,

now was probably not the best time to bring it up, not until Meghan had a few more Diet Cokes in her system or until Rad took care of her sexual frustration.

The thought suddenly dawned on me that maybe Oliver Wentworth wouldn't remember me—or wouldn't remember me with hard feelings. I pushed myself up in bed, feeling a tiny twinge of hope. Just because I'd thought about him around a thousand times over the past six years didn't mean *he* had. Men got over things quickly. Like ex-girlfriends. And chicken pox.

A controlled environment like idiot Tim's wretched party might just be the perfect setting for a reunion to take place. I couldn't help imagining what Oliver Wentworth might look like today—which caused my heart to do two complete somersaults. Sarah said he was a "hottie."

Well, duh. If he was a supreme hottie back when I knew him, what did the man-sized Oliver look like?

Absolutely gorgeous, of course.

My stomach did a belly flop when I remembered that Roger planned on making an appearance at Tim's. Roger and Oliver in the same room, breathing the same muggy San Francisco air. Cue nightmare.

Slamming my eyes shut, I flopped back on my pillows.

Chapter Thirteen

Bruce reached out like he was about to touch my hair, but then stopped. "It looks different," he said as we hovered over a first draft, large print ad for a Tahoe casino that was spread across the conference room table. "Nice."

I noticed his hand move again so I gave it the eye. Our team had just gone through a rigorous Code of Conduct training, and he dropped his meaty paw.

"Thanks." I tucked some loose strands behind my ears.

"And you're—" He leaned across the table and actually sniffed the air in front of me. "Is that new perfume?"

Me thinks someone needed another COC refresher.

I cleared my throat and straightened, making sure he couldn't see down my shirt. "It's aromatherapy, regular perfume irritates my skin."

He sniffed again. "What do I smell on you?"

"Grapefruit and wild orange."

Moron Bruce actually cocked an eyebrow and growled.

What a pig. It made me shiver and pull back even farther.

"Hot date tonight?"

"Party at a friend's," I answered, unwilling to divulge personal information to a guy who was as sensitive as a steaming pile of Sydney's poo. "No big deal." I circled a mis-spelled word with my red felt-tipped pen.

Bruce glowered down at the circled word, and we fell into silence. When we were done, he rolled up our drafts and settled his gaze on me. "Whoever you're out to catch better watch out—he's about to get hooked, baby."

Gross.

I tried not to let him spoil my mood. I'd been cheerful all day, and I was seldom overly cheery at work. I wasn't sure if it was because it was Friday or because Claire hadn't scowled at me since before lunch or if I was actually looking forward to Tim's party.

At T-minus two hours until the end of the workday, the evening plans were finally set. Sarah—who I didn't have the heart to ditch—was going to call me when she got close to the office, and then we were meeting Roger and Meghan at an Italian restaurant a few blocks from my building. From there, we would head to North Beach and Tim's place.

My stomach twisted anxiously as I swiveled in my chair, unable to focus on the assignment on my screen. I tapped a pen against my keyboard then struck the X key over and until it filled the whole Word document. I pushed back my chair and stood, pacing a track around my tiny cubical.

Out the window, I could see a corner of the Embarcade-ro that lead to AT&T Park. I stared at it for a while, remem-bering the time Oliver won us tickets to a Giant's baseball game. I was jazzed at finally being at the stadium, but I'd been twitchy and paranoid through our whole date, knowing the camera was bound to sneak a shot of us together and Roger would find out about it. What an untrusting coward I'd been. Had I grown out of that?

Since Oliver, I'd never had to test love, or rather, test how I would do in another intense relationship. Would I lose balance again? Or had the mistakes I made six years ago taught me a lesson?

Done pacing, I sat at my desk and checked emails. A message from Krikit. I couldn't face it, so I scrolled through Pinterest and Instagram, trying to keep my mind busy. Around five thirty, I grabbed my purse and headed for the ladies' room. Leaning over the sink, I studied myself in the mirror.

Huh. I tilted my head, a little surprised by how non-dead I looked.

Despite not sleeping soundly the last week, the habitual circles under my eyes had miraculously faded, and thank goodness for new BB cream from a tiny shop in Japantown that worked like magic. The coral blush sweeping up my cheeks was in full bloom, probably because I couldn't make myself calm down.

Normally a bit frizzy and hyper from humidity, my dark hair was swingy and glossy for a change. I'd taken the time to run a screaming-hot flat iron through it that morning and added this spray stuff my beautician back in Dallas had been begging me to use. Wistfully, I ran my fingers from scalp to tips, wondering if this was what Jennifer Aniston's hair felt like.

This was the best and most put-together I'd looked in a while. Meghan warned me that she was going to cast an anti-intimidating glamor on me. Maybe she hadn't been joking.

Properly dotting it on my upper lip first, I applied then

smacked the shiny tinted gloss I brought along for the occasion. The lady at the Clinique counter said it brought out my creamy skin tone. When I was done, I blew a kiss at my reflection, causing another self-inflicted blush to spread across my cheekbones.

I couldn't help strutting as I made my way back toward my cubical. A welcomed burst of self-confidence put an extra sway in my strut, and I was actually excited about what tonight had in store. More importantly, I was smiling ear to ear.

I knew this because I felt the exact instant my smile dropped.

"All you *blankety-blanks* better get your *blankety-blanks* out of the *blankey-blank-blank* and do the *blankety-blank-blank-blank*!"

Wow. Bruce was in rare form, having to actually make up new profanity as the standards were insufficient for the occasion.

"Do you *see* this *stack*?" He was shouting into the face of a trembling junior sales exec assigned to the Vondome account. My account. "They all have to be postmarked by *tomorrow*. Signed, sealed, *delivered*. And *where* are my *proofs*? We're not leaving until they're done *all over again*."

The sales exec looked like she was ready to cry. I was about to tiptoe to my cubical and grab my jacket when came the one word I dreaded the most from Bruce:

"Rachel!"

Okay, so I wasn't great at my job—I was first to admit this. But I was trying, I was learning, and no one busted their ass more than me; late nights and long hours under the tutelage of Moron Bruce. Taking this job had been a huge step that I wasn't certain I'd been ready for.

But this thing with the missing Vondome proofs—that was *not* my fault. Any other night, I would've been fine with working late and taking Bruce's verbal abuse. But tonight?

First, I placed a call to Meghan. "We told you to quit that job!" was all she had to say. Next, I texted Sarah. She was already en route to the office to do some filing until I was ready to go. I told her to stay away, far away! If Bruce saw her, she'd be trapped. Lastly, I called Roger to let him know I'd be late and the three of them should eat without me, but to keep their cells close so I could call when I was done.

Vondome was my project. I worked extra hard, extra efficiently, helping anyone I could from every department involved, running the stairs from floor to floor, hoping to speed the process along.

Around eight o'clock, the building's AC decided to shut off. Heat from the concrete jungle below hit like steam from a sauna. My hair went simultaneously flat and frizzy. Mascara and eyeliner pooled under my lower lashes, causing the *extremely* sexy "raccoon eyes" effect.

Everyone was sweating and ornery and aggravated. No one wanted to be working late on a Friday. My last phone call—with the last of my hopes of getting out alive—was to Roger around eleven. I got his voicemail, which made me feel even worse.

The pathetic, whiney side of my brain took over. *They're all off having an amazing time without you*, it said.

In a city of over eight hundred thousand, it seemed like I was the only car driving east on Market Street as I headed home at midnight. I didn't know who I loathed more: Bruce for being a moron, or myself for believing that my sucky personal life actually had the chance of taking a turn.

Chapter Fourteen

The next morning, everything felt achy and off, though nothing specific. I was hungover without the benefit of alcohol to drown the memory. My head pounded and rang, worse than when you're flying in an airplane and your inner ears won't decompress.

Around nine, I lost all hope of lying in bed any longer when the sound of "Back in Black" seeped out from under my brother's bedroom door. The AC/DC meant Roger was in a good mood. And that just plain pissed me off.

That must've meant he'd had a good time at the party last night. He was obviously awake, so I could've knocked on the door and asked him what I'd missed. I stood outside his room, going as far as making a fist.

But my palms got all clammy just thinking about what he might say.

Unwilling to remain in brooding solitude, I located Sydney's leash and together we hit our favorite dog/bike/

jogging trail that wound around Golden Gate Park. There was no way I was jogging, though. I could barely stagger.

The sunshine seemed extra bright for so early in the morning. The grass was green from recent rain, and the sky shone bright blue. It might've been a lovely day had I the desire to enjoy it. Helmeted bikers whizzed past, as well as a procession of random exercisers either on foot or on various wheeled contraptions. It took genuine stamina to hit the hilly miles of the park, especially this morning when everything felt uphill.

Not far into our walk, Sydney stopped to sniff a rock, so I took the opportunity to plop down on the grass off to the side of the trail. Leaning back on my hands, I yawned so wide it hurt the corners of my lips. Too many days of restless sleep and self-induced mucho stress were catching up to me.

My sweat-dried then slept-on hair was loose and hanging wildly over my shoulders, probably matching how hideous my unwashed face felt. Meghan had told me once that she loved the natural Rachel; that I looked best with wavy "beach hair" and hints of last night's makeup. But everyone knows only supermodels can pull of that "morning after" look.

As I sat there taking a breather, watching Sydney scratch around a cluster of purple flowers, I observed the parade of runners trotting past. They looked trim and fit, taking the hills with no problem, while I felt my backside sink deeper into the ground. I decided to let one more pair of beautiful, Special K-eaters pass before puppy and I returned to the flow of traffic.

I hadn't thought to bring sunglasses and was squinting into the sun while noting the oncoming couple. She looked all healthy and springy, and the guy was tall with nice shoulders. I moved farther off the trail, about to let them pass. Until I heard a familiar voice.

"Nooo. Stop." Followed by breathless laughter. "You wouldn't! You *swear* you wouldn't!" Megs. I couldn't help snorting, wondering how long it had been since she'd willingly exercised on her own.

Knowing Meghan, if I didn't pull her focus, she probably wouldn't notice me. But since I'd already scooted off the grass, I took the high road. Sort of. I extended one leg across the path in a pretend attempt to trip the approaching duo. Seeing my barricade in the nick of time, they knocked into each other, nearly falling onto the grass beside me.

Catching Meghan's startled expression set me into a fit of mad giggles, and I rolled back on the grass, cackling out loud and clutching my stomach. Nothing like a good belly laugh. Meghan marched toward me, while her guy was turned the other way, leaning over to pick up the baseball cap that had fallen off his shaved head.

Ahh, so I was about to meet the infamous Rad.

"Devil woman," Meghan hissed, glaring down at me. "You could've *killed* us."

I couldn't respond because I was still caught in the throes of giggle hysteria as her shadow darkened my view of the morning sky.

"Fine, laugh away," she continued, while Sydney barked at her protectively. "Your little doggie can't defend you. I know where you live and I've seen where you sleep." Her face finally broke into a smile and she grunted a laugh, tightening her ponytail. "It's awfully early for you to be up, isn't it?"

I rolled onto my knees and wiped the corners of my eyes. "Funny, I was about to say the same to *you*. I didn't think you knew this trail existed. You never come out here when I want to go for a run."

"Yes, I do." She kicked my shoe, which was probably supposed to be a subtle request for me to play along, though Meghan had never grasped subtlety. "I run here all the time. *Remember*?"

I shaded my eyes from the sun and coughed a laugh. "Uhh, sure, Megs. Whatever you say."

It was right about then that I glanced past my best friend's shoulder and took note of her running date, who was standing frozen in place, purple Colorado Rockies baseball cap between his hands. Staring at me.

You know that scene in *Jaws* when that little boy is getting devoured by the shark amid a geyser of blood? Spielberg did that cool "forward tracking, zoom out" shot on stunned Police Chief Brody's face. Everything around him is pulled forward while *he* seems to be pulling away. Spielberg said the purpose of the shot was to give a sense of dizzying vertigo or a "falling away from yourself."

Which was exactly how I felt. I was falling away, but with perfect tunnel vision of the subject.

Pressure built inside my head. It was going to explode in the blink of an eye...in the blink of a pair of very familiar metallic gray eyes.

The guy made a sound that, in any other circumstance, would've sounded like a low, hissing curse word. But I knew it was my name he'd quietly hissed between his teeth.

"Hey. *Rach*." Meghan kicked my shoe again, harder.

I shifted my eyes back to her, woozy and dazed. "Huh?"

"Why aren't you blinking?"

I blinked twice for her benefit, causing my mascara-smeared eyes to burn. I blinked again and looked past her shoulder at Oliver Wentworth. Six years older, but I'd know him anywhere, those eyes and mouth, those shoulders and hands. I even knew his knees.

"*Rach*," Meghan repeated, causing me to flinch. "This is Rad."

Oliver took a step toward me. I recoiled, sinking deeper into the grass.

"You know," Megs added, sotto voce, "the one I told you about."

"Hi," Oliver said to me, sounding a little winded and a little...something. He wore a bright blue T-shirt, the sleeves straining over his biceps, and long black shorts, the word *Creighton* printed in white block letters over one knee. I found myself studying his workout gear longer than necessary, because it struck me as really odd that I didn't recognize either piece of clothing. Which—I know—made no sense.

I couldn't move. Couldn't breathe. Polite convention dictated I was to shake his hand or whatever, but, "Um, hello," was all I had.

"Rachel and I grew up together." Meghan lunged into a calf stretch then pointed her toes, probably something she'd seen on an exercise DVD. "She was *supposed* to be at Tim's last night but got stuck at work. I think I told you that."

"Only about ten times," Oliver said, looking at me and lifting a pleasant smile.

No, it wasn't pleasant—dammit. It was heart-stopping, just like in college whenever his silvery eyes settled on me.

My head felt heavy but light, and the pit of my stomach

was a cyclone of heat. How did my body remember exactly how to respond to his presence? After my heart was done with its stopping, it went into spasms, trying to beat its way up my throat.

"I did *not* tell you ten times, Rad." Meghan swatted his arm playfully.

I'd almost forgotten she was standing there. Between us.

Oliver's eyes left me and slid to her. He smiled dotingly. I knew that smile by heart, but I'd never witnessed him giving it to another girl. It was so out of context it made my stomach twinge with jealousy.

"I'm coming over tonight, remember?" Meghan said to me.

"Right." I shifted my weight to stand, but feared my legs were about as sturdy as rubber bands, so I stayed put, petting manically at Sydney's head. "To do what?"

"Rog is helping me with my Spanish accent for an audition. Gotta nail these lines. Her brother Roger is like a super genius at languages," she explained to Oliver.

He looked at me again. "Your brother Roger. Huh." He scratched his chin. "Wasn't he the student body president at USF? I think I ran into him on campus once."

Hi. I'd like to die now.

"Uh." I rubbed my nose. "Yeah, that's him."

Had he really forgotten who Roger was, or was he trying to be funny? Or torture me?

"I keep forgetting you went there, too, Rad," Meghan said. "Such a small world."

"Getting smaller by the minute." After the side note, Oliver looked away. Had his face turned just a tiny bit pink? It was probably from exercise. I didn't need a mirror to know my face was an extremely attractive beet red. "Meghan, we should keep moving if you want to make it five miles." He shifted his weight back and forth like an athlete whose muscles were cooling, forcing me to take quick note of his leg muscles. Good grief.

"Oh, yes." Megs jogged in place, her springy ponytail bouncing up and down. "Gotta run those five miles."

More than ready for them to leave, I tried to steady my heart and my breathing, but they were both out of control. It was too hot. Too stifling. Was San Francisco in the middle of a heat wave? I pressed a hand to the back of my neck then ran it across my throat and clavicle, again and again.

"So, Rach, I'll see you—" Meghan's gaze whipped back to me in a double take. "Rachel," she whispered, leaning toward me. "What are you doing?"

I flinched at her accusatory tone. "Nothing. I didn't do anything."

"Have you seen yourself? You're all dewy and tousled and…" She snickered through her teeth, lowering her voice another notch. "And you're touching yourself…like you're thinking about sex."

I dropped my hand from my throat. "*What*?"

"Seriously." She nodded at me. "Is that one of Roger's T-shirts? It's way too big, and since when do you go commando upstairs? I can totally see your…"

I fisted the front of my shirt, pulling it back in place from where it had slid off my shoulder, covering the part of my boob I'd just displayed to the world.

"Better." She straightened and returned to the trail. "Bye, Rach," she chirped. "Call me later."

I lifted a hand to wave good-bye then glanced in Oliver's

direction. He was bent over, facing the other way while petting Sydney, who'd wandered from my lap. Before I could even exhale, he pivoted a one-eighty, and our faces were two feet apart.

"Nice to *see* you, Rachel." His gaze flicked from my eyes to the top of my V-neck that I held together in one fist.

I felt a charge at the back of my neck, under my hair, in the air around my head. Without another word, he straightened and jogged away.

It wasn't until Sydney pulled on her leash that I realized I hadn't moved. When I managed to make it to my feet, it was much warmer outside. How long had I been paralyzed on the side of the trail?

Securing the leash in one hand, I pressed my other hand over my eyes, trying to decide if what just happened actually did happen, or if it was one of my funky dreams. I stared down at the patch of grass where Oliver had been standing. Could I still see shoe imprints?

So, Rad was Oliver. Perfect.

My best friend had the hots for Oliver. Double perfect.

Welcome home, Rachel.

Besides Chris Pine and that one singer in Backstreet Boys, Meghan and I had never gone after the same guy. Not that we were now. I'd known Oliver a million years ago, and I probably hadn't made the best second impression by lounging on the grass, looking—as Meghan insinuated—like I probably used to look right before Oliver and I had...

Gah! Way to stay classy, Rach.

Chapter Fifteen

The classic rock continued all morning. After an extra-thorough shower in an attempt to scrub the events of the running trail off my skin, I left home, driving without a destination, though it wasn't a surprise when I ended up across the bridge at *Another Time & Place*.

A lovely punch of spice and citrus invaded my nostrils as I entered the store. Simply being in the same room with so many aromatherapy wonders was enough to ease my tensions. I grabbed a few sticks of beeswax candles, but what I was really after was more oil.

"Hey. Rachel, right?" Spring came out from the back.

"Hi. And you're Spring. Hard to forget a name like that."

"We've got my mother to thank." She rolled her eyes. "So what can I get for you? We've got some—" She stopped at the sound of something crashing behind her. She glanced at the set of salon-style double doors that led to the back office, but didn't move to investigate.

"Do you need to check on that?"

"That?" She waved a hand. "No, I know what that is. It's nothing."

"Springer." A man's voice came from the back, then the swinging salon doors swung apart. "Have you seen my other— Oh, hey." It was the argyle sweater guy from before. He wasn't in argyle today, but a suit. Or rather the bottom half of a suit. His top half consisted of an unbuttoned, untucked white shirt with a dark blue tie hanging loose under the collar. Why did it seem I always stumbled upon these two in the middle of…I don't know.

"Wasn't aware you had a customer," he added, going to work on the buttons.

"This is a store. Of course I have customers." She glanced at me. "I have a paper due and we were, um, ya know, editing."

"Cool." I nodded, not needing gory details. "Hi." I waved at the guy, thinking it would be more awkward if we tried to pretend like I didn't notice him standing there half dressed.

"Henry, this is Rachel," Spring said. "One of my highly valued Naturally Pure customers."

"Nice to meet you." He finished the last button. "You're into oils, too?"

"Yeah. And aren't you into cranberries?"

His glance shifted to Spring. "Honeycutt." He narrowed his eyes at her. "You will so pay for that later." He kissed her on the forehead, gave one of her little braids a tug, then disappeared into the back.

I looked at Spring and we both laughed. "Sorry," I said. "I hope I didn't embarrass you—or him. It was too easy."

She waved me off. "Believe me, Henry Knightly doesn't get embarrassed. His sister runs a relationship blog and I'm pretty sure he tells her everything. Anyway, he shouldn't be such a cynic about the holistic lifestyle." She leaned against the counter. "And *he's* into oils, too. He just won't admit it."

"I had a boyfriend who loved Citrus Joy on me. He said it made me smell like Fruity Pebbles."

"That's hot." Spring moved to the display. "You should totally stock up."

I pictured Oliver's face from this morning, when I'd caught him not-so-subtly checking out my wardrobe malfunction, and his secretive smile that followed. Then I gave myself a mental head-thwap. No, Rachel. Just—no.

"We're not together anymore."

"Too bad. I'll bet the chemical remembrance of childhood sugar cereal was a ginormous turn-on for him."

"Yeah, it was." The weight of a small mountain sat on my chest. Just then, my cell rang. "Sorry." I pulled it from my purse and checked the face. Sarah. Speak of the freakin' devil. I declined the call.

It wasn't *her* fault, but simply looking at the name on my caller ID made me twitchy. A few seconds later, my phone pinged with voicemail. I walked toward the display of jewelry while I played the message, gnawing on my knuckle.

"Hi Rachel. It's Sarah Wentworth. I just wanted to see how you're doing. So sucky you got stuck at work. We really missed you last night. Really. My brother dropped by—I told you he was, right? I met a lot of new people. Meghan and your brother and Tim. Seriously, everyone's so friendly. Thanks again for inviting me." A pause. "So, I was wondering, I mean, I know it's Saturday and I'm sure you already have plans tonight, but if not, do you want to hang out? No biggie. Give me a call back when you can."

Why did she have to be so damn sweet?

"Bad news?"

I glanced at Spring rearranging pamphlets on the front counter.

"Your face," she added. "It's all frowny."

"Not bad news. Just…weird."

She narrowed her eyes. "Hmm. That's worse than bad. Guy trouble?"

"Sort of." I shrugged. "Well, yes. *Definitely* guy trouble."

"They're such children, aren't they? I mean, seriously, if you don't agree with everything they say, even if their facts are *clearly* wrong—"

"I can hear you, babe," Henry called from the back.

Spring lifted her chin. "I know you can, babe," she replied. "Here." She handed me a bottle. "Try some Jubilation. It's an elevating blend." She leaned her elbows on the counter. "I actually met the chemist who invented it, and she told me it's meant to duplicate the release of endorphins and pheromones, like a burst of straight estrogen."

I opened the bottle and took a sniff. It was interesting, familiar. "Endorphins? Like after you exercise?"

"No, more like after you…" She lifted an eyebrow.

"Oh."

"Yes, *oh*, as in…"

"Ohhh," I repeated, catching her drift. I took another whiff. "I can't put my finger on what it smells like, but it reminds me of…"

"I *know*." Spring grinned. "That's the point."

"Spring." Henry held open one swinging door, fully dressed, tie in a perfect Winsor knot. "I better not find any of that on your nightstand."

"Of course not, babe." He nodded and disappeared. "I don't need it," she added in his direction. Then she looked at me and whispered: "I really don't." She fanned her face. "So this guy problem you're having, what's the deal?"

I sighed, desperate to discuss it with someone. Spring was safe, she wouldn't know who I was talking about. "Okay, well, long story short, someone I dated ages ago is back in my life. But not really back, just kind of back."

"In a good way?"

"I'm not sure yet. It didn't end well with us—at all. And now I'm accidentally friends with his sister, and when I ran into him this morning for the first time in six years, I inadvertently flashed him my boobs, and I'm pretty sure my best friend is in mad lust with him."

"Frack," Spring said. "Good thing I have an oil for that."

I smiled. "I thought you might."

A short while later, I left with another stash of oil and the address of a good bar in Nob Hill. Henry's recommendation. I sat in my car and sandwiched my cell, needing to reply to Sarah about tonight.

Meghan was coming over later for takeout, then to practice her conversational Spanish with Roger. Unless she had a sudden date with "Rad," of course—gah. My stomach clenched. There was no reason Sarah couldn't come over. I scrolled down my missed calls and rang her before I lost my nerve.

Back at the apartment, I scoured my bathroom top to bottom. Later, I booted up my laptop, sifting through my Yahoo inbox. A nice long email was waiting from Krikit. I replied thoroughly to my sister's message, even attaching a few choice photos of George Michael, in case she was having a bad day.

Just before the girls were due to arrive, I rang the neighborhood Chinese place and ordered an array of greasy-delicious food therapy. An hour later, half of the food was gone.

"What does your fortune cookie say?" Meghan asked Sarah from across the coffee table where we gathered. "And remember, you have to add 'in bed' at the end of the fortune."

I gave her a look. "Are we thirteen?"

She tossed a wonton at me. "It's part of the fun, loser."

Sarah was looking down, silently re-reading her mystic message.

"What does is say?" Meghan repeated, noting our new friend's blush.

"Umm." Sarah shifted. "It says, 'Excitement and intrigue follow you closely wherever you go.'"

"*In bed*," Meghan tagged on.

"That totally bugs." I stabbed my half-eaten egg roll with one chopstick. "That's not even a fortune. A fortune is supposed to forecast something to come, not tell you what's currently happening."

"Does yours forecast anything?" Sarah asked Meghan.

"It says, 'A closed mouth gathers no feet.'"

"*In bed*." Sarah shrieked, and the two of them dissolved in laughter. "What's yours say, Rach?"

I cracked open my cookie with one hand, already sensing the fortune was going to be something I didn't want to hear. "Umm." I squinted, pretending to focus on the teeny font. "It says, 'If you want a rainbow, you must put up with a little rain.'" I lifted my eyes while wadding the tiny slip of paper into my fist.

"In bed?" Sarah said, confused.

"Yeah." I twisted my lips and shrugged. "Doesn't make sense. Who wants ice cream?"

"That's a crock," Meghan cut in. "That's a Dolly Parton song."

My neck felt hot and splotchy. Dammit. I knew I'd heard that phrase somewhere. So much for coming up with my own fortune on the fly. Some creative writer I was turning out to be.

"Crappy fortunes, right?" My voice sounded high and strangled, and I slipped the wadded paper into my pocket, knowing I'd probably black out if I attempted to read to them what my fortune really said: "A past love will send you a sign of affection."

In bed.

Nice joke, cookie.

After a single knock, Giovanna barged through the front door. Without so much as a hello, she strode directly to us, sank to the floor between Sarah and me, and started picking at the leftovers on our plates. It was after nine at night, yet she wore round, black sunglasses and her dark hair was in a twist on top of her head, looking *very* Holly Golightly.

"Hungry much?" I chuckled.

"Starving."

Sarah, who'd yet to meet Gio, leaned away, looking rather terrified at our local goddess of fabulous.

"Didn't you go out to dinner with what's-his-head?" I asked, sliding over the plum sauce so she wouldn't have to reach. "Enrico, was it?"

"*Enzo* was tonight," Meghan corrected.

"Didn't he feed you, Gi? Oh, sorry." I waved around the table by way of introduction. "Giovanna, Sarah. Sarah, Gio."

Sarah tried to smile. "Nice to, umm…"

Giovanna never stopped chewing, but was courteous enough to lift her sunglasses, make eye contact with Sarah, and nod. "Too petrified to eat," she finally said, and then added something in French I didn't understand. A drop of soy sauce was smudged on her chin.

While Sarah and I cleared the plates, Meghan disappeared into Roger's room to practice Spanish. When she finished an hour later, Roger took all the leftover food and made himself a late-night picnic in the kitchen, heckling us when the conversation turned to Pitt versus Clooney. Gio was on her back under the coffee table, sunglasses still in place, snoring softly, while Sarah was in my room looking through my books, leaving Megs and I to sprawl across the couch and flip through my DVR.

"You didn't tell me you knew Rad," she said.

The remote control slipped out of my hand. "Did he say we knew each other?" I asked in my best totally casual voice.

"He said you met freshman year."

"Long time ago." I made a show of pointing the remote at the TV, but the channel wasn't changing. Then I noticed it was pointing backward.

"That's what he said, too." Meghan reached for the bowl of pretzels between us. I pushed it over. Sarah reentered the living room carrying three novels. "He said he was surprised he even recognized you."

Sarah plopped on the couch next to me. "Are you ladies talking about a *guy*?"

For the life of me, I did not know how to answer. Even Meghan appeared uncharacteristically tongue-tied as the question—and the name of its answer—hung in the air.

"Um, your brother." I rubbed my nose. "We were saying—"

"You know Ollie, Rachel?"

I shrugged, feeling all sorts of weird. "Kind of." My cheeks were about to burst into flames, so I did some slow yoga breath through my nose, trying to stop the oncoming blush, which probably made it worse. "We met at USF—a *long* time ago," I added, even more casually, waving my hand in the air to display the appropriate breeziness.

"Seriously?" Sarah slid closer. "Why didn't you tell me you knew him when we were talking about him at dinner the other night?"

"I didn't know it was... I wasn't—"

"That's Rad's name?" Gio startled us all. After the boatload of carbs she'd just inhaled, I thought she was down for the count. "Ollie?"

"Oliver," I corrected automatically, then concentrated on the remote again. Wowzers, there're just *so* many buttons, weren't there? "I guess he goes by Rad."

"That started when he transferred to State," Sarah said. "We never call him that at home." She swished her long, chestnut hair. It was the same color as Oliver's before he'd shaved it off. And her eyes were the same light gray and shape as his. I was so clueless.

"Which poor star of *Ocean's Eleven* you talking about now?" Roger asked, appearing out of nowhere. "Or do I want to know?"

In a burst of what could only be called a "desperate attempt to change the subject," I flung the remote across the room. It hit the wall and the batteries flew out. "Oops, slipped." I slid to the floor, fumbling for the four double-A's.

"My brother, Oliver," Sarah said to Rog.

So much for distractions.

"He was at Tim's last night," she added, "and he was friends with Rachel in college." She looked at me with a big smile. "I love how we all know each other!"

I glanced up from all fours to see Roger peering down at me. We exchanged a brief glance while I felt puke lapping at the back of my throat. Not a word. Please.

"So!" I exclaimed—mostly because I didn't have another remote to throw. "Megs! W-why don't you break out the karaoke?"

"Only if you change the lyrics for me."

"Fine, sure," I said. "Which song?"

She rubbed her chin. "I want to make it hard for you this time. How about Maroon Five's *Misery*."

Happy with the successful change of subject, I sat cross-legged on the floor. "Okay, it's now titled 'I am Rotisserie,' and it's about a chicken in a restaurant window. Wait." I held up one finger. "Only it's not a chicken, it's a woman, and she's naked…naked in a restaurant window, covered in herbs." We all burst out laughing, even Rog. "Give me a second to come up with the chorus."

"Did you know Ollie writes music sometimes?" Sarah said. "He used to make up funny lyrics all the time. He'll think this is hilarious."

My laughter cut off mid-cackle. Oh, please never mention my name and naked chickens in the same sentence to Oliver!

"I'm gonna text him about it right now." She grabbed her phone and snorted a laugh. "Rotisserie. You're so funny, Rachel."

Chapter Sixteen

Work wasn't my favorite place to be the next few days. In fact, it was pretty impossible to concentrate on anything advertising-related. My mind kept going back to the jogging trail and my naked chicken song and watching Sarah text her brother all night.

During one of my lunch breaks, I started free-writing a scene—not set at the hilly trails of Golden Gate Park, but the paved and shady running paths along Katy Trail in uptown Dallas, where I used to go after work with the rest of the yuppie population. The chick in my story wasn't only sporting last night's melted makeup and frizzy hair when she ventured out to walk her dog the "hideous morning after," but she was also wearing last night's wrinkled cocktail dress—which I found much more funny than her brother's holey T-shirt. And she actually did trip the jogging couple, whom she didn't know. But also, she ended up leaving with the guy in the purple baseball cap.

My story: my happily ever after.

By the end of my lunch hour and the end of the twenty-page short story, I was giggling at the exploits of my girl hero, a Texas version of Bridget Jones. I'd forgotten how much fun creative writing could be. If only I could make my day job as enjoyable.

Claire's assistant buzzed my office phone. Last-minute meeting in five minutes. I grabbed my notebook and headed for the conference room, though for the next hour, I kept wondering why I was still invited to these things. No one ever listened to me.

"Rachel, what have you got?"

I looked up from the notebook page I'd been doodling on to find Claire and four other copywriters staring at me. "Oh, um, well…" I glanced at what I'd just written but then shook my head. "Pass."

Claire arched her thin eyebrows. "If you have an idea, by all means, speak up."

Silently, I read the tagline I'd scribbled then I couldn't help it, I pressed my lips together to hold back a very inappropriate laugh.

"What is it?" Claire dropped her pen. "You've got us intrigued."

"It's nothing. I was just free writing and—Bruce!" Suddenly, my notebook was gone and Bruce the Moron had it in his mitts. The fifth grade bully stealing my lunch.

He chuckled after scanning my scribbles. "Looks like she's more *creative* than we thought. Wait'll you hear what sweet little Ray-Ray thinks should be the branding for a ten-pack of high-end emery boards."

I sank into my chair and held a hand over my face, prepared for the oncoming mortification.

"Well, Rachel?" Claire said. "Tell us your tagline. Now." Why she hated me, I had no idea.

"Because"—I coughed when my throat went dry—"because sometimes…" Oh, hell. Get it over with. The rest of the tagline came out in a rushed mumble.

"What was that?" Bruce cupped his ear.

I blew out a breath and sat ramrod straight. "Because sometimes a girl likes it rough," I said, louder and more pronounced than necessary.

It was dead quiet, and I wondered how many trips it would take to my car to load my personal belongings after Claire fired me. Another hitch in the ten-year plan.

A weird snickering came from the other side of the table. It was Claire, laughing behind a hand. "Well, I admire your, uh, imagination, Rachel, but we should perhaps save that for another—more fitting—product." She swiveled in her chair, grinned, and recrossed her legs. "Now, who has the guts to follow that creative genius?"

I exhaled, never so relieved in my life. Aside from a couple of the douchy ad execs asking me out for drinks and snickering about how I liked it rough, the rest of the day flew by. It was Thursday, which meant Meghan and I were meeting at Pluckers for dinner and trivia night. Which also meant I'd taken public transportation to work instead of my car. As per our two-month tradition, I would hop a cable car up to Russian Hill and Meghan would drive us home at the end of the evening.

At 7:03 p.m., I'd claimed a coveted inside seat on a northbound cable car when my cell rang.

"Get off at Bay Street instead of Lombard," Meghan instructed before I'd finished clipping on my Bluetooth.

"Why?" Bay was only two stops away, so I grabbed the overhead bar, hauled myself to my feet, and did the monkey hand-over-hand toward the standing platform, trying not to fall over when the car came to a bumpy stop at the top of a hill. "You wanna meet somewhere else?"

"You know those awesome Victorians on Stockton across from that park with the weird tree where we saw that group of trannies?"

I laughed, knowing exactly where she meant. "Other side of Coit Tower?"

"Meet me there. The pink Victorian with the tall-ass stoop and blue stained glass on the third floor."

Just as I grabbed the vertical brass bar near the outside running board, the guy behind me started shoving against my back. There was no need for that, the car wasn't full, the next stop wasn't for another few minutes, and I wasn't in the mood to fall four feet and face-plant across the train tracks. I felt the need to turn and knee him where the sun don't shine.

"Megs," I said, suddenly annoyed by everything, "I'm starving. I thought we were eating."

"We are—chill." Meghan laughed, then she was talking to someone else. In answer to that someone's question, she said my name. The car jerked to a start, making my teeth rattle. I gripped the bar as my upper body swung out over the running board into empty space, wind whipping through my hair.

"Fine," I said after the car's momentum swung me back inside. "As long as I'm fed within eight minutes of arrival. I think I'm about to faint from hunger. I skipped lunch. Stupid Moron Bruce." I made a point of glancing over my shoulder at pushy guy. "You won't *believe* my day. Rachel needs fuel."

"Don't worry." Megs was whispering now. Noise from the street made it hard to hear so I pressed a hand over my Bluetooth. "And he cooks, too. Bet you didn't know *that* about him at USF."

"What?" The hand over my ear started to shake. "Meghan. Where exactly am I meeting you?"

The stoop had fourteen steps. I knew because I counted them three times from across the street. Pink Victorian: check. Blue stained glass on the third floor: check. Tall-ass stoop: check. It was part of a duplex, connected to a mint green house, mirroring the architecture exactly.

The minty house was cute, with a darker shade of green around the windows and outside moldings. But its twin—the pink house—was gorgeous. Instead of just plain paint, the six-inch moldings were carved wood, painted in intricate designs of blue, yellow, and purple. None of the windows were curtained, and the third floor's was not only blue stained glass, but it actually looked tie-dyed.

Even though the sun was almost set, the October air was humid, causing a drop of perspiration to trickle down my spine. This shook me awake. The last thing I wanted was to appear flushed-faced and moist like on the running trail, so I crossed the street and up those fourteen stairs.

The front door was dark mahogany with worn, thick grooves down the wooden grains. It was probably not the original door, though it looked ancient and well preserved. There were two built-in mailboxes, one labeled "Rennaker" in block letters, and the other read "Wentworth" in neat dude script that I found eerily familiar. I lifted a hand to knock, but lost my nerve.

Did I have another choice here? How about running away? Possibly. Jumping in front of oncoming traffic? How would that look?

Feeling another tingle of sweat under my hair, I made a fist and knocked.

When he opened the door, what would his reaction be? I braced myself, feeling way too unprepared to come face-to-face with the only guy I'd ever loved. Before I could tell my pounding heart that everything was cool, the doorknob started to turn from the inside.

Crap. Here we go.

It was Meghan. She grinned, looking happy and well groomed, while I hadn't brushed my teeth since breakfast and had crazy cable car hair. An automatic jolt of jealously, of my best friend, shot through me. It was a completely unfair emotion, but I couldn't help it.

"Get in here." She grabbed my arm.

There were a million ambiguous questions I wanted to hiss at her, like, "How could you do this to me?" and, "Don't you know how stupid I feel?" But I simply allowed myself to be pulled in.

The scent of fresh paint, new leather, and woodsy-smelling furniture was my first impression. The vestibule was small but bright, with a narrow staircase along the duplex wall for tenant number two. Apparently Oliver resided on the first floor, because Meghan led me past the second entrance and into the living room.

A dark brown couch and loveseat surrounding a coffee table were the only furniture. Victorian duplexes were never overly spacious, but these walls and ceiling were bright white, loft-style trendy, contrasting perfectly with the huge picture windows and original hundred-year-old wooden floors. I couldn't recall what Sarah told me her brother did for a living, but it seemed he wasn't struggling.

"Posh, right?" Meghan whispered. I realized I was ogling, so I quickly adjusted my expression to impartial. "These were refurbished four months ago. You should see the garden on the roof next door. There's an outside amphitheater with an awesome view of the bridge. Mucho romantico."

I opened my mouth but then shut it and made an "mmm" sound.

Off to the right of the living room was a small dining room table with four chairs, a pass-through window, and an open door leading to the kitchen. That was where noise was coming from: running water, a blender whirring, and the radio tuned to USF's student station. Meghan walked us that way, but I flinched and pulled back. So much for playing it cool.

"Hey, don't worry. You're not crashing our date or anything."

My stomach dropped—I hadn't even considered *that*.

"When I called Rad earlier, I told him we'd be up this way tonight. I invited him out, but he said to come over."

"Yeah, cool." I nodded. "I'm just going to put my stuff down. You go on ahead."

Meghan winked like we were in on the same scheme, then disappeared into the kitchen. I backed up, bumping into the couch behind me.

I swallowed hard, feeling a variety of distress. I let my purse slide off my arm and onto the floor but then picked it up and found my tiny bottle of Citrus Joy. If ever I needed to feel "elated," it was now. I shook a few drops into each palm, then wiped my hands over my throat. I took a deep breath, trying to slow everything the hell down.

Still worried about overheating in my layers, I peeled off my suit jacket. Underneath it, I wore an almost-too-sheer-for-public, pale pink camisole, and I briefly fretted that I'd look too post-coital wearing only that. But with my jacket removed, I felt so much cooler and lighter, and much less likely to go into heatstroke, so I kept it off.

I tugged at the bottom of my gray pencil skirt that ended just above my knees. I wished I wasn't still in my work clothes, and silently cursed Meghan for the hundredth time in ten minutes.

"Rachel."

I gasped and spun around, teetering on one high heel. Oliver stood in the doorway of the kitchen. His blue dress shirt was unbuttoned at the top, sleeves rolled up, and the tail of his still-knotted tie was tossed over one shoulder.

He looked…absolutely…making me want to…

"Hi." I swallowed, forcing myself to forget what I'd just been thinking. "Thanks for the invite." I wasn't sure why I was thanking him. In fact, I had no idea what I was doing there. "We usually go out to the"—I jerked my head to the side, pointing somewhere east—"on Thursdays."

"Meghan invited me to join you, but I didn't feel like going out. Do you mind?"

I lifted my eyebrows. "Mind?"

"Coming here…with…" His gray eyes glanced toward the kitchen. "I get the feeling she doesn't know."

"Yeah."

He blinked. "Oh. You *do* mind."

"No. I mean, no, Meghan doesn't know anything." I bit my lip. "I never told her about…"

He nodded, saving me the embarrassment of having to explain further. He glanced toward the kitchen again; apparently he didn't want to be overheard, either.

What was *his* excuse for wanting to keep our history a secret?

While pondering this thought, I took my first real look at the guy who was now called Rad. He was still nice and tall, a good six-foot-one. His face and his once-lanky, pre-man body had filled out, but not to the point of looking like he'd let himself go. On the contrary, he looked strong and fit and was probably in the best shape of his life. Those funny 1970s pop culture T-shirts he used to wear were replaced by dress pants, a dress shirt, and tie.

His metallic eyes were framed by long, dark lashes. It didn't surprise me that his wavy chestnut hair was shaved off. The Oliver I knew was a little insecure about his hair, but I'd always loved it. I loved touching it, running my hands up the back, curling my index finger around the longer strands in front. Understanding his insecurity and wanting to help, I used to gush on and on about what great hair he had, how it was my favorite physical trait about him.

What a silly, *juvenile* thing to do.

Now, hair or no hair, Oliver didn't look unsure about anything. He stood straight with a definite expression of confidence and intelligence. And yet—with his tie boyishly flipped over his shoulder like that—he also showed a hint of the devil-may-care liveliness I remembered.

I cleared my throat. "The subject never came up with her."

He tilted his head. "In six years?"

"Yeah." I touched the strap of my top, feeling flushed again.

"Oh." Oliver dropped his gaze to the floor. "Understood. You can have a seat. Dinner will be a few minutes." He turned and disappeared into the kitchen. I heard him and Meghan talking while I stood trapped in my personal nightmare.

What was understood? What was he talking about? What had I said to explain anything?

I hadn't moved when he came back out. He regarded me for a moment—still leaning on the back of his couch—before he tossed three black placemats on the table and slid three bowls into place. A moment later, he looked up.

"I didn't know." His eyes lowered as he straightened a spoon next to a bowl. "I mean, I didn't know what you'd like to eat. I hope gazpacho's okay. Mine is spicy," he explained, or maybe warned, as he set down another spoon, "I make it with jalapeños."

"That sounds good."

"I just have to add the ice and…"

I couldn't keep from chuckling under my breath.

"What?" He took a step forward.

"You—following a recipe. You used to burn toast on a regular basis."

He slid his hands into his pockets. "We both sucked on that front back then."

"I know." I laughed. "If it weren't for the cafeteria and free pizza delivery, we'd have starved."

He looked like he was about to say something else, but instead, he pulled back a slow smile. "Rachel Daughtry," he said, then ran a knuckle under his chin. Such a familiar gesture.

For a moment, it felt like time froze then whizzed us back six years. I was standing before the Oliver I knew, the one I was in love with. Every hair on my body, every nerve ending was experiencing total recall of exactly how I used to feel about him, and exactly what I used to do to express that.

Exactly.

My knees swayed and my vision blurred. Before I fell over, I tightened my grip on the couch behind me.

Oliver stood a few feet away, hands in his pockets. "Sarah told me—"

"What's next, Rad?"

We both flinched when Meghan appeared with a bread basket.

"Um." He closed his eyes and pressed a thumb along the bridge of his nose. "Nothing, thanks. I'll finish up."

The moment he was gone, Meghan slid to my side. "I could freaking die," she whispered in a rush. "He is absolutely the hottest thing I have ever seen. A gorgeous man cooking for me." She fanned herself. "Total sex fantasy, right? I'm marrying him, I swear I am."

"Yeah." I lifted a wobbly smile, staring toward the kitchen.

"I've no clue what he's making in there. He was chopping stuff and dropping it in a blender. He called it something Italian, but I can't—"

"Gazpacho." My gaze was fixed over her shoulder. All I could see were cabinets and shadows of someone moving. "It's a Spanish soup. Tomato-based. Served cold."

"Huh. Well, even if it tastes like floor, I'll praise him out the yin-yang." She glanced toward the kitchen with a hungry expression. But not food-hungry.

Coming here was a huge mistake.

"Do you know where the bathroom is?" I asked, needing a couple of minutes alone.

"Down the hall." She pointed. "I've already scoped out the place. If he wasn't so hot anyway, I'd marry him for this apartment." As I turned to leave without replying, she hooked my elbow. "I was kidding. You know I don't care about money. I care about what's under those suits he wears."

"Yeah." I offered one noncommittal chuckle. "Good one." Feeling a little wonky, I slid my arm out of her grip. "I'll be right back."

Unlike Meghan, I did not snoop around Oliver's bathroom. It was a half bath anyway, which meant he most likely never used it. If I was after personal evidence of what the twenty-four-year-old Oliver Wentworth was like, I wasn't going to find it behind the single cabinet in that bathroom. Instead, I kicked off my shoes and leaned against the sink, counting backward from three hundred, while inhaling the oil dabbed at the inside of my elbows.

I wasn't ready to go back out, but didn't want anyone to hail the fire department thinking I'd fallen in, so eventually, I slid into my heels and made my way toward the dining room. En route, I stopped to study an oil painting hanging in the hall. It was on canvas but not framed. With deep blues and golds, it reminded me of Van Gough's "Starry Night."

"She's awfully quiet." Oliver's lowered voice came from around the corner. He and Meghan must've been waiting for me at the table. Voices sure did carry in these old houses.

"I know." Meghan sighed, her voice just as low. "She wasn't always. She used to be hilarious, actually. But something changed. They talk about the freshman fifteen, well, she gained *ten*, but in *years*. I'm not surprised you said you barely recognized her the other day."

"Huh," Oliver said, then I heard him pop open a bottle.

"She came back that summer a different person," Meghan added. "I had to practically drag her around with me. It was sad."

I was afraid to move; hardwood floors in these houses creaked louder than a coffin at a haunted house.

"Did she…" Oliver's voice was quiet. "Did she ever tell you why?"

"She hardly talks about freshman year at all. Want me to pour the wine? Like I said, she was a different person, all anti-social and serious."

Oliver was silent. I was dying to see his expression. "Did she date?" he asked after a few moments.

I stiffened, not wanting to hear Meghan's answer, whatever it might be.

"We were both really busy in school. I remember her going out sometimes." She chuckled softly. "Actually, we used to joke that she had a secret boyfriend stashed somewhere. But she's never been like that. Now it's like she sees dating as a job—no fun. She's cynical about the whole thing."

"You've never asked her why?"

It was quiet. I wondered why Meghan was taking so long to answer.

"I've set her up with a few guys but she's not interested."

I was beginning to feel hot in the face. I couldn't believe Meghan was openly discussing my personal life—practically right in front of me. None of it was untrue, but still.

I heard a chair scrape back. "She's got this ten-year plan for the future that she's sworn by since we were eighteen.

With that and the way she works herself to death at that stupid ad agency where they treat her like crap, it doesn't seem like she intends to get serious with anyone. Unlike me, I *love* dating. And I especially love when my dates cook for me."

Yeah.

I grabbed the knob to the bathroom door and pulled until it slammed shut. The painting I'd just been admiring shook on its hook.

"Rachel?" Meghan's voice held the tiniest hint of guilt. "That you?"

"Who else would it be?" Oliver answered. By the time I'd rounded the corner, he was pushing back from the table to stand. "Oh good, it is you. Otherwise I have a major mice problem."

"Just me," I said, trying to not appear like a girl who was way overworked, treated like crap, was cynical and sad about relationships, but had *never* had a secret boyfriend. I wasn't sure how that was supposed to look, so I just smiled and tucked some hair behind my ears. "Need any help?"

"We were waiting for you." Meghan slid into the chair across from Oliver. There was an empty chair beside her and beside him. For a moment, I didn't know which to take, until Megs glanced at the one beside her. I took the hint.

While Oliver ladled the soup and Meghan poured the drinks, I kept my mouth shut. Since Oliver had already noticed how non-talkative I was tonight, why spoil the illusion. So I listened to their conversation, enjoying the soup very much.

I'd had authentic Spanish gazpacho when I was younger. With the jalapeño peppers and what tasted like a splash of Worcestershire sauce, Oliver's was better than what I'd had in a granny's *cocina* in Seville.

"Where did you learn to cook, Rad?" Meghan asked, sawing off a hunk from a loaf of sourdough.

"College." He shot a quick glance my way and reached for his drink. "*Late* in college." He set down his glass without drinking, then ran a hand over the top of his head.

"Is that when you started shaving your head?" Meghan leaned her elbows on the table. Before he could answer, she continued with, "How often do you have to shave it?"

"Every other day."

"That's how often I shave my legs."

I wasn't sure why I decided to chime into the conversation with how often I shaved. Meghan and Oliver stared at me, each displaying a slightly different quizzical expression.

"I mean, I shave every day, but just one leg. Then I shave the other the next day. It's more Zen."

The words hung in the air like a bubble over my head.

"It was a joke," I said. You can always tell that a joke has fallen flat when you have to explain it. I was about to slide from my chair onto the floor then crawl away when Oliver burst out laughing.

"Every other day." He ran the back of his hand over his mouth. "That's funny—*clever*. You're still—" He cut himself off and his smile immediately vanished. In fact, the lightning-fast glance he shot me held anger more than anything. He grabbed his empty bowl and disappeared into the kitchen.

I watched him go. Oliver used to laugh at all my jokes, especially the ones that were particularly lame, like on the day we first met in the cafeteria and I'd made that super-lame crack about running for both Congress and the Senate. He claimed one of the things he loved best about me was my wit. He called my sense of humor sexy. Was he thinking the same thing now? And why would that suddenly piss him off?

"*Rachel.*" Meghan's hiss jerked my gaze away from the kitchen. "What the hell?"

"What?" Did I have that glazy "thinking-about-sex" look about me again?

"You're talking to Rad about your legs? In the *shower*?"

"Oh." I shook my head and reached for my glass. "S-sorry."

"Are you all right? You're acting weird."

I exhaled, wishing I'd told her about me and Oliver a zillion years ago, or at least before tonight. It felt too late to come clean now, like I'd been lying all this time on purpose.

"I'm okay." I held up my glass and clinked it against hers. "Too much caffeine, not enough sleep. Same old shizz."

"Well, no more shaving talk, okay? If Rad's going to think about anyone's naked legs, they should be *mine*. And stop being so funny and—"

Oliver came back to the table with some napkins and sat down, just as abruptly as when he'd left. It might have been just me, but it felt like he was giving me the cold shoulder. Which was fine, whatever. I wasn't supposed to be pulling his attention. It wasn't *our* date.

For the next little while, Meghan had us engrossed in a story about the director of her current movie project. She hovered over the table, drawing a picture of the complicated set. Just as I leaned forward, I shifted my gaze to Oliver. His elbows were on the table and he was also leaning toward Meghan's sketch. But his eyes were on me.

When I met his gaze, he didn't look away, as though he'd been expecting me to look at him. There were questions behind his gray eyes—I recognized the strong, silent expression. In that moment, I was willing to answer anything he asked of me. His lips began to peel apart like he really was about to say something. My heart beat in my temples, waiting. But he cleared his throat and looked away, tugging at the neck of his shirt, pushing up his sleeves.

This was a nervous tick in the Oliver I used to know. But how could that be now? He was cooking dinner for Meghan and I was the pathetic third wheel.

It took a few moments for me to realize I was still staring at the side of his face. I swallowed and glanced toward Meghan, nodding at whatever she was saying.

Maybe it was the silvery moon cresting through the picture window behind him or his zesty-delicious soup that lingered on my tongue, but that look we shared shook my soul like the '92 earthquake.

I'd broken up with Oliver while I was still in love with him and never got over it, never really moved on. Every other guy who'd come into my life, guys I might have fallen for, could never fight their way in. My heart had been closed off ever since that sunny spring morning freshman year.

If I wanted to move on—which I did!—then I needed to write an ending to the Oliver Wentworth chapter in my book. Complete, total, healthy closure…before he married Meghan and I hated them both.

After this personal epiphany, Meghan didn't have to tell me twice to stay quiet and let her shine. I was too afraid to speak, anyway, nervous that I'd blurt something totally inappropriate. So I learned even more about her movie and some of the backstage romances going on. The girl really did share everything.

"Damn." Oliver looked at the clock on the wall. "It's almost midnight. I've got a conference call tomorrow so I'm working from home. I didn't think about how late it was getting."

"We should go." I pushed out my chair.

"Already?" Meghan glanced at her phone. "It's not that late."

"You can stay, I'll go." And now, please. Nothing more awesome than being a third wheel at the end of a date.

"You're going alone?" Oliver moved into my line of sight, looking unexpectedly concerned after practically ignoring me for the last two hours.

"I'll take a cab, it's cool."

"Do you think that's safe?" He looked at Meghan. "I thought you drove."

She didn't reply for a moment, probably trying to decide if she wanted to grab some alone time with her man at the cost of painting herself as an inconsiderate friend. Despite her earlier gossip session, Megs was not inconsiderate.

"I did," she said, brightly. "You're right, Rad. It's not safe to be alone this late at night. Rach, we'll both go."

I was about to point out that I used public transportation all the time, day and night, and I carried a king-sized can of pepper spray in my bag for such occasions. But I didn't want to ruin Meghan's chance at showing what a giver she could be.

"May I use your bathroom first?" she asked, probably wanting to make sure she hadn't left any closet doors unsnooped-through. After Oliver pointed her in the right direction, she added, "I think I need that soup recipe, Rad. I've been meaning to cook more at home. Maybe take a class.

Wouldn't that be fun?"

He disappeared into the kitchen and I sat on the arm of the couch. The room was empty and quiet and I felt conspicuous with only the sound of the ceiling fan above my head to break the silence.

"Too bad," Meghan's voice continued, though her footsteps slowed, probably stopping to investigate some closet. "Too bad you don't cook, Rachel. We could take the class together, but you hate touching raw food."

"I remember that," Oliver said, leaning against the kitchen doorway, looking all gorgeous and intense—like in my dreams. His voice was low, meant only for me to hear. "*You* were the one who burned our toast in the morning, Rachel. If I recall."

My stomach filled with butterflies and I took in a deep breath, ready to begin some kind of dialogue about our past with this hunky guy who lived in a pink house.

"We ready?" Meghan reappeared, fresh as a daisy. "Good night, Rad. Thanks for"—she smiled and wound a curly lock of her hair around a finger—"you know, everything."

"Sorry again that it's so late." His eyebrows pulled together as he glanced at the floor, looking and sounding apologetic. "The night got away from me, there was something else I wanted to—"

"It's no problem for me, since I'm not due at the studio until noon," Meghan said. "Rachel's the one with the early schedule."

"Don't remind me." I automatically started kneading my left temple. "I'm going to be dead tired in the morning and I have such a busy day with—" I cut myself off, knowing I did indeed sound like I was "working myself to death."

"Ya know what—screw it." I grabbed my purse and jacket. "I officially decide to play hooky tomorrow and go to the beach or the wine country. No wait, there's that twenty-four-hour spa in Calistoga with the volcanic mud baths. I'll start my weekend early and head there tonight." I slid into my jacket and pulled open the door. "Thanks for dinner. I'll see you guys later."

Before either of them had the chance to speak, I was out the door and down all those steps, heading toward the bus stop, finger on the trigger of my pepper spray.

True, I'd been meaning to try out that mud spa, but my exit had more to do with not wanting to witness how Oliver and Meghan said good-bye.

Chapter Seventeen

For a while, I didn't see Oliver very often—the odd museum outing or group trek to Alamo Square to picnic at the feet of the "painted ladies." Though I did receive steady, unrequested updates from Meghan and Sarah. *Ollie* was busy at work again. *Rad* said the funniest thing the other night. Once, Roger was sitting right next to me on the couch during one of Meghan's updates.

"She doesn't know?" he said to me after she'd left.

"No," I said.

"Have you two—"

"No."

More often than not, when I did see him, he was monopolized by Meghan or otherwise engrossed in conversation. We were never alone. He never came around. Sarah—his sister—had my phone numbers, knew where I lived. If he wanted to see me or talk to me, he could have. But he never reached out. Then again, neither did I.

The rare moments when we did happen to be sitting next to each other in a taxi van or happened to be at the bar waiting for drinks at the same time, he was polite, but no more stolen glances across the room. Whatever I'd felt at his house that night…I'd imagined it.

Oliver was over me.

Worse than that, it was as though we had no history at all.

A group of us were meeting to watch the parade and lion dancers in Chinatown one Saturday afternoon. I'd made sure Oliver wasn't coming before I'd agreed, and was surprised when I saw him standing on the curb along the parade route on Grant Avenue, leather jacket and jeans, sunglasses, and a huge smile as he chatted with Meghan and a few of our other friends.

I sucked in a breath, adjusted my purse strap over my shoulder, and joined them, doing my best to stay on the other side of the group from him. It was easier for me when I didn't give him the chance to snub me. Later, at Dim Sum Heaven, I had no choice of proximity, since I was last to our table and the waiter had to pull over an extra chair, right next to Oliver. After weather and traffic was all I got out of him, I stopped trying. Halfway through lunch, my stomach felt all knotty and I couldn't stop wringing my hands. After the third time I caught Oliver glancing at them with an annoyed expression, I kept them in my lap.

"You didn't eat the chicken, did you?"

I had to look twice to make sure he was actually addressing me. He glanced at my twitchy hand when I reached up to take a drink. It was red and splotchy.

"There're sesame seeds in that dish."

Someday
MAYBE

I flipped my hand over. Hives. I'd always had a minor allergy to sesame seeds, but I'd been so preoccupied by trying not to talk to Oliver that I'd forgotten to check what I was eating.

"Is your throat closing?" he asked in a quiet but rushed voice.

I swallowed, testing it out. "No."

He pushed back from the table a bit to get a better look at me. His eyes doing a quick assessment of my body made my heart thud. "Is the rash just on your hands?"

He was running down the checklist we'd done half a dozen times when I'd had an allergic reaction. I pushed up my sleeves. "Stops at my elbows."

"Do you have your Benadryl?" I nodded and went for my bag, but Oliver was already reaching for it. "Can we get some water here?" he asked as a waiter breezed by. Then he pushed my cup away. "No more black tea. You need to flush it out."

I was peeling the tiny pink pill out of its wrapper, about to thank him for being so observant and calm and kind, but when I looked up, he was moving to a chair on the other side of the table, switching places with his sister.

Disappointment weighed down on my shoulders. He wouldn't look at me.

"Hey." Sarah slid into Oliver's vacated chair at my side. "You okay?"

"Fine," I said, feeling a chill and nausea in my stomach that had nothing to do with allergies.

"Ollie said to…to keep an eye on you." She glanced at the pill in my hand. "Make sure you took that with two full glasses of water."

Tears pressed against the backs of my eyes. Taking extra-long to keep my chin tipped while swallowing the Benadryl, I blinked them away. For the rest of the meal, I kept trying to catch his attention. It finally dawned on me that, with Sarah at my side now, he was done worrying about me. After that, I couldn't look at him, either.

The following weeks brought a string of new dreams. There was the one when I fell down Alice's rabbit hole and, instead of Wonderland, I was in the first car on the Titan Scream Machine at Six Flags. As the car climbed the first hill, I realized I wasn't strapped in. My subconscious literally threw my sleeping body out of bed to wake up. Because, as everybody knows, if you die in your dream, you die for real.

Then there was the reoccurring dream that sent me hiking through dark woods trying to find my way to the white castle. With that rusty tin cup in my knapsack, I continued on until I came to a high stone wall. I needed to get to the other side, but as I looked down at my feet, I was wearing flip-flops. Not the proper gear for climbing straight up, even in a dream. The ground below was covered with thorns and sticker bushes.

"Trust me," my dream-self heard from the other side of the wall. *"Reach out and trust me. I'm here."* Like most interesting dreams, my alarm clock always woke me before I could find out who I was supposed to be trusting and reaching for.

A week before Christmas, Meghan, Gio, Sarah, and I were at my apartment watching one of Meg's "movies" while picking at two different cheese logs and cheering each other to good health with homemade holiday cider—Giovanna's Canadian recipe which was guaranteed to grow hair on our chests. Yikes.

"This job," Meghan reported as we watched her in a re-enactment of the Bubonic Plague, "paid my rent for three months *and* Scorsese's second-cousin-twice-removed direct-ed it." She glared at the screen. "But all the body makeup gave me a rash so I couldn't play Mary Queen of Scots the next week." She downed a Classic Coke then tossed the can near the vicinity of the trash.

"She was inconsolable for weeks." Gio patted her shoulder.

"It should've been my big break." Meghan accented her foul mood with a very unladylike belch. "Where's all the chocolate?"

"You ate it." I lounged back on the couch. "Aren't you supposed to be paleo these days?"

Megs lay prostrate across the floor, her arms out, stretching for her purse just out of reach. After a few moments of searching through its contents, she threw it aside and grabbed her jacket. "Ah-ha!" The look on her face was ecstatic as she pulled a Snickers from an inside pocket.

"I hope she gets cellulite for Christmas," Gio mumbled, staring at the TV where some actor in splotchy makeup was barfing in the bushes. She grabbed the remote. "We've seen this three times."

Sarah scooped up a handful of popcorn, then slid across the couch cushions toward me. "Did Ollie tell you?"

"Tell me what?" Meghan asked, even though Sarah had clearly addressed me.

Of course Oliver hadn't told me anything; we'd barely exchanged twenty words since lunch at Dim Sum Heaven. It wasn't entirely his fault. Just because we happened to be in love when we were practically kids didn't mean we had to be friends now. So much for my plan to be adult about it and make proper closure with transparent communication to everyone.

Sarah gazed at me wide-eyed, waiting for my answer. Why she considered her brother and me to be such *great* friends was a mystery.

"No, sorry," I said to her, glancing at Meghan who was giving me a look. "I haven't talked to your brother about anything."

"Really?" Sarah frowned. "Well, anyway, he has to go to Vancouver in January, but when he gets back, he's heading to L.A. for a week."

"I didn't know his job took him to other parts of the state," I said. "We're from Santa Barbara, Meghan and me."

Sarah laughed. "I know that. We've got friends in Pasadena—that's close, right?"

I nodded. "About an hour away."

She smiled bigger. "Ollie and I are taking vacay and we were thinking you guys should come, too. You can show us your old stomping grounds."

"Los *Ang*eles!" Meghan sang with an accent, snapping her fingers above her shoulder like a flamenco dancer.

"Road trip!" Sarah squealed.

"Vacation?" I said it like I'd never heard the word before.

Sarah rose to her knees, firelight catching the auburn in her hair. "Two of Ollie's college roommates live in Pasadena; they're like brothers to me, and there's a huge festival that whole week."

"Get Happy." I'd read about it a few weeks ago, actually tagged it in my Yahoo news feed. "It's an annual street fair. There's a pub crawl, a scavenger hunt, and a 5K color run. All proceeds going to charity."

"Sounds like a blast." Meghan sat on the coffee table across from us. "I'll check with my agent, but I don't think rehearsals are 'til the end of January."

"Wish I could go, chicas." Gio refilled her cup by dunking the entire thing into the pitcher of holiday cider. "But I'll be in Atlanta for trade shows."

When I didn't chime in, all three looked at me.

"There's no way I can leave work for a week."

Sarah widened her eyes like a puppy. "Did you take off extra days for Thanksgiving?"

"No."

"Are you taking time off for Christmas or New Year's?"

I shook my head, feeling awkward and pissed off; pissed off that I had the suckiest job in the world.

"Sounds like a done deal to me," she said.

"Yeah, me too." Though Meghan didn't sound as enthused. "You've been talking about doing something charitable, right?"

"Peer pressure, Rachel." Giovanna pointed at me, a curtain of her black hair covering half her face. "Just. Say. No."

I considering for a moment. "Well, I guess it's been six months and I haven't taken more than a few days off, and it's probably time I check in on Krikit to see if she's lit anything on fire."

"So you're in?" Sarah asked.

"Don't stress, Rach." Meghan pulled out her phone. "If

you can't come, you can't come."

I frowned as she disappeared into the kitchen to make a call. "Sarah," I said in a low voice, "are you *sure* your brother's okay with this?" I glanced toward the kitchen. "With me coming, I mean?"

"Totally. He told me twice to make sure I invited you."

"Okay." I didn't know what to make of that, but I nodded and walked into the kitchen. Meghan was leaning against the fridge, typing on her phone. "Hey. Are you okay? Do we need to make a chocolate run to—"

"What's going on with you two?"

I blinked when she cut me off. "Me and Sarah?"

She put a hand on her hip. "Don't play dumb. You and Rad."

My hands felt cold and tingly. "Nothing, Megs." I made double fists behind my back in case my hands started to shake. "He barely speaks to me, barely *looks* at me."

"It's called sexual tension, Rachel. Anytime I'm around you two, the room screams with it. Am I imagining that?"

"Meghan, it's not—"

"Don't think I haven't noticed the way *you* look at *him*. So I'm either blind or crazy. Either way, you're not being a very good friend."

She was dead right. I didn't realize I'd been obsessing over him in the guise of gaining closure. Which wasn't fair. He didn't want me and I didn't want him—but my best friend did. If I didn't stop this crap, I really might damage our friendship.

"I'm sorry." I touched her arm. "But I swear to you, there's absolutely nothing going on between us. I'd promise to stay away from him if that would help, but honestly,

I don't know how to stay away from him more than I am."

She twisted her lips and stared at the floor. "I like him, Rach."

I smiled supportively, but my stomach hurt.

"He's confusing." She snorted. "Typical guy, right?"

"Maybe he's busy with work. When you first met, he probably had more free time."

"Maybe." Meghan smiled and seemed relieved by my explanation. Lovely how I was trying to convince my best friend to not give up on the guy I was trying to get over.

Damn. My *brain* needed a vacation, if nothing else.

In my gut, this particular vacation felt like a bad idea, but after confirming practically in blood that I was going, I did everything I could to get out of it, keeping Meghan's feelings in mind.

Adding to this stress, work was beyond hectic. With Claire finally on my side after the emery board brainstorming session, I was offered more responsibilities. Which was great—if staying in advertising was what I wanted.

I'd just gotten out of a long meeting when my cell rang.

"Are you packed?" Meghan asked. "We leave first thing in the morning."

"Locked and loaded," I confirmed, happy to no longer hear suspicion in her voice.

"Got your license? Health insurance card, passport?"

I stared down at my phone. "Megs, what do you think is going to happen, exactly? We're going to Pasadena."

"Just preparing for anything. So you're completely ready?"

"I still have to stop my mail." I opened a browser window to do just that while I was thinking about it.

"Roger's in town. Can't he grab your mail?"

I didn't reply right away. A few weeks ago, I'd submitted a short story—the one with my Texas-style Bridget Jones—to *Self, Women's Health*, and a couple other women's magazines. I'd also emailed ten resumes. No one needed to know that yet. I just wanted to see what options I had. I didn't need Rog to see a bunch of rejection letters addressed to me from New York.

Plus, there were other considerations when I thought about amending my ten-year plan.

Oliver had snuck into my nightly dreams. Sometimes he was a minor character who'd pop in then fade into the background. Other times it was just him, talking to me, sitting in a chair, standing in a room, sometimes rehashing conversations we'd shared six years ago; but always kind, always reassuring, even when I wasn't, as if he knew something Dream Rachel didn't. Those mornings, I would wake up energized and buoyant. It usually took me a few moments to realize it wasn't real.

Chapter Eighteen

I hadn't been on a road trip in ages and was actually looking forward to the five-hour drive. But once we were inside Oliver's SUV with Meghan in the front seat, it was "Rad" this and "Rad" that. I couldn't help it, he didn't look like a Rad to me, and if I heard "Rad" one more time, I might vomit.

Settling in, I crossed my legs and rested the side of my head against the window. Sitting kitty-corner from him, I had a straight-on view of Oliver's profile behind the wheel.

Rad. What did that name even mean?

A Rad didn't have corded muscles in his neck like that. I stole a glance at Oliver, and right on cue, he swallowed, working those sexy neck muscles. I shifted, recrossing my legs. And no one called Rad could ever have a jaw sharper than a Ginsu knife. Oliver said something to Sarah then rubbed his jaw. It was sprinkled with stubble today. I felt my lips peel apart, throat going dry. And that perfect profile of Oliver's, those lips of his could *never* be mistaken for—

I blinked, getting a full frontal view of his face now. He was turned halfway around, saying something else to Sarah in the backseat beside me, but he'd caught me in a full-on stare.

"Did you say something?" he asked.

My mouth was obviously still open, lips parted, so I shut it first then said, "Me? No."

He turned back to the road but shot me another quick glance, running a knuckle under his chin. Did he know I absolutely loved that move? Or *used* to…I *used* to love that move.

Seriously, Rachel.

I grabbed my jacket, wadded it up into a ball to use as a pillow, and slammed my eyes shut. I could still hear Meghan's "Rad" comments—puke—but I least I couldn't see anything.

But that didn't mean I wouldn't dream. Before I knew it, my eyelids were heavy and I nodded off… We weren't in his car anymore, but in his bedroom back in college. I could smell his soap, the wet towel from his shower. There were those neck muscles again. I was closer to them now. That jaw I'd kissed a million times, and yes, his lips. I had to touch those lips.

It wasn't exactly a snore that startled me awake. I'd actually mumbled something else in my sleep. And if it was a name, it sure as hell wasn't "Rad." Everyone in the car was talking, though I hadn't yet opened my eyes, making sure no one had heard me, if I had indeed said aloud what I'd called out in the dream.

Megs was on her phone, talking to her mother, it sounded like. And Sarah was telling Oliver about a painting she was replicating for a class. All clear. I cracked one eye open. From my position, I wasn't in plain view of Oliver's profile anymore, but I could see his reflection in the rearview mirror. For a second, I thought I must still be dreaming, because he was looking at me. But since I was squinting, I couldn't be sure, so I cozied into my jacket/pillow, like I was rolling over in bed, and took another peek. We must've been driving through a town, idling at a stop light, otherwise, our driver's gaze could not be focused on my reflection—instead of the road—for so many seconds together.

Slowly, I opened both eyes, a millimeter at a time.

We were looking at each other now, just us. And no one else knew. It was like time stopped. *"I love to watch you sleep,"* he'd once told me. *"But watching you wake up, that's my favorite part."* My heartbeats faded, then sped up, hard and fast. After a moment, the corners of his eyes crinkled, like he was smiling at me. At my reflection, just waking up.

"The light's green. Ollie."

Oliver blinked—once like he was coming out of a daze, and a few more times, like he was embarrassed at being caught by me.

"Thanks," he said to Sarah, then he cleared his throat, definitely not looking at me when he started driving through the intersection. He wiped the back of his hand over his upper lip, then across his forehead. Oliver was sweating.

I sat up and stretched, feeling a little bit gratified. So, I wasn't the only one who'd gotten caught up in the past.

The winters around Los Angeles County were milder than in San Francisco. After the five-hour drive—two of which I'd been napping—I was instantly exhilarated by the bright, breezy, sunny day that welcomed us in Pasadena.

Oliver pulled up to our hotel. It was typical southern California decor: orange stucco buildings surrounding a pool with sky-high palm trees. It looked trashy but charming. Before Oliver could put the car in park, two guys wearing black hoodies jumped out of nowhere and started pounding on the hood. Meghan screamed and huddled with me in the backseat. When Oliver laughed and honked the horn, I relaxed, though from the way he was pointing at the guys and gesturing out the window, I was even more confused.

"Oh, it's Ryan." Sarah stuck her tongue out at the hooded guy by her window. "And Nick." She hid her face in her hands, reverting back to her tween self around her big brother's buddies.

The night before we left, Sarah gave Meghan and I a quick dish on Ryan and Nick—complete with a peek at their Instagram photos. They'd been roommates with Oliver at Nebraska State and were both cute. Ryan on the hipster side, Nick on the Nordic God side. Though you couldn't tell everything from pictures.

"Okay, smartasses," Oliver called through the windshield to the guys rocking the car. "You scratch it, you buy it."

Meghan glanced at me with raised eyebrows. I shrugged in reply and looked out my window, enjoying the show. The one I took to be Nick slid across the hood of the car, landed, then positioned himself like a sniper. This caused Oliver to double over laughing. Ryan pointed both hands at Oliver, mouthing something I couldn't understand, but it looked like he was singing. Evidently the rest of us were not in on the inside jokes shared by the former roommates.

Oliver was laughing to the point of tears now and I couldn't help staring at him, at his whole face alight like the carefree boy I used to know. The sound of his laughter made my heart duck and cover from the avalanche of memories... us laughing together like that.

Out of my peripheral vision, I caught Nick moving to my window. When I turned, he stopped cold and took a step toward the car. "Hi," I mouthed and waved one finger.

He slapped a hand over his heart like he'd been shot and stumbled backward. Everyone inside the car went quiet. I chuckled, self-consciously. "Is he all right?"

"Dang." Sarah looked at me, her eyebrows lifted. "What'd you do, Rachel?"

"Waved."

The two guys were in a football huddle now. Nick's blue eyes—that were way bluer than in pictures—found me over Ryan's shoulder. Instagram filters did the guy no justice. He was *Vampire Diaries* pretty. No wonder he'd moved to L.A.

Oliver muttered under his breath, then opened his car door, nearly hitting Nick in the face. I didn't move while watching the three buddies reunite. They looked so happy as they bumped fists and did those awkward-looking guy half-hugs. When all three looked at me, my face got hot and I glanced away.

"Rachel." Meghan stood outside my door. "Let's check in."

"Yeah, coming." I nodded, still feeling several sets of eyes on me.

We were a rowdy bunch, our voices, bodies, and luggage taking over the hotel lobby. Because of the Get Happy festival—and Meghan's inability to make a reservation—we lost one of our rooms, so we three girls were left sharing one. "It'll be like the dorms again," Meghan cheered. I volunteered to take the rollaway cot for the first night.

After check-in, Nick fell into step with me, offering to get my bags.

"My contribution to the week is I'm taking us to the Lakers/Spurs game Thursday night, the day after the 5K," he said, as he rolled my suitcase down the hall. "I couldn't get us all in the press box but the seats are good, first level behind the bench." This set everyone chattering. "Have you ever been to a game?" he asked me as we fell to the rear of the group. "You should see Kobe Bryant. Amazing athlete. Especially live."

"Dallas has a pretty solid team this season. Nowitski's a shoo-in for MVP." I flipped my hair in a way I'd seen Gio do. "He averages twenty-five a game; twenty-seven on the road. But we should actually worry about Garnett in the west. He's hot since the trade. And Kobe is so five years ago."

Nick stopped walking and stared at me.

"A friend of mine knows Mark Cuban." I shrugged, coyly. "When I lived in Dallas last season, I sat courtside twice and twice in his suite. He gave me the inside scoop."

Nick looked like he was about to simultaneously drool and cry. I flipped my hair again and walked ahead, laying on the flirty coy. At least, I hoped it was flirty. It had been so long.

We hadn't been in our room ten seconds before Sarah started in. "So, hello. Nick is *totally* smitten with you, Rach." She tossed her bags on the bed.

I unzipped my suitcase, trying not to smile. "What are you talking about? We just met."

Meghan, who was unloading her pre-measured bottles of cayenne pepper, honey, and sea salt water into the tiny hotel room fridge, let loose a dramatic wail. "I have *never* heard you talk like that to a guy. You were flirting with him in front of everyone."

I rolled my eyes. "I was not."

"You were. You touched his arm and flipped your damn hair. I saw you."

"So did I." Sarah sat on the edge of the bed. "Don't you think he's cute?"

"Duh. Of *course*." I made myself wait a couple of beats so I didn't sound as giddy as I was starting to feel. Nick wasn't just cute; his *face* should've been in magazines instead of his words about West Coast sports. "Which is precisely why he wasn't flirting back. No one that good looking would be *smitten* with *me*."

"What do you mean?" Sarah asked.

Meghan screwed open the top of one of her water concoctions, took a tiny sip, and gagged. "What Rachel means is"—she jabbed a thumb my way—"she's got it in her head that she's not pretty. Whatever *that* means."

"Rachel!" Sarah gasped dramatically. "You've *got* to be *kidding*."

I really hoped I wasn't about to witness an argument about how pretty I was or wasn't.

Sarah stood with her hands on her hips. "Sometimes I can't stand to look at you."

I laughed. "My point exactly."

"That's not what I mean." Two blotches of pink appeared on her cheeks. "I mean, you're so beautiful, everything about you." She stretched out on the bed, propped up by an elbow. "It's a little intimidating."

"Ha!" Meghan pointed at me. "I told you."

"Guys—stop." I busied myself with hanging up my clothes I didn't want to get wrinkled. "This is a pointless topic."

"Okay, okay." Meghan unpacked her toiletries, lining bottles and zipper pouches on the desk. "Sarah, tell us everything we need to know about Nick."

"He's from Omaha. He's the only boy with a bunch of sisters."

"Cute." Meghan tapped her chin. "Rachel needs better female influences in her life."

"Hey!" Sarah frowned indignantly, but went on. "I'm not sure what he was studying in school, probably journalism or communications. *LA Times* hired him straight out of college."

"Impressive."

"We already knew that," I said.

"Hush—this doesn't concern you." Meghan pinched the air in front of my lips. "Go on, Sarah."

"He hikes."

"Nice." Meghan nodded.

"And surfs."

"Sexy."

"And I don't know this for sure, but I think Hemingway's his favorite writer."

Meghan hmm'd and nodded clinically. "When was his last serious relationship?"

Sarah bit her lip, thinking. "It ended less than a year ago. His cow ex is already engaged."

"Cow," Meghan agreed.

"He's single and looking—*that* I know."

"Any latex allergies?"

"Meghan." I nudged her hip with my bare foot. "Do you

really think I need to worry about latex tonight?"

"A modern woman is always prepared." She plopped on the foot of my bed and cracked open a Diet Coke. "I don't think there's anything left to discuss. Nick is perfect." She rolled onto her back and lifted her chin to look at me upside down. "All yours, Rach."

"I appreciate your confidence." He was cute, *very* cute, and sure, I'd only been around him for twenty minutes, but he seemed smart and funny and, yes, he *had* been flirting with me. I wasn't that out of practice.

I'd been meaning to move on from Oliver, get past that whole mess. But was it a wise idea to move on from him with one of his best friends?

Chapter Nineteen

That evening, while the group headed to a swanky-chic restaurant in downtown L.A., I rented a car and drove fifty miles east. I needed to pop in on Krikit as soon as possible. I was spending six days in Pasadena, but each second I didn't see my sister was a second she would make me pay for it when I did visit by watching videos of eighties pop music.

Before I could unload my bag, a scream rang out from inside the house. I sprinted through the front door to find my sister in the kitchen. "What's wrong?" I exclaimed. "Where are the kids?"

"It's *gross*." Krikit lifted up on her tiptoes, pointing to a corner by the sink. "Kill it, Rachel. Get the gun."

I looked toward where she was pointing, expecting to see a hungry coyote who'd wandered in from the hills.

"Krikit." I exhaled. "It's just a little pill bug." I grabbed a paper towel off the counter and scooped it up. Krikit whimpered softly as I walked past her toward the front door. Once outside, I opened the paper towel and let the little gray guy slide onto the porch. It stayed curled up in a tight ball, waiting. But it never got the change to uncoil because the heel of a hot pink trainer came down, squashing it flat.

"Krikit!"

"And so is your old lady." She glared at the tiny stain then looked at me. "Sister!" I was pulled into a hug. I laughed, relaxing into it. "I'm so glad you're here. Just wait, Paul's going to say 'I told you so' if I don't clean this up before he gets home."

Once she released from our hug, she tugged my sleeve, pulling me into the house. "I was making fried chicken and the bread mixer went all crazy."

"How did flour get in the bottoms of all the glasses?"

She leaned a hip against the counter. "Before I could shut off the mixer, the oil was bubbling and I'm not any good at actually frying anything, but I promised Paul I'd learn to fry chicken for his birthday next month. Now there's flour everywhere and I scorched the bottom of my new pan from Williams-Sonoma—it's sitting on the back porch. The kids are down the street, and Paul'll be home in two seconds and there's no dinner." She glanced at the drawer next to the phone, the one I knew was crammed full of paper menus. "I guess we're having pizza again. Would you mind calling? I need to sit for a second."

When she stopped to breathe, I laughed. "And so is your old lady?"

"That bug was pissing me off. How dare it disturb me when I'm trying to fry chicken?"

"I don't think it's fair to blame an innocent bug for the fact that all Daughtrys suck at culinary arts."

"I guess." She wiped her hands on her jeans. "So. Rog really didn't come with you? He hasn't been home since last summer."

"His home is San Francisco." But she went off on a tangent about how home is where you grew up and why does he never come visit. I listened patiently while crouched on the floor, sweeping up flour. No, I couldn't cook worth a crap, but I could clean.

"Meghan didn't come with you?" Krikit peered into the framed mirror over the stove, etched with a saying about how a happy home is a dirty home. Whatever got her through the day. "I ran into her mother last week. I guess Meg's got a new guy?"

The dustpan slipped from my fingers and fell to the bottom of the tall, metal trash can, clanking all the way down.

Krikit pulled out a chair and sat at the table. "Have you met him? He's probably so hot, like one of those guys on that one show. Ya know which one I mean? She has good taste when it comes to looks. I bet she marries this one, right? Rachel. What are you doing?"

I caught myself staring into the trash can, sweeping the air. "I've met him, yes. His name is Oliver." I cringed, wishing I'd referred to him as Rad. It was easier to think of him by that non-name when I thought of him with Meghan. "She's known him five months, I guess." I rescued the floury dustpan, not making eye contact with Krikit. "He's a computer programmer. And yes, he's hot, like Chris-Pine-in-*Star-Trek* hot."

It made me queasy to utter that last sentence, but the celebrity description detail would pacify Krikit. I walked to the sink and washed my hands, sneaking little glances at my sister. "Can I ask you something?"

"Shoot." She tossed me a towel to dry my hands.

"Why did you marry Paul?"

She snorted. "Rude, much?"

"No, Sorry. Paul's great." I paused, wrapping my arms around my middle. "I meant, why did you get married so young? You were twenty. I ask because I have a...a little problem and I think your answer might help."

Krikit slowly met my eyes then pushed out a kitchen chair with her foot. "Sit."

"Thanks."

She played with the napkin holder before answering. "I was ready to get married, but it was a timing thing, too. Things were rough at home. Dad was out of work, you probably don't remember."

"Of course I do."

"Then you understand what I mean. Paul became everything to me. It felt safer to be with him—someone all my own—than with Mom and Dad when there was all that instability and tension. Paul and I had to trust each other, take a huge leap of faith together. Believe it or not, I did a lot of growing up those first years."

"What happened since then?" I smirked and nudged her leg.

"Doodoohead."

I ran my palms over the table. "It is funny. We shared the same situation but it affected us the exact opposite."

"How do you mean?"

I hesitated, but it felt right to finally talk to my sister about it, though she didn't need to know every detail. "I had a boyfriend freshman year."

"I didn't know that."

"No one did. Anyway, it got really serious really fast. I became, like, consumed with him. I started skipping classes just to be with him. It was pretty unhealthy, and then I freaked out because he didn't fit into my"—I paused to cringe—"my plan."

Krikit lifted her eyebrows. "Your *plan* plan. The ten-year plan?"

I nodded. "Yeah. We weren't on the same level about everything back then, which I know now was a ridiculous expectation. I was a total control freak."

"Was?" my sister said after a snort.

I smirked back. "I'm handling it better now. I've had to kind of roll with the punches at my new job. It's been humbling. Back then, though, the thought of dealing with potential instability scared me to death."

"It's good to be scared about the future when you're young. That probably means you weren't ready to take whatever step was next."

"I was the same age as you. *He* was ready." I rested my chin in my hands, my shoulders slumping. "We loved each other, and I hurt him bad."

Krikit reached out and fingered the ends of my hair. "Forgive yourself for what you did when you were a kid. You made a mistake—"

"I did." *A huge one*, I almost added. Conflicting emotions spun inside my head. My relationship with Oliver had been so important—life changing. But I still couldn't think of it without feeling sad. I rubbed my arms, worried that I might cry.

"You're supposed to make mistakes at that age—lots of

them," Krikit said. "You're supposed to fall in love and screw up and cry and get arrested and sleep with your lit professor and go public skinny-dipping and fall in love again. Lather, rinse, repeat."

When I tried to laugh, a sob/cough hung in my chest. "It still hurts when I think about it."

She put a hand over mine. "Seriously, forgive yourself. It's been how many years?"

"Almost seven."

"Seven years. Rach. That's so long. It's like a whole dog's life, right?"

That sob/laugh finally broke out. "I think you've got that backward."

"My point is, and not to discount your feelings or anything, but to this guy, your relationship was a fleeting life experience, something he sulked about for two months tops, and only when he drank beer alone. You've dated since then, haven't you?"

"A little."

"You need to get back out there. That's part of forgiveness, giving yourself permission to really move on and be happy with someone. You deserve that."

I turned to smile at her. "You're so wise, sis. I'm in awe at how self-possessed you are."

Krikit jumped when a car door slammed out front. "Crap, Paul's home. Quick—pretend the house got broken into and robbers burned the chicken, 'kay?"

"Yeah. Scratch that awe."

The next evening, I'd texted Meghan from the road that I was stuck behind a wreck and would be arriving back in Pasadena pretty late. I was surprised to see Nick in the hotel's deserted lounge when I finally rolled in.

"Hey." I met him under a chandelier made out of deer antlers. He closed his laptop and stood. "I told Meghan for everyone to go to dinner without me. They didn't wait, did they?"

"Just me."

"Oh." So maybe his flirting last night really did have some intention behind it. "Cool." I smiled, hoping I didn't look too travel weary. I hooked the strap of my overnight bag over my shoulder.

"Let me take that."

"Thanks." I passed him the bag. "Do you know where they went to eat? I can drop off my stuff if you want to meet up with them."

"I don't—not really." He lifted a little smile. "It was pretty noisy with everyone today."

"Not surprising. We're a rowdy bunch." There was a bit of an awkward pause. "Well." I shrugged, not knowing what else to say. Had my flirting skills already dried up?

"Are you thirsty?" He pointed toward the hotel bar.

"No."

"Hungry?"

"Starving, actually. I always lose weight when I visit my sister. It's a nonstop obstacle course."

Nick laughed and slid one hand in his pocket. "Sounds fun. We should have gone with you. Over here." He led me toward a couch sectional in the corner of the dim and deserted breakfast dining room. "We can have room service delivered here, if that's okay."

"Sounds great. I was dreading going out tonight, too. Just a little."

"Maybe we both needed a night off." We sat, separated, each of us on our own couch.

Nick's blue eyes seemed even brighter today. They squinted a little whenever he smiled at me, making me feel warm and…wanted. *Forgive yourself*, Krikit had said. *Give yourself permission to be happy with someone else.* I deserved happiness. I deserved someone who smiled at me—and not just in rearview mirrors. Someone who made me feel warm and waited for me in the hotel lobby under deer antlers.

Thirty minutes later, I was finishing my first half of a turkey wrap while Nick polished off a California club. Still tan from his recent trip to Miami, he'd been telling me how his job flew him from sporting event to sporting event, depending on which he covered for the paper. Sounded glamorous, particularly to someone who was lucky to take two minutes during working hours to look out a window at the foggy bay.

I learned about his family in Omaha. His sisters and his dogs. The summer he backpacked through Italy. As the hours ticked by, and we both reclined, our heads slid to the touching ends of our respective couches, only two armrests apart. He asked about my job and life. It felt nice to talk to someone who seemed interested.

I nearly jumped out of my skin when a blue fingernailed hand touched my shoulder.

Meghan hovered over our heads, grinning. "Well, well. What are you guys doing out here?"

"Nothing." I sat up and smoothed my shirt. Oliver and Sarah stood under the deer antler chandelier. The way Oliver's eyes were fixed on me gave me the strangest feeling, like I'd been caught doing something inappropriate. "I got in late. We were hanging out."

"Late?" Meghan arched an eyebrow. "Rach, it's one a.m."

Nick was on his feet, too, rubbing the side of his face that had been mushed into the couch. "Rachel was keeping me company since neither of us wanted to fight the, uh, traffic." He talked to them while looking at me. The twinkle in his eyes made me giddy, like we were in on a secret.

As I fell asleep that night, I had to keep forcing myself to picture how Nick had smiled at me when we'd been waiting for the elevator to take us all up to our rooms, instead of how tense Oliver's shoulders seemed as he left us to take the stairs.

Chapter Twenty

"I believe I'm officially done drinking for the night."

Nick propped an elbow on the bar and looked at me through lazy, half-lidded eyes. "It's only seven o'clock."

"And we've been to eight bars so far."

"It's for a good cause. Plus, it gives you a chance to show off your seventies fashion." He touched the sleeve of my "flower power" T-shirt.

When I'd agreed to the trip—which also meant agreeing to participate in all the festivities, including the twelve-hour pub crawl—I'd forgotten that the theme for this year's "Get Happy" festival was Disco Days.

"I think the fates were aligned so I'd miss that entire decade." I swiveled around on my bar stool and displayed my bright yellow clogs. "I can rock four-inch heels, but these puppies are killing my feet."

"Your *shoes* are *fab*," Meghan said as she breezed by wearing a tiny lime-green dress and white go-go boots.

"They make your entire outfit." She bumped my arm. "Let's go, time to crawl, y'all."

"Ugh." I rolled my eyes good-naturedly and slid off the stool.

"Are you cold?" Nick asked after we'd been walking a few blocks. "The tip of your nose is red, and I know it's not from alcohol. I've been monitoring your intake."

I rubbed my nose with the back of my hand. "I probably should've worn something more than a T-shirt."

"You look cute." His blue eyes did that cute squinting thing. "Like when we were on the couches the other night."

I felt an oncoming blush, so I turned to pretend window shop at a closed store. Meghan, Oliver, and the others passed me on our way to the next bar. I saw wind chimes through the store window, and candles, reminding me that I needed to go to *Another Time & Place* to restock my essential oils when I got home.

"Here." Nick draped his white polyester *Saturday Night Fever* jacket across my shoulders. "Keep it 'til you get back to the hotel."

His face was so pretty. Women would kill for those cheekbones. "Thanks." I slid my arms through the sleeves, still warm from his body. "I guess I am cold...*was* cold."

He fastened the three buttons of the jacket then put the collar up. "Even cuter."

When I smiled, my teeth chattered with another shiver. The next thing I knew, Nick's hands were on my waist and he was pulling me in.

"Better?" he asked, wrapping his arms around me.

I was too caught off guard to reply, so I froze against his chest and kind of patted his sides like I was a TSA agent.

Someday
MAYBE

He was being so sweet, and he was warm and strong and too pretty for human eyes. It had been a really long time since I'd felt a man's arms around me, so long that I couldn't remember what to do.

"Much better." Though I wasn't as relaxed as I should be. "What happened to our nice pre-spring warm spell?"

"SoCal. If you don't like the weather, wait a day and it'll change."

"I think that original quote was describing Facebook."

Nick shook in quiet laugher, then squeezed me once and let go. "You smell nice. Like a walk in the woods."

"Good guess. It's lavender, verbena, and cedar. I blended it for this trip." I pushed up the sleeve of his jacket to expose the inside of my wrist. When his nose touched my skin, I felt a zing. Gotta love that zing. "I hoped there'd be occasion for a man to want a whiff of me."

"Rachel." He dropped my hand and stared hard at me, as if trying to convey what he couldn't express verbally. When his expression broke into a sexy smile, my stomach turned a cartwheel. "Come on, we better keep moving before I make a scene."

"Promises, promises," I said.

He took my hand, looping my arm through his.

Three days into our six-day trip and Nick was never more than an outstretched arm away. I wasn't used to the attention. But I liked it.

A few crawl stops later, we hit a bar that had a restaurant. Our group took a table in the back. Nick was parked at my left with Oliver at the head of the table, our elbows bumping every now and again. My side was to him most of the meal because I was trying very hard to put my efforts into Nick.

"You really shouldn't drink so many of those," Ryan said to Meghan after she slurped down her third glass of Diet Coke.

"You don't say." Her voice slurred sarcastically as she arched an eyebrow. "I suppose it would be okay if it had a shot of rum?" Meghan wasn't a big cocktail drinker. If she was going to alter her mood, she preferred her beverages be stimulants rather than depressants.

"Megs only intakes carbonation when she's *not* on Gwyneth Paltrow's pomegranate diet," I said, jumping to her defense.

"My skin felt glowy for days."

Ryan rotated all the way around to face her. "There've been studies for years on diet sodas. The cola beans, the aspartame, they actually eat away at your intestinal tissue—"

"Eww." Sarah squealed.

"Excellent dinner conversation, buddy." Oliver raised his glass.

Ryan looked down at his plate. "It's unhealthy. So is crash dieting—which you haven't stopped talking about for three days."

"You sound like my *mother*." Meghan, herself, sounded testy and a little tipsy. She flagged down our waiter and asked for another refill. "Do you think I enjoy having to whiten my teeth every six months like a chain smoker, and getting the worst migraines you can imagine when I'm not within two inches of a straw?"

"Then do something about it," Ryan said. "I can help."

"Are you drunk?"

"Megs," I whispered, trying to catch her eye.

She scoffed. "Not all of us are born with the perfect body

like *Rachel*."

"What?"

"Never mind." She took one long pull from her straw, excused herself from the table, and stomped away on her platform heels.

Nick was the first to break the silence. "Note to self. Do *not* mock Meghan's junk food habit, no matter how disgusting. Better remember that, Rad, or you're in for a hell of a life with that one."

Oliver pushed away his plate. "What's that supposed to mean?"

Before he could get an answer, Ryan said, "I was trying to help." He gazed toward where Megs had disappeared. "In every other way, she's amazing and perfect and—" He cut off.

Huh. Maybe we'd all been pub crawling for too long.

Our table turned awkwardly quiet. I stole a glance at Oliver who was fingering his chin, looking faraway and lost. I would've had to be a heartless zombie to not see the trouble behind his gray eyes.

"It's cool," I said to Ryan. "She'll be all right. I mean, after she's had another refill." There was nervous tittering around the table. "So...how 'bout them Lakers? Who still misses Shaq? Raise your hand."

Nick chuckled and draped his arm across the back of my chair. "Never liked the Lakers. Not since I was a kid."

"Me, neither," I admitted, lowering my voice. "It must be a beating living in L.A."

He nodded, sagely. "I have to write about it every week during the season. We can always hope their injury list keeps growing and their defensive plays—"

"*Quiet*," I warned. "That kind of talk is grounds for an old-fashioned California firing squad." I leaned toward him, dropping my voice to a private tone. "If you're lucky. I shudder at the alternative, though it could be kinda fun."

Nick laughed out loud. "This woman is trouble," he announced to the table. "She says too much for her own good, but when she holds back"—he nodded at me, his eyes looking all smoldering—"it's even better."

"Har, har, whatever," I said, waving him off.

While loading my fork full of chicken enchiladas, my gaze moved to Oliver. He was watching me with a curious, almost confused expression. I did not move my eyes away, meeting his questioning gaze while asking a few unspoken questions of my own.

"Hey, Rad," Nick said. Oliver blinked and broke our stare. "Rad, did you know—"

"Did *you* know," Oliver cut in, "that I haven't gone by Rad in two years?"

Nick stared back, his mouth frozen in mid-word.

"The only reason Meghan used that name in the first place is because she heard Tim say it, and now everyone in San Francisco calls me that."

"Not everyone," I said before I'd processed the thought.

Oliver rotated his body to face me. "I know." It was the closest we'd been—physically—since we broke up. "Thank you, Rachel, I've noticed." His voice was so kind and so solid, making warmth and butterfly wings engulf my stomach, my chest.

His gaze remained on me, neither of us breaking contact this time. In the back of my mind, I could tell the others around us had moved the conversation along, but Oliver kept his eyes on me. After a moment, he cracked into a smile.

"What?" I asked, my voice barely a whisper.

He shook his head. "I was just thinking about that weekend."

"Weekend?" I repeated, leaning an inch closer.

"Yeah. The weekend in your dorm when we didn't watch *Dawson's Creek.*"

I knew exactly what he meant, and when his smile was replaced by an expression of intensity and longing, I knew what that meant, too; I remembered it from six years ago. Or was it seven? For a moment, the world broke apart, and it was us...

• • •

MARCH, FRESHMAN YEAR

After trudging up four flights of stairs, I arrived home exhausted and starving from back-to-back study sessions, a huge exam, and an oral presentation in my journalism class. So ready to tear off my stupid, dressy skirt and collapse into bed, I almost didn't notice Oliver waiting for me in my dorm room. At first sight, I panicked. My roommate was bound to come in and bust us. Then I remembered she was gone for the weekend. The moment I met Oliver's eyes—the knowing look behind them—I realized that was his plan.

"Hi." I was happy to see him, but almost too tired to react. "This is the best surprise—"

"Shh." He took my backpack and set it on the desk, peeled me out of my jacket one sleeve at a time, then wound his arms around me, lifting me off my feet, my shoes falling off in the process. "I know what a long twenty-four hours you've had." He kissed me lightly. "Now I'm here to take care of you."

"You don't have to—"

"I have your favorite pizza, the third season of *Dawson's Creek* on DVD, and I found some of that oil you were out of."

"Cinnamon Bliss? Wait, you don't even like *Dawson's Creek*."

"But you love it." He sat on the foot of the bed, cradling me on his lap like a baby. "I know you've been going since last night, so what would you like first? We can eat, or you can crash out—I don't mind." He placed a hand on my cheek and eased me against his chest. "I'll rub oil into your feet if you want."

It was overwhelming. Without him doing a thing, I'd never felt so taken care of. It was then that I realized it wasn't just a freshman fling. Oliver loved me, like *real* love, like when no one is looking and when you have nothing to gain but you give and you love and you sacrifice and cherish. That's what he was offering me as he held me against his beating heart.

"I want to do all those things." I stroked the back of his neck. "But first I want to kiss you."

He dipped his chin so I could press my lips to his. "Done, sweet pea. Now what? Food? Yoga pants?"

"I want you to kiss me."

He smiled and met my mouth, sending pulses of heat through me.

"Next?"

"What if I asked you to kiss me all day and all night?" I rotated around so I was on my knees, my skirt sliding up as my legs straddled him.

"Then I would never stop." As he kissed me, his hands rested at the sides of my neck then moved down, landing on my thighs. They slid under my skirt, cupping my butt, hoisting me closer. Heat burned through the layers of cotton between our skin. "All day and all night?" he whispered over my mouth.

"That's all I want."

"I'll kiss you here." He pressed his lips to mine. "And here." They moved to my jaw, down my neck. "Here." He moved his hands to my sides, boosting me higher, pressing his lips between my collarbones.

I smelled his hair, the blinding endorphins that made me never want to breathe in any other scent that wasn't him. I sucked in a gasp as his hands slid inside my shirt, holding me right below the ribcage.

"Here." He kissed the top of my shoulder, then as he rotated me around to lie back, he deftly pulled my shirt over my head. "Here." He knelt over me, resting his palms flat over my bare stomach, then touched his mouth between them, planting kisses all over my skin. "Beautiful," he whispered as he moved.

"Oliver." I held the back of his head, torn between letting him take his time with me or climbing on top of him.

After one more kiss, he lifted his head. "So beautiful." We locked eyes in a way that made something deep inside me break apart. "Whatever you want, Rachel. Whatever you need, you know I'm here. Always."

My heart banged in my chest, and more love than I'd ever known I had inside sang through my blood. "Come here." I pulled him to me. "I'll always remember this moment, always." I moved him over me, feeling the firmness of his love, the solidness of his body. "I love you," I whispered. "No matter what I do or say. Never forget."

• • •

"I haven't forgotten." Oliver's silvery eyes locked on me, though the vision of us together all those years ago had dissolved.

"Neither have I." Was everyone in the restaurant witnessing this? I almost didn't care.

He placed a hand on the table, an inch from mine. "I've been meaning to talk to you about that."

"Me, too." Though there was no way we were referring to the same thing. How could we be?

"When we get home?" Before I could answer, he smiled—at me, only me. And I'd never seen anything more beautiful in all my life. "Rach." He brushed his finger over mine.

"Who's ready for dessert?" The glasses and dishes rattled when Meghan returned to the table, all smiles.

I blinked and my lungs sucked in a gulp of air. Oliver did the same, shooting me one more look before sitting back in his chair. I pulled my hand off the table and wiped my palms on my jeans. Oliver did the exact same thing.

"I was talking to the hostess," Meghan continued. "She said their baked flan is major killer." She elbowed Ryan. "No caffeine or trans fat, slugger." She fluttered her fake seventies eyelashes at him. "Rad, scoot over here so we can share. Come on."

Our entire table began chattering about dessert. I glanced at Oliver, he glanced back at me. What were we supposed to do now? To break the tension, I grimaced at him, showing my bottom teeth. "You like flan," I whispered.

He chuckled under his breath and put a fist over the exposed side of his mouth to shield it from the rest of the table. "You know I hate it, Rachel. You also know I prefer the taste of Fruity Pebbles over everything."

He pushed back from the table and took the spot next to Meghan. It might've been exactly like the Chinese restaurant after he'd helped me with my allergy attack and then left me without a word or even a look. But this time, every few seconds, I could feel Oliver's eyes on me. And every time I met his gaze, he smiled.

Chapter Twenty-One

"Meghan?" My voice sounds like it is underwater. "I can't see you, are you all right?" The clinging mist surrounding me begins to lift. I am back at the stone wall that I've yet to scale, though this time, I am finally atop. My breath catches when I see Meghan on the other side, lying on a rock, limbs contorted, not stirring. I spring from the wall. My legs cannot move me fast enough through the tall grass. "Wake up!" I'm screaming but afraid to touch her blue, bloodless face. "Meghan, please. Please don't!"

"Don't *what*?" The living and breathing Meghan hissed from the other bed. "You're dreaming again, Rachel. Roll over and go back to sleep before Sarah gags you like we've been plotting for the last half hour."

"It's okay, Rach," Sarah's soft and sleepy voice lifted over. "Nightmare."

"I know." I listened to each bang of my heart as I stared

at the ceiling until the sun shone through the hotel blinds.

"Here comes—"

Nick was about to say *yellow*, but he was cut off when a guy stepped from the sidelines of the designated running path and tossed a bucket of yellow-dyed cornstarch in his face.

"Bah-ha-ha." I snorted, having to slow my jogging pace so I could double over. Blue, pink, green, and purple powder fell out of my hair like rainbow dust. We had one more kilometer to go and my once-white tank top and shorts were well on their way to being a spectacular kaleidoscope of colors.

Oliver jogged up to my side. He wore mirrored sunglasses and was completely coated in color. As he was about to pass, a cloud of yellow exploded over his head.

"Ooh, *nailed*." I laughed.

He turned to me and, noticing my conspicuously-yellow-free ensemble, hooked an arm around my waist and swung me toward the sideline, directly in front of a guy with a full bucket of yellow.

I squealed, ready to block my face, but the whole idea of this 5K was to end the race without a speck of skin or clothing showing white. So I lifted my chin, extended my arms, and pranced through the cloud of yellow like it was a finish line.

Oliver's arm stayed around me, so I both heard and felt him break into laughter. "There's the good sport I know."

I snorted a laugh, inhaling a nose full of cornstarch.

"You all right?"

"Do I have anything on my face?" I rotated inside his arm.

He brushed my cheek with his free hand." Maybe one spot right here."

At some point, we'd stopped jogging, and were face-to-face, with me held to his chest. It didn't feel like my feet were touching the ground.

"You're falling behind, yo." Ryan trotted in place at our side.

"Dude, for the last time, there's no falling behind," Oliver replied. "This isn't a timed race." He still didn't release his grip on me, even when we started to run again. If I could've seen behind his mirrored shades, I was sure I would've caught an expression of defiance.

Now was not the time to have our little talk, however, so I forced myself to step out of his arms. He kept a hand on my elbow for a second, then dropped it.

"How's the new business going?" Ryan asked him, taking the spot between us.

"Good." Oliver didn't even sound winded. "Coming together, slowly."

I thought Oliver worked for a big software company. "What new business?" I asked, trying to jog around Ryan. I couldn't see Oliver's eyes, and then I couldn't see him at all when a huge group of women in pink tutus trotted between us singing "Breaking Up is Hard to Do" in four-part harmony.

"What's he talking about?" I asked Ryan.

"He's quitting his job."

My footing stumbled. "What? Why?"

"So he can branch out on his own with this software idea—website support." He wiped his forehead with his sweatband. "I was helping him at the beginning, getting started with a business plan." He chuckled under his breath. "If you can call it a plan. He was kind of all over the place, still nailing down projections, marketing, branding—simple things like product names. Starting a new tech business in this economy, though. Pretty risky, if you ask me."

I searched for Oliver in the crowd beside me, in front of me, but he was nowhere. "Why would he leave his job if it's such a risk?"

Ryan shrugged. "Guy never seems content with what's he's doing, always looking for something better or what's next. I think he has like one investor, but that's it."

"Can you start a business with only one investor?"

"No way, not with what he says he wants to do."

"Does he have any other capital?"

"Dunno. Not that I know of."

"Well…" I knew I was badgering Ryan with questions, but I wanted to understand. "Why then…why is he doing this without a business plan or financial backing?"

Ryan shrugged again and panted; he looked winded. "Have to ask him."

I jumped over a crack in the sidewalk. "Yeah," I muttered, not liking the sound of any of this.

We had a bit of catching up to do to reach the rest of the group, which was difficult enough with my heart pounding like I'd already crested Lombard Street.

Why would Oliver leave his awesome job? Okay, so I didn't know how awesome his job was, but it seemed stable and he was always busy, and being relied upon because you're responsible and good at what you do was a kind of awesome. So why? Didn't he know eighty percent of small businesses failed in the first year? Why would he knowingly do something without a plan for the future or a…

Oh. My pounding heart took a dive.

Oliver was still that nineteen-year-old who didn't have a care in the world. Pick a major, or don't; it doesn't really matter. Go to this school, go to that school. Quit your job, start a company. Move in with Rachel, let her walk away.

I pumped my arms faster, fueled by betrayal I knew was irrational and unfair, but it was still there.

"Where'd ya go?" Nick asked as I was about to sprint right past him.

"Oh, uh, yellow." I displayed the front of my tank top as explanation for my lagging behind, and not that I'd allowed Oliver to put his arm around me and laugh with me and touch my face. What was my problem? I normally wasn't a glutton for punishment, so why was I hell-bent on making the same mistake of wanting a guy who wasn't right for me? And my best friend was totally into him, and I was trying to get over him, and I had this amazing guy—right here, right now—interested in me. Just because Oliver and I'd had another *moment* at the restaurant last night didn't mean I should screw everything up.

"Ah, yes, yellow." Nick smiled and we jogged in silence until we caught up with the others. Our group made its way through the center of the shady street of downtown Pasadena, nearing the finish line.

"I'm covering the LA/Dallas game Saturday night," Nick said to me. "Should be a good matchup."

Meghan jogged a few feet ahead of me beside Oliver,

her ponytail looking like something out of Rainbow Brite. I kept my eyes glued on her, still unable to shake last night's dream, how real it had felt. But then I thought about what Ryan had told me, and I couldn't stop my eyes from roaming Oliver's way. I didn't know what to make of it or of him. My legs were tired and my burning lungs were ready to burst and I couldn't think straight about anything.

"Yeah, should be a good game," I replied to Nick, picking up my pace so we were directly behind them. I wanted to grab Oliver by the elbow and demand answers. But I couldn't think of even one question.

Nick kept talking. "You lived in Dallas for a while."

"Yeah."

"You went to many Mavericks games?"

"Sure." Whenever Meghan laughed, she bumped her shoulder against Oliver's. She swatted his arm a lot, too, and she was constantly grabbing him. Was she always so touchy?

"Aren't you an NBA fan?"

"Sure." Oliver hooked an arm around Meghan's shoulder as they laughed.

"You should come with me."

Now Megs had her arm around *him*. I inhaled sharply, extremely winded, glad the finish line was only a few yards ahead.

"Yeah. Maybe." I stared at Meghan's bouncing ponytail and wondered if it was always so springy and stupid.

Nice, Rach. Way to be a friend. Now stop thinking about him. Just stop.

"Hey, slow pokes." Sarah met us at the other end of the finish line. I think it was Sarah—she was so covered in colored cornstarch that I couldn't make out her features. "We finished before half the runners, so the party's not for another twenty. Want to check out the water hazard over there?"

"Totes!" Meghan jumped up and down, clapping. She was still so full of energy, it made me want to take a nap.

"That's not a water hazard." I followed behind the rest of the group, working out the stitch in my side. My feet, and parts of my heart, felt like they were full of led. "It's a fountain, part of the campus. We're not supposed to be over here. See the barricades?"

"It's *glorious.*" Meghan sprinted ahead of us. "Isn't this the most gorgeous weather? If it rains tonight, all my wishes will come true." The cement ledge of the fountain was knee-high and looked like a large reflecting pool. Meghan jumped onto the ledge, lifted up on one sneakered toe, and twirled around. "Just look at those lovely clouds!" Her chin lifted as she whirled in another ballerina-type spin. "Rad? Didn't you tell me this is how the sky looks in Hong Kong right before it rains?"

"Something like that," he said, though I could only see the back of his head.

The closer I got, the fountain looked more like an Olympic-sized swimming pool. The thing was huge. It probably wasn't very deep, but Meghan definitely shouldn't be doing a Britney Spears dance routine on the high ledge.

"Megs, be careful."

"What?"

"Rachel?" Nick was at my elbow again. Or had he been there the whole time. "Were you listening?"

"No, I wasn't." I half-turned his way while still watching Meghan's little dance. I couldn't help envying her fearless inhibition.

"Rachel." Nick took my arm and slowed my pace. "I said I think you should come with me."

I blinked a few times and looked at him, really looked at him. "Sorry. Where?"

"Dallas." His hand cupped my elbow and we slowed again. "The game's Saturday and you'll be back in San Francisco Sunday night." He lifted a small, intriguing grin. "Come with me. Two days, just you."

Before I could reply, Oliver stopped dead in his tracks and spun around. I couldn't tell which of us he was focused on because of his sunglasses, but when he whipped them off, it was pretty clear he was looking at me.

Mostly so I wouldn't run him over, I stopped walking, too, and so did Nick. Oliver stared at me, Nick stared at him. I didn't know where I was supposed to look.

"Rad?" Meghan's lilting voice swirled around us. "Rad? I said, do you dare me?"

"Seriously, Rachel?" Oliver's words sounded like a growl. "You'd go with him to Dallas before you even *talk* to me?"

The nerve. I growled right back. "Are you quitting your job?"

He blinked and blue powder drifted from his lashes. "What?"

"Are you?"

"Hey...do you dare me, Rad?"

Oliver put his hands on his hips. "I don't know yet, Rachel. Probably."

"Yeah." I scoffed. "You do that."

"What does it matter—"

"Have you thought it through at all? Or is this another

thing you'll decide when you feel like it?" When he didn't respond, I added, "And yes, I'm going to Dallas."

Oliver's eyes narrowed but didn't move from mine.

Until the splash.

Meghan was at the bottom of the fountain.

Sarah screamed, Oliver swore, and we raced toward the water where Meghan had sunk like a stone. A moment later there was a second splash as Ryan jumped in after her. He disappeared immediately over the high ledge. The water looked about three feet deep, but when he pulled her to the surface, Meghan's eyes were closed and her forehead was bleeding.

"She's not breathing," he panted.

"Pull her out!" I shouted, images of last night's dream shrieking through my mind. "Hurry!"

"Pull her out!" Oliver's voice echoed mine.

"No stairs." Ryan grunted to his feet, holding Meghan in his arms. The water was getting deeper. "Edge is too high." Without another word, he sloshed his way toward the other side where the ledge dipped down.

Oliver was shouting to 911 through his cell while a crowd of helpless, rainbow-colored onlookers headed our way. The bridge to the other side seemed too great a distance, especially with my leg muscles shaky and spent. By then, the medical crew from the race sprinted toward the fountain. It was better to wait where we were.

"He's giving her mouth-to-mouth," Nick reported. "He used to be a lifeguard." Sarah came up behind me, wedging herself between Nick and me. Oliver put a hand on my elbow, then his arm went around my shoulders.

After what seemed like a million years, I heard the most

wonderful sound of gasping. "Is she okay?" I called across the fountain.

"She's breathing," Ryan called back. He leaned over Meghan again. "Now she's swearing like a sailor."

I covered my mouth with both hands, stifling my combination laugh/sob. Just as I felt I was about to break into hysterics, Oliver's other arm pulled me to his chest, holding me so close I almost couldn't breathe.

"It's okay." He ran one hand down my back, his other hand cupping my head. "She's okay, Rach."

Without thinking, I wrapped my arms around him and squeezed as hard as I could.

Part Two

*"She hoped to be wise and reasonable in time; but alas!
Alas! She must confess to herself that she was not wise yet."*
~Jane Austen's PERSUASION

Chapter Twenty-Two

The castle is closer; practically in full view. But why am I alone? I'm not supposed to be alone. The patch of grass where I had once seen Meghan's lifeless body is grown over, as though it's been years. I clutch the shoulder strap of my trusty knapsack and make a beeline toward those lofty spirals.

"Faster," someone whispers. "It won't be here forever." I recognize the voice. This is the first time he's appeared in one of my dreams.

"I am going faster," I reply to Nick, who is now walking beside me. "But the grass is too tall."

"It's not the grass that's slowing you." When I look down, I am standing knee-deep in the middle of a lagoon. Cattails, ferns, and water lilies cover the four banks that surround me.

"It's getting deeper," I say and stop walking, grateful to finally have someone to talk to. "What next?"

Nick puts his hands on my shoulders and turns me away from him. "You're asking the wrong person."

"It's not him." It's a new voice now. "Not Nick."

Someone from the shore throws me a white life ring. It easily slips over my head. "Just hold on and I'll pull you in," the new voice calls. I hold on with both hands. My fingers must be wrinkled and pruny by now. One minute, the water was knee-deep, and the next it's over my head. I don't even know which direction to swim. So I tread water. I pant, knowing it has been too long and relieved that the life ring was offered by the formless, faceless stranger. I am dragged to a set of cement stairs leading up and out of the mossy lake. When I reach the top, I don't cough or sputter because I am not short of breath or injured in any way. In fact, my heart is light, my mind is alert. I have never felt better.

The last of March's winter melted from the tree branches. Not quite full-on spring yet, but the excitement of newness and rebirth and change was definitely on the horizon. I wheeled my office chair to the mouth of my cube entrance, so I could look out the walls of windows. The morning sky was gray and dull—not matching my mood.

Nick cracked a joke and I laughed. It wasn't the funniest pun around, but he was a sweet guy and deserved a girl to laugh. We were on the phone confirming plans. Tonight, his flight would land at SFO at 7:00 p.m.

Weird how things could just…work out. Nick was buddies with Oliver, and he'd be crashing at Oliver's place over the long weekend. But Nick wasn't coming to San Francisco to hang out with his college buddy. He was coming for me.

The morning after Meghan's accident in Pasadena, he left for Dallas alone. With so much on my mind, I couldn't remember saying good-bye to him. Two days later he called.

And fairly regularly after that for the next two months.

He was smart and he made me laugh and I felt good when I thought about him. Without much of an effort on my part, he was growing on me, wrapping around my limbs like ivy. With no other weeds in my garden as competition, I'd become his willing post.

Oliver and I never had that talk. Why should I bother? Krikit was right. I needed to forgive myself for childish mistakes and move on—the mistake of *lying* to him, not of breaking up. He'd stayed in Pasadena until the end of the week. One night at the hotel, he tried to get me alone, but I had no intention of hearing about his big plans to squander his future. It was *his* life.

Meghan's injury wasn't too serious, though serious enough to keep her in Ryan's bedroom after she was released from her overnight stay at the ER. Ryan managed to drill it into her impressionable head that it was her dietary lifestyle that caused her body to go into shock and not properly absorb the stun of the fall into the water. Despite his doting bedside manner and overwhelming devotion toward his patient, our friends in San Francisco were surprised when word traveled north that they were in love. Though I already knew—Meghan could never keep even the smallest details a secret from me.

"You should see her now." Nick chuckled. "I didn't know her very well before, but from what you've told me, she's a changed woman."

I twirled the phone cord around one finger. "I know." I laughed back. "Whenever I talk to Megs, it's all about macrobiotic and fiber and whatever scientific study Ryan's working on. She sounds so...calm." I slumped in my seat as Bruce stomped past my cubical, trailed by a string of his expletives.

His lurking and stomping and swearing didn't bother me as much as it usually did. Maybe because I'd heard back from three of the companies I'd sent resumes to. I'd also written a few more short stories to go with my tale of the running trail. I might just have a series on my hands. I now had options I hadn't had before. And that was empowering.

"Megs is playing this role pretty close to the vest," I continued to Nick, "but I can tell she's never been happier."

"Ryan, too." There was a smile in Nick's voice. I could picture it. Such a nice smile.

"I have to go now. See you tonight."

"Yes, you will." That smile again.

I smoothed down my collar, then slid on some of Gio's jangly bracelets to complete my outfit. Nick would be here any minute. I didn't try to stifle the flutter this thought caused. I relished it.

"Hey, Trouble," Roger said with a big smile, his shoulder propped against my open bedroom door.

"Hey, Double."

"So, how does this work?" He crossed his arms. "Do I answer the door when he knocks or make myself scarce? I don't have a shotgun, but I can improvise."

"Funny. Stay and meet him. You should."

He leaned against my dresser. "Is it serious? I thought you two were just talking on the phone."

I caught his reflected eye in the mirror. "We're talking seriously."

Roger chuckled. "Got it. Do you want me to stay out of the apartment tonight?"

"We're not coming back here to...if that's what you mean." I tried not to feel completely mortified by talking about the subject with my brother. "We're going to dinner then he's bringing me home and staying at Oliver's."

Roger's eyebrows shot up. "Oliver Wentworth? That's where your boyfriend is staying?"

I toyed with my bracelets, fixated on the word *boyfriend*. It was way too early for that label, but it did sound nice for future reference. "Yes."

"Awkward."

I eyed his reflection, not needing to ask him why. Roger was privy to enough of our history to know it was going to be horribly awkward for me, thank you. But I wouldn't give him the satisfaction to tease me about it. Plus, I was a grown-up, dang it.

He dipped his chin and chuckled.

"Don't be a doodoohead," I said. "Nick's known Oliver way longer than he's known me. There's nothing awkward."

Roger did stop laughing, slid his hands in his pockets, and looked at the floor. "Listen, Rach, there's something you should know. A few months ago, I ran into him—Wentworth."

This was not news to me. "At Tim Olson's party the night I was stuck at work." I exhaled, completely unaffected. "I know."

"Before then. I knew he was here before you moved back. I knew he was hanging out with Meghan."

I pushed out a dark chuckle, recalling that *extremely* awkward scene on the jogging trail, me loafing on the grass with crazy hair and zombie-girl makeup, being completely blindsided at the sight of my gorgeous ex.

"Gee, Roger, a little warning back then might've been nice."

"Yeah." He rubbed the back of his neck. "I left you a voicemail about it, but I should've followed up with you."

"Oh." My mind flashed to that second, "Rach, we have to talk," moment. "I got your voicemail, but I thought I'd hallucinated that part of the message so I deleted it."

"Do you often hallucinate voicemails?"

"I think you're missing the point."

He sighed and sat on the edge of my bed. "He's not a bad guy."

"He wasn't a bad guy in college, either. You barely got to know him." I whirled around, the past falling in on me before I could stop it. "One dinner and your mind was made up that he wasn't good enough for me."

"I never said that."

"Yes, you did, when you showed up at my dorm the next morning."

He shook his head. "You're rewriting history, Rach. I never said that because I never thought that about him. I was worried about you."

I didn't want to rehash this. Not tonight.

"But I was even more worried afterward," my brother said. "You were a mess."

Well, it was nice to know someone actually noticed.

"I blamed myself for a long time."

The words, "Good—you should!" sat on the tip of my tongue, but I couldn't speak them because they weren't true. I closed my eyes and sighed, then sat beside him, pushing back memories, reeling them in again.

"It wasn't your fault. I didn't handle things well back then. I had this…hang-up." I laughed darkly, remembering how I'd yelled at Oliver in the middle of the color run. "Apparently, I've *still* got it. But I didn't know how to talk to Oliver about it. Instead, I ignored it and kept falling in love with him."

Roger shifted on the bed. He didn't want to rehash this, either, but the time had come.

"It was always there, though, the fear that he wasn't right for me in the long run. When I was with him, I couldn't balance our relationship with my goals. You remember how close I came to failing that semester?"

Roger nodded. "But you got back on track. You've always been a planner."

"Yeah. My romantic downfall." I shook my head. "I knew it would come to a head the night you two met, when we had dinner."

"I was an asshole, way too overprotective. Sorry. I didn't dislike *him*, but you were nineteen."

"I know. Believe me, there wasn't a single worry you had that I hadn't already obsessed over. But yeah, I was nineteen and I loved him and ninety percent of me wanted to be with him, but it was the nagging ten percent that made the decision."

"You didn't tell him why?"

"No." I rubbed my nose. "Instead, I kind of threw you under the bus."

"Me?"

"It was easier to say you wouldn't allow me to date him, so I lied about the whole thing, blamed you for it—right to his face like a damn coward." I broke off when my throat grew thick.

Roger stared at the floor for a moment, scratched his head, and laughed. "No wonder. That night I ran into him at the party, I got the impression he didn't trust me, kinda hated me."

"I'm sorry. Oliver's got a long memory, too."

"I kept catching him staring at me. When I finally realized who he was, I went up to him."

"You didn't." The back of my scalp shivered. "What did he say?"

He shrugged and rubbed his jaw. "I don't know. We just talked for a minute."

"Again, Rog, it would've been nice if you'd told your sister."

"Guys don't share every nuance of information like women do." He shrugged again. "It was no big deal. We talked it out."

"Talked it out?" I repeated. "What did you say? How did he look? Did my name come up?" I jumped when there was a knock on the front door. Nick. Shit.

No, no, I should *not* have allowed my thoughts to stray down the Oliver road. Nick was here. Yes, good. Nick with the great hair, who paid attention to me and liked me and had a job he loved. I was happy to see him—I was ready to see him. So ready.

"I'm glad things are cool with you guys now." I rose to my feet, dabbed vanilla oil along my collarbones, and grabbed my jacket. "But Oliver's not who flew four hundred miles to spend the weekend with me."

When I pulled open the door, a rush of relief hit. Nick

looked better than ever. Very Brad Pitt a la *A River Runs Through It*. I quickly introduced him to Roger at the door, but didn't want to linger. I couldn't erase the picture of my brother and my ex "talking it out."

The moment we were outside the closed door, Nick spun around and wrapped me up in a hug. "I have to imagine this every time we talk on the phone."

I hugged him back. It felt nice.

He spoke into my hair. "How've you been?"

"Good." His body was warm and he smelled of after-shave I couldn't place. "You?"

"I'm happy I'm here, Rachel." He gave me a squeeze then let go.

"Me, too. You look hungry."

He cocked an eyebrow. "You are the queen of subtext." He kissed the corner of my mouth, keeping his cheek pressed to mine for a moment after. "I'm very hungry, but not for food." Butterflies fluttered in my stomach, and I couldn't help exhaling a silly giggle. "Well, you asked." He drew back and looked into my eyes.

We were healthy adults, obviously attracted to one an-other, and we'd been chatting on the phone for two months. What would have happened right then if Roger hadn't been on the other side of the door?

"We should, um…" I nodded toward the street. "Reservations in twenty."

Nick lifted a grin. "Okay. I'm pretty jet lagged, anyway."

• • •

Beside the overnight sporting events for his job, Nick hadn't visited San Francisco since he was a kid. The next day, he wanted to see Fisherman's Wharf—a place I'd described to him many times over the phone. We walked around all day, in and out of cafés and shops and bookstores, even Ghirardelli Chocolate Company, Meghan's favorite, a sort of a fond *aide-memoire* to our friend.

The pear trees and dogwoods were beginning to bloom after a long winter of bare branches and crunchy leaves. At the start of the day, Nick scooped up my hand in his, which felt strange at first, but as the day progressed into evening, it was as easy as our conversation.

But conversation could take a girl only so far.

I was restless and stirred up, and I'd been stirred up for weeks—since Pasadena. Nick had barely touched me when he'd dropped me off last night. My body felt like a genie's lamp, needing a good rubdown, or like a cat's scratching post. And Nick was right there.

"Do you know what I like about you?" he asked when we stopped to lean over a stony footbridge, twinkle lights reflecting in the water.

"My sparkling wit?"

His hand slid to the small of my back, his shoulder against mine. He smiled at my reflection in the water below. "I can read everything on your face."

"Yeah?" I faced the real Nick, more than ready for him to relieve my restlessness. "Whatcha reading now?" I lowered my gaze to his mouth then cocked an eyebrow.

Some bad line, Rachel. But it worked.

Finally, a real kiss. Though at first, I didn't know what I was doing, like kissing a hottie was a secret procedure reserved for lucky people. I hadn't been lucky in years. But there I was, enfolded in the arms of a strong, sexy guy who cared about me, someone I trusted and liked. Yes, I liked him.

"You're shaking."

I lowered my chin and giggled softly, not remembering the subtleties of how to chitchat after a first kiss. Chitchat was overrated.

"Do you want my coat?"

"I'd rather you warm me up this way." I kissed him this time. It was soft and romantic and made my heart beat fast and my palms tingle. It was everything off the checklist of what you'd read in a romance novel: the two of us under the moonlight, forcing people to walk around us, the taste of chocolate on both our tongues. Before I knew it, the shops were closing for the night, and we were the last to retrieve our car at the valet stand.

Nick double-parked on the hill outside my apartment. "Roger's home." I peered at the glowing light of my living room.

"We better say good night, then."

I grabbed his rental car keys and hid them behind my back. "How can you?"

"Am I going to have to wrestle you for those?" He tucked a piece of my hair behind an ear. "I think I might like that. Or we can always"—he fingered a lock of my hair— "take a drive."

Take a drive. That was code for "find a deserted parking lot and tear each other's clothes off in the backseat like oversexed teenagers."

The thought was certainly tempting, and when he kissed me again, pressing me against the car, it was very hard not to start the process right there on the sidewalk. But a voice inside my head wouldn't let me. No, it wasn't in my head...it was the voice from my dream telling me it wasn't Nick.

For such a tiny voice, it rang louder than the fog horns on Golden Gate Bridge.

"It's late." I handed over the keys, my breaths jagged and loud—not matching my action of pushing him away. "You want to check out Bodega Bay in the morning?"

Nick exhaled a soft, frustrated moan. "Sure. But you're driving this time."

"Fun." I smiled at the prospect. "I've got a convertible."

He opened his car door. "You'll pick me up at Rad's place?"

The happy little campfire in my chest was suddenly dowsed. "Right, s-sure," I said with a big smile that gave me a sudden headache. I hoped against hope that things would not be awkward, like Roger implied, even though there was no way in hell they wouldn't.

Chapter Twenty-Three

I had to knock three times. I wasn't thrilled to have to be there in the first place, climb those fourteen stairs. But since I didn't see Oliver's car anywhere on the street, I was fairly certain he wasn't home. The door finally swung open. Nick had a phone to his ear.

"I tried to catch you on your cell."

"Oh." I pulled my phone from the outside pocket of my purse. "I must have turned it off."

"I need to finish this conference call." He looked properly apologetic as he stepped back and waved me in. "It's work. Is that cool?"

I glanced past him. The place appeared otherwise empty. "No problem."

Nick promptly disappeared down the hall and I leaned against the couch, taking an uninhibited examination of Oliver's living room. The smell of fresh paint from the only other time I'd been there had faded. It now smelled like pinecones and—I sniffed—cinnamon? Or more specifically, Cinnamon Bliss essential oil. But that was insane.

The walls were bare except for five framed pieces of art-work. Paintings and drawings. The signature "S. Wentworth" was scribbled across the bottom of the first painting. Huh. All the pieces were Sarah's. I knew she was an artist, but she'd never shown me her work. If she was self-conscious about her talent, she didn't need to be. Her paintings were beautiful.

Undaunted Courage and a recent biography of Steve Jobs were opened and dog-eared on Oliver's coffee table. Beside them sat a black spiral notebook. I ran a finger across its cover, wondering if it was one of the great-great dece-dents of that notebook Oliver used to carry around with him back at USF. He was always writing in that thing. I was tempted to accidently push it off the table at the exact angle to make it fall open so I could get a peek inside, but I swiv-eled on my heel and walked away.

An acoustic guitar without a case leaned against the wall in the corner. I hadn't played for years but something drew me to the instrument. I picked it up and strummed a few chords. It was in perfect tune, meaning Oliver—or who-ever's it was, Nick's? Sarah's?—had played it recently. My wandering fingers doodled up and down the strings, not playing anything specific. The doodles took shape, morphing into a song, the catchy, upbeat Motown classic turned mel-ancholy under my fingers.

The floorboards of the vestibule creaked. I looked up to see Oliver standing at his open front door.

"You play. Why didn't I know that?" It didn't sound like a question. He shut the door with his foot.

I set the guitar against the wall. "Nick's on the phone, so I'm waiting for him."

"Lucky Nick." He cleared his throat, and slowly, almost cautiously, entered his own living room. He tossed his jacket over a chair. "It's been a while, Rachel. Two months."

"Yeah." I pulled at my ear. Where the hell was Nick?

"Last time we talked, you were angry."

Very observant. And he could hardly say what we did at the end of the color run was "talk." If he really wanted to talk to me, he could have. Okay, maybe he'd tried once, but—gah! It didn't matter now.

I hadn't seen him since Pasadena and noticed he wasn't shaving his head anymore. His chestnut hair had been growing back for two months. Maybe he decided it was time for a change. Women did that all the time. He also looked slightly more tired since the last time I'd seen him. Maybe he was dating someone and out late every night, or up even later right here playing her love songs on his stupid guitar. Well, good for him.

"Was I angry?" I eyed the couch to sit, but didn't move. "I don't remember."

"I do. You asked if I'd quit my job, and I asked if you were going to Dallas with…" He jerked his head toward the back of the house. "But that wasn't what I wanted to talk to you about."

"*Did* you quit your job?"

"What?" He looked baffled, just like he had when I'd asked him the first time. "I still don't have a firm plan about—" My scoff cut him off. Oliver crossed his arms, confusion turning to annoyance. "What was that?"

"Nothing." I glanced at the couch again, then down the

hall. "It's just…you're exactly the same. You don't *plan* for the future."

It was Oliver's turn to scoff. "Don't I?"

"Obviously not. And some people need that. Some people need to feel secure in what's coming."

"Life doesn't come with a crystal ball."

"There're ways to take some of the risk out of the equation." I shrugged, tired of dancing around the subject. "Though I guess some people don't give that a second thought, even if it affects someone else."

He pointed at his chest. "Are you talking about me?"

"*You—*" I lowered my voice when it echoed off the hardwood floors. "You have a good, steady job and you're willing to throw it away."

His eyebrows shot up. "I don't know who you've been talking to, but you have no idea what you're saying." He took a step toward me. "There's always risk in life, especially when it comes to careers. Yes, I'm starting my own business, if that's what you're referring to, but I'm being smart about it. And believe me, this is *nothing* like before, Rachel. You of all people should realize that I learn from my mistakes. All of them."

Then why didn't he realize what he was doing was reckless? These things could take years to plan and organize. Not preparing for the future killed relationships, hurt even the strongest ones. I was living, breathing evidence. Oliver was smart, I knew this, but I didn't understand why he couldn't see he wasn't being smart now.

"I…don't know what else to say." I blew out a breath, frustrated, trying *not* to be frustrated. Being frustrated showed I cared. And I didn't care. I couldn't. "We shouldn't be talking about this, anyway."

Nick was in the next room, I was wearing sexy new underwear, I was armed with both latex and latex-free, and it shouldn't matter to me what Oliver was doing about his job.

"Then what should we be talking about, Rachel?" He took another step toward me. "The weather? Politics? Or that weekend with me in your dorm that you swore you would never forget?"

Heat flooded my chest. Painful, exquisite. Reeeeally unhelpful.

"I…I noticed Sarah's paintings." I pointed to one. "They're excellent."

Oliver stared at me with arched eyebrows, then he exhaled and ran a hand over the top of his head. "She doesn't think so."

I blew out my own slow breath. At least he was willing to drop the subject before it got any more heated.

He slid his hands in the pockets of his black suit pants. "I had to steal these from her portfolio. She hates that I hung them up, but I told her it's therapy, preparation for when she's in all the Soho galleries."

I laughed under my breath and moved to another piece. Art was a safe subject. "I especially like this one. The greens and blues remind me of a dream I had the other night. All swirling and nonsensical, like a storm, disaster over the horizon, fear of the unknown, but in a good way."

"Here's where we differ again. I see a pattern in the chaos, a path leading out." His voice drew quiet. "Life after the storm, in a *very* good way."

I peeked at him from the corners of my eyes, then back at the painting. "I could analyze all day. Roger tells me I'm too literal, but Meghan claims I'm blind about what's right in front of my face."

Oliver placed a hand on the mantel, placing himself between me and the painting. "What's in front of your face now?"

Before I could answer, we both turned in the direction of Nick's voice rising to a laugh down the hallway. I felt Oliver's eyes on me, but I glanced toward the front door out of there.

"In my opinion, things for you look clear." He dropped his hand and stepped back.

I had a pretty good idea that he was referring to Nick, and I felt the strangest urge to explain myself, explain *why* I was with another guy—a guy who wasn't him. That's absurd, Rachel. Unproductive. Still, I couldn't help asking, "What things?"

The conversation derailed when Nick entered the room. He was whistling and grinning like he'd landed a golden stock tip. "Hey you." He rested a hand on my shoulder, giving it a little massage. "Hope you haven't been bored."

I looked at Oliver, waiting for him to say something, *anything*, to finish a damn thought for once in his damn life.

When he didn't, I filled the silence with, "We were talking about Sarah's paintings."

Nick examined one. "Kid's got an eye."

"Rachel and I don't agree on what this one symbolizes." Oliver gestured at the swirls of green and blue.

"Huh." Nick tilted his head as his gaze swept over the painting. "No clue."

"I think it represents chaos and disorder." I pointed at the painting but glanced at Oliver.

"And I see optimism," he said, at the exact instant Nick planted a kiss on my cheek. "But I'm probably wrong."

I couldn't look at either guy. Why did it feel like all my options were suddenly gone? Was I marrying Nick? Were we even an official couple? No! Just because Oliver said *he* thought my future with Nick looked clear shouldn't mean crap.

It was my life, I could do anything I wanted, be who I wanted, be *with* who I wanted, choose if I stayed at NRG Interactive until I rotted and became the next Scary Claire, or tear up my stupid ten-year plan and start over. It was up to me. I had to make the choices, or suffocate.

• • •

I gripped the steering wheel after shutting off the radio. Would San Francisco stations ever stop playing "Time of Your Life" by Green Day? The real title, "Good Riddance" felt more fitting, anyway.

"My head's not in a good place right now."

Nick actually chuckled. "Pretty cliché line for a writer, Rach."

"Sorry." I decelerated behind a logging truck on the way back from our touristy day in Bodega Bay that had been cut short due to my unexpected announcement. "I know it's bad timing. I mean, you came all the way here."

He put a hand over mine, the same hand I'd clung to last night that had slid through my hair and down my back. Its touch did nothing for me today.

"I wanted to come. We needed to be in the same room to see what was really between us."

"Yeah." I stared at the white dividing lines on the highway.

"And there's nothing?"

"Not enough and not now." I flipped my hand over so I could squeeze his. It was a gesture, nothing more, and I slid it out from his after a few seconds.

For the last two months, Nick had been my way out, or rather, my way *back* to living life again, maybe even finding love. He was fun and easy, and I really liked talking to him on the phone, emailing him, IM-ing during the workday. Plus, he was gorgeous and into me and he smelled really good and…

"I have issues," I said.

"We all do. I get it, Rachel. You've been hurt. You're not the first."

"I was the one who did the hurting," I said. "I think I'm still doing it, to the same person. While I'm trying to figure out why or how to stop, it's probably not a good idea for me to be with anyone. And it's kind of a long time coming." Almost seven years.

Chapter Twenty-Four

A few days after I'd dropped off Nick at the airport, I called Sarah and Giovanna to meet for lunch and some serious girl time.

"Nick's hot. You're cray-cray." Gio flipped her glossy black hair then dug into her salad. "If I was in your shoes, he'd be on his knees."

I smiled at my beautiful friend. Sometimes it was hard not to tie her down and give her a Mohawk. "Thanks for the support."

"I think what Gio means"—Sarah passed me the pepper—"is we're a little surprised. I thought you liked him. Was there no chemistry?"

"Plenty of that." I licked the back of my spoon. I'd ordered nothing but soup because my stomach felt queasy and my jaw ached like I'd been clenching it for hours. Maybe I had a cavity or an oncoming sinus infection. "I did like him. It's complicated. *I'm* complicated."

Gio snorted. "Since when?"

"Shit, guys. I miss Meghan. At least she humors me."

"Sorry, *cheri*." Gio put a hand over mine, her accent coming out. "Tell us all about your *many* complications, Rachel Daughtry."

I needed lunch with my girls to take my mind off Nick, but also to take my mind off the dream I'd had last night—the creepiest one yet. Though it cut off before anything tragic happened, it was weird. I'd never come so close to dying in a dream before or…or knowing that I was about to die.

Halfway through lunch, I dropped the next bomb. "I'm considering moving back to Texas." I'd planned the statement to sound both casual and exciting. Mostly though, I just needed to say it out loud, see how it felt released into the atmosphere. "*The Dallas Morning News* is hiring. I've been in touch with my old boss and…"

Sarah dropped her fork. Giovanna looked like her chair was on fire.

"I'm *thinking* about it." My voice held much less conviction now.

"Well, stop." Sarah slammed her palm on the table. "You can't leave, too."

"Rachel." Gio looked beautifully miserable. "I think I'm gonna puke."

"I said I'm *considering*, keeping my options open. Options are good. Choices are good. Life without choices and chances is smothering, right?" When I got nothing but blank stares, I stopped. "Forget I brought it up."

I grabbed my drink, the ache in my jaw giving me a headache. I got a few more skeptical glares across the table at lunch, but nothing more was said on the subject until I was dropping Sarah at her dorm.

"I know why you want to leave."

"It's not about *leaving*, per se." I set the car in park. "But a change might be nice, something unplanned."

"You don't do unplanned."

"Oh." I blinked at her. "Maybe I need to start."

"I don't want you to go," she said, biting her thumbnail. "This just seems so spur-of-the-moment…moving, taking some new job. Is that what you really want to do?"

I looked away from her and stared at the gauges on my dashboard. "Just because I don't have a complete plan set in stone right this second doesn't mean I'm not working on it. What I'm doing now, or what I'm *thinking* of doing, will put me in a position to have more choices later." I ran a finger over the cruise control button. "And I'm sorry, I don't really want to move, either, but sometimes stepping into the unknown is necessary. Sometimes you need to take risks—*smart* risks. That's the only way to grow."

Sarah scoffed and folded her arms. "You sound exactly like Ollie."

I stared at her, slack jawed, my latest inhale stalled mid-breath.

Oh. Crap.

Was this the same as what Oliver was doing?

No. No, no, no.

Well, I guess I didn't know exactly *what* he was doing. I'd never given him a real chance to explain why he was making these choices and taking risks that seemed unnecessary. Unnecessary *to me*. He told me he was being smart about it, and I hadn't believed him. Hadn't even bothered to hear him.

I closed my eyes and pressed the heel of my hand to my forehead. It was burning, pounding.

No, no, no. It couldn't be the same.

Currently, my job at NRG Interactive was more stable than ever, yet I'd considered leaving that for something new, taking a risk. But it was a calculated risk, not a spontaneous move because I was bored or felt like blowing my life savings and ruining my life.

Was Oliver preparing himself the same way?

And what about those stories I'd submitted to *Vogue* and *Best* and *Redbook*? What was my plan if something came of that? Did I need one right this instant?

Of course not. But now I could see the value in taking a chance on the unknown, preparing for that by being responsible and wise in the meantime.

My skin crawled as I remembered what I'd said to Oliver about that very thing. Accused him of being reckless and thoughtless, screwing up his life. I'd projected my fear onto him. Just like when we were nineteen.

I flinched when Sarah moved to take off her seat belt, feeling shaky and unfocused. *I* was the one who'd screwed up, not him.

"I know it's Sunday and you have a million things to do," she said, "but will you come inside for a minute?"

I swallowed, wanting nothing more than to be alone to finish my disgraceful self-analysis. But it was obvious Sarah wanted to talk. "Sure," I said, and followed her inside. Her dorm room was chilly and smelled like honeysuckle candles. It was a different layout than mine had been. Good. The very last thing I needed was any more blasts from the past.

"Would you like some tea? I always drink chamomile

after a meal."

"Yes, thank you." Tea sounded soothing to my churning stomach, but the formalness between us felt odd. I folded my arms tightly, feeling like I'd stepped into a trap by coming inside.

"Sugar?" She held two blue ceramic mugs with hand-painted daisies.

"Sure."

She sat on the loveseat across from me, cupping her mug with both hands, but not drinking or speaking, hardly moving.

"Mmm, it's good." I took a few sips. "Maybe this will help me sleep tonight. I'm still having those dreams about—"

"Do you remember"—she cut me off, maybe not realizing I was speaking—"when I told you about… Umm, I feel stupid. This is hard."

"Sarah, what's on your mind?"

"Yesterday, I was at Ollie's apartment doing my laundry. He knows I'm kind of seeing this one guy—it's no big deal, but he got all bossy and brotherly and warned me not to lose focus on school."

How ironically familiar.

Sarah stared down into her mug, rotating it between her hands. "He told me some things about his freshman year. That was the summer I was fourteen." She lifted her chin and peered at me. "I told you about that, how my family got into goal setting and stuff around that same time."

Talk about a blast from the past. I rubbed my nose and nodded.

"But I didn't tell you about *before* that, what Ollie was like right when he came home from USF. He was quiet and angry, depressed—not at all like he used to be. I think my parents wanted to send him to counseling."

I set down my mug. Pain lashed at the back of my throat when I tried to speak. "I didn't know that."

"Well, they didn't have to. Ollie changed on his own. Once he decided to live at home and transfer to State, it was like the first of his black clouds lifted. It wasn't just USF he didn't want to face, there was a girl there."

"Sarah—"

"I'm naturally curious, Rachel. Later that day, when Ollie left for the gym, I found the box under his bed that has his yearbooks, the one from freshman year."

I picked up my mug only to put it back down. I tried not to look at Sarah but couldn't look away.

"All the pictures of you are circled." She took a slow sip of her tea. "He must have bought it before your breakup. You wrote in it. Two pages."

"I know." I cringed when I heard my voice break.

"You *wrote* in it." Accusation was in her tone now. "You wrote in Oliver's yearbook, Rachel, like you were in love with him."

"Yes." I laced my fingers together and squeezed hard, trying to hold everything together, my emotions, especially. "I should've told you."

"Yeah, you should have," she snapped. "I'm really mad at you, Rachel. Well, I mean, I was, I wanted to be." Her voice turned calm, then her tough façade dissolved completely and her eyes twinkled. "You and Ollie." She leaned back and grinned. "I bet you were the hottest couple on campus."

I blinked, still teetering on the brink of tears. "What?"

"Oh, yeah. I can totally see it. You were freaking perfect for each other, still are. You were apart for all those years then thrown back together. Meghan would call that fate." Her eyes lit up. "Let's call her, get her take."

"Not a good idea."

But she was already pressing buttons on her cell. The phone was on speaker when it rang.

"Sarah," I hissed in panic. "Meghan doesn't know about us."

She stared at me and set the phone on the middle of the coffee table. "What?"

"I never told her anything—"

Meghan's crackly voice chirped, "Hello?"

Chapter Twenty-Five

I held my breath and stared at Sarah, begging her silently not to spill my secret. Meghan was with Ryan now, and I knew I'd 'fess up about Oliver at some point, but on speakerphone in front of his little sister was not the optimal time.

"Meghan, hey. It's Sarah." She nodded at me.

"And Rachel!" I tried to sound bright and chipper.

"Hey, peeps. What's up?"

"Umm." Sarah and I shrugged back and forth at each other. "Umm. Rach was going to tell you about…about…"

"About a dream I had last night." I sank to the floor and slid the phone closer to me.

"Cool," Meghan said. "Tell me."

"I dreamed that my teeth were falling out." I held a hand up to my jaw, still sore from clenching my teeth or whatever.

"Dude. That's harsh."

"So? What does it mean? I've lived for months without your dream analysis, and my mouth has been aching all day."

I rocked my jaw, gingerly. "What's your take?"

"I always heard hair falling out is fear, and teeth falling out is insecurity."

Sarah frowned and touched her hair.

"Oh." I felt another painful twinge in my jaw. "What am I insecure about?"

"Beats me, Rach. Maybe Nick?"

I laughed. "That's *stupidity*, not insecurity."

"What else are you dreaming? Still about the rusty cup and that castle?"

I shuddered at the memory. "Stop joking—you *died* in that dream once, Megs."

"Died?" Sarah slid to the floor across from me. "You didn't tell me that."

I nodded at the phone between us. "The next day is when she fell in the fountain."

"Rachel." Sarah gasped.

"Calm down, you guys," Meghan soothed. "Rach, you're obviously caught in a psycho-cosmic, heightened-sensory moon phase. Maybe you have the *touch*."

"I don't have the *touch*. It's just my subconscious freaking out, right? You've said it a million times."

"Don't blow off the subconscious. Part of subconscious is *conscious*—waking reality. Your dreams come from somewhere, something already experienced, or hoped to be experienced. The subconscious isn't all that creative."

"She's right," Sarah added sagely.

"Seriously. I'd pay extra close attention if I were you. Your subconscious thinks something is about to happen and it's bursting to tell you."

"If you're trying to scare me…" I was only half joking.

"Inform me immediately if you have any dreams about me or Ryan. I will need complete details. Start keeping a journal."

"Yeah, okay." But my mind slid to the dream I'd had earlier in the week.

I always, *always* heard you can never die in your own dream; that whatever situation the dreamer is in, they will wake before the certain death-blow is executed. So then, what does it mean if you dream you are *going* to die? If the dream is so vivid, so meticulously detailed, that—even if you hadn't seen it three nights in a row—you could storyboard every scene perfectly?

And what if you knew exactly when it was going to take place? Your death. Down to the minute.

Meghan was the only person I could've talked to without sounding crazy. But even *I* thought death premonitions were outlandish. So I focused back on my teeth-falling-out dream. If it meant insecurity, I could live with that. I reached for the little bowl of almonds on the coffee table and set it on my lap, but my hand froze halfway to my mouth when there was a knock on Sarah's door and Oliver walked in.

He wore jeans and a nicely fitting sky-blue button-up, and had his chestnut hair grown in even more in the four days since I'd seen him?

Hmm. So, this was the guy brave enough to face life without a plan, to take risks and leaps of faith. I knew where he was coming from now, that rush that comes when thinking about the huge, scary, exciting possibilities of the future. He was brave because he *had* planned, he'd probably been planning how to start his own company for years, probably ever since his father had taken that same leap.

This was the guy brave enough to look at a painting that confused me, and see optimism, hope, the path to a better life. The dude manly enough to live in a pink house like a boss. He was a loving brother, a good friend, and a hard worker. He'd grown into a better man than I could've imagined, even when I'd been in love with the boy.

And dang, he was hot.

And single. So was I.

"Oh." I sat up straight.

"Oh." Oliver glanced back and forth at us, maybe wondering why we were on the floor. He set down a shopping bag. "I was just dropping off—"

"Is that Rad?"

Oliver peered down at the phone on the coffee table. "Meghan?"

"Heeey!"

"Uh, hi." He stood over the phone, his hands in the back pockets of his jeans. "How's it going?"

"Great." I heard Meghan's smile. "Just catching up with my girls. Rach was telling us about a dream she had last night."

Oliver looked at me, one eyebrow lifted. "I'd like to hear about that, too."

I felt like this was the time to flash him a smile and do a sexy hair flip or something, but I didn't appreciate how it looked like he was about to laugh. Okay, I didn't believe in *all* of Meghan's mumbo-jumbo, but at least I was open to the idea.

"Nope. We're all done discussing that." I stared at the wall straight ahead and tossed an almond at my open mouth. I missed and it bounced on the coffee table. I tried again.

Bull's-eye. "And I was just about to—*ow*! Ohhh, son of a—"

"Rachel." Oliver was beside me.

"Rach?" Meghan, this time. "Hello? What's happening?"

"She's holding her cheek," Sarah reported.

"Insecure, my ass," I muttered around the pain shooting up my face, encircling my entire head. "I just broke a tooth."

"No *way*." Meghan sounded a little too happy. "Rach, do you realize what this means? Your teeth are falling out!"

"I'm aware, Megs." When I tried to stand, Oliver had me by the arm to help.

"No, I mean your dream came true—in the very literal sense. Do you know how lucky you are? Okay, tell me about the castle one again. What did the tin cup look like? I want every detail."

"A little busy now," I mumbled. It hurt worse when I talked or even moved. "Where are my car keys and phone? I have to call my dentist. Ow—crap. I have no idea if he's open on the weekends."

"Mine is," Oliver said. "It's only a few miles. I'll take you."

There wasn't much choice. Before leaving, he grabbed a bag of peas from Sarah's freezer and instructed me to hold it where it hurt. His arm was around me as we walked down the stairs and across the street to his car. I tried not to breathe in the smell of his shirt or acknowledge the feel of his hard muscles against me, how perfectly I still fit inside the crock of his arm.

"Thank you," I said as we both buckled in.

"Happy to help." Before pulling into traffic, he made a quick call. I could see his dentist right away.

I wanted to speak again, maybe casually bring up Sarah's

painting. Super-casual segues into talking about us. "Oliv— ohh."

"Don't talk. We'll be there soon."

Blerg. I exhaled and sat back, adjusting the makeshift icepack against my cheek. Not too much time later, after handing over my insurance card, I only had to wait a few minutes before being called into the examination room. Two shots and too many drills later, I had a temporary crown and found Oliver in the waiting room.

"You didn't have to wait. I could've—"

"Shh, this is hilarious." His eyes were fixed on the TV mounted to the wall, his expression as animated as a little boy watching SpongeBob.

"Is that Jerry Springer?" I sat beside him. "I thought he went off the air."

"No way. He's a legend."

"I didn't know you watched daytime talk shows."

"I don't." He glanced at me, a little smile tugging at a corner of his mouth. "Well, sometimes." He leaned back and toward me so our heads were almost touching. "See, that guy"—he pointed at the TV—"he just found out his sister is really his mother."

"That story's been done."

"Right, but he also just found out that his other sister is really a dude."

"Is that why he's hitting him over the head with a chair?"

"Yeah." Oliver's eyes twinkled adorably. How could I have ever thought anyone's eyes were as adorable? "And see that couple on the other couch, the ones not beating each other over the heads? One of them has a secret." He looked at me. "But we don't know what it is. Ah, damn. Commercial break."

I laughed at his disappointment. "It'll be a little while for the dentist to send over my prescription. We can wait for the show to come back on if you want."

"Naw." He ran a hand over his chin, but his eyes flashed toward the TV.

"No, it's fine. My afternoon plans of eating an entire bag of apples just went down in flames."

He swiveled around to me, head tilted as if noticing me for the first time. "Are you okay now? Your mouth."

"No taffy for a while, but they say I'll live."

"Good." He flipped his cell in his hands. "Sarah's been calling."

"I'll text her." After sending a quick "all clear" message to both Sarah and Meghan, I put down my phone.

"I'm glad you're so close. Your friendship means the world to my sister." His gaze held on me for a second, and my heart stopped. *Please say something.* Was I talking to him or me? The music of Springer returning filled the small waiting room, and Oliver's silvery eyes left me for the screen.

I blew out a slow breath then said, "Secret time," though my heart still pounded with the need to unload a few secrets of my own.

Oliver chuckled. "Best part of the show."

The camera pulled tight on a woman's face. It was one of those talking head interviews and she went on to tell her husband (and the rest of the planet) that she was leaving him for another man.

Ahh. Such beautiful drama. God bless America.

She was leaving him to be with her childhood sweet-heart—the boy next door, the man she loved twenty years ago but never got over. She'd been 100 percent faithful to her husband until running into her ex-flame, and they both realized they were still in love.

I was glued to my seat, afraid to even breathe. Oliver wasn't moving, either.

The husband on the screen huffed and puffed but finally left the stage when the new/old boyfriend came on. I was transfixed as I watched them kiss in front of everyone.

"Do you think it's true?"

I flinched at his voice. "W-what's true?"

He turned to me but kept his gaze on the floor. "That she loved him all that time, Rachel? Even when she was married to another man?"

"No way."

We turned to see a guy, another patient, in the waiting room. I thought we'd been alone.

"No way, what?" Oliver said.

The guy pointed at the TV. "No woman holds a torch for that long. She's either lying or they've been hooking up the whole time."

"Not necessarily." This came from the receptionist who'd poked her head out her little window. "Women stay faithful way longer than men. It's in our genetic code."

"So is cheating," the guy shot back. It was like watching a tennis match.

"Women's senses are tied to emotions, *feelings*. We're more sentimental. Men are usually way more visual."

Wow. She was certainly opinionated. I'd heard that philosophy before, though I didn't necessarily agree with it.

"A woman can hold the memory of love way longer than a man," she continued. "Most guys have to be in the presence of who they love to get that really strong stimulation. But women…" She paused, looking a little choked up. "We never forget."

"Wanna grab a drink later?" the guy asked.

She smiled. "I'm off at six. Now come on back, the doctor's ready."

I stared after them, about ready to make a joke to Oliver about how we'll see them on Springer in a year.

"Let's go," he said gruffly, standing and walking to the door. "I'll drop you off at Sarah's."

My chest felt hollow and the heaviness on my shoulders weighed me down as I watched his retreating back. We'd been close to…something, the subtext was written on the wall. One of us just had to say it. But the whole drive back to the dorms, Oliver kept his left elbow propped on the side of the door as his fist scraped back and forth over his frown. He did *not* want to talk.

Chapter Twenty-Six

I've reached the shore. And, not surprisingly, am completely dry and carrying my trusty knapsack. Still panting, I look around, searching for the person who threw out that life ring and pulled me in. I look down. Footprints in the sand. Which I follow. Down a path, up a switchback. Oliver is leaning against a tree. "You made it," he says. "I didn't know how long I would have to wait." He smiles as he approaches. The way he looks at me makes every bone in my body ache to kiss him. "Give me this." He slides the knapsack off my shoulder. When it hits the dirt, that small, rusty cup rattles. "You don't need it anymore. You don't need this, either." I'm confused when he removes the strap of another knapsack I've been carrying. "All this time. How heavy these must have been for you." When I look over his shoulder, impossibly, we're in London, standing on the bridge facing Big Ben. The hands of the big clock are moving too fast, making me dizzy. It's Saturday the fifth; I know this because the date is flashing on a marque.

*Oliver still smiles. "Let me have this, too." He removes anoth-
er bag of my heavy burden. His smile turns crooked. "You're
practically naked now, Rachel." He is eyeing the front of my
body. As he reaches for me, the clock chimes. It's so loud that
the sound feels trapped in my head. I slap my hands over my
ears like a little girl. When Oliver's arms go around me, the
pain strikes. He is whispering my name, repeating it over and
over. He doesn't know I'm in pain. When he pulls me up, I see
the blood bubbling out from under my skin, seeping across
my s`tomach, dripping down my hip...*

I hit the floor. It didn't take long to realize I'd flung myself
out of bed, tangled in sweat-soaked sheets. I rolled over and
checked myself. No pain, no blood. Just a dream.

But it was *that* dream. Again.

I tried to shake it off while I showered and dried my
hair. Why had it hurt when dream-Oliver held me?

I tried to shake it off at breakfast. After nearly puking
up a piece of toast, I tossed the rest and checked my tem-
perature. A tiny fever, but not enough to skip work.

I tried to shake it off as I sat in my morning meeting,
taking notes for Claire who was out of town. Where was the
blood coming from? And why didn't dream-Oliver know I
was in pain when he touched me?

Everyone had projects, freeing me up to pace around
my cubical, on the brink of retching up my toast. Five nights
in a row, I'd had the dream. Every time, right before the pain
would hit, Big Ben would chime the same hour, every night,
and the date would flash across the marque: Saturday the

Someday
MAYBE

fifth.

Today was Thursday. The third.

I tried to shake it off when Moron Bruce dropped off a client folder. While staring at the same out-of-focus sentence, I nibbled on my pen. It slipped and stabbed my brand-new crown, making my mouth throb almost as badly as when I'd chipped it in the first place—the day after I'd dreamed that my teeth were falling out.

After the tooth dream, Meghan had told me to keep careful track of all my dreams. But the only other dream I'd had in a week was the one when I died. In two days.

Without bothering to shut my laptop, I grabbed my purse and rounded the corner toward the elevators. If it hadn't been for that damn tooth dream and my subsequent trip to the dentist, I wouldn't have been as freaked. But now…

Roger was in Japan for another week. Sarah must be on campus or her dorm. Who the hell knew where Gio was, because all the way home, no one was answering their phones. I slammed the front door shut and peeled off my binding work clothes, leaving a trail to my room. Sydney was a loyal dog, but she wasn't enough to still my racing mind.

"Meghan," I gasped into my cell, cold sweating now. "Call me when you get this message. You were right, I-I think I'm… Just call me, please."

Call it instinct, the *touch*, or plain old female intuition, but the knot that wouldn't leave the pit of my stomach told me I shouldn't be alone. So I threw on clothes and grabbed my keys. Not until after I'd parked and climbed out of my car did I consider how ludicrous it would sound.

I froze on the sidewalk outside the pink house and gazed up the steep stairs to his door. So completely ludicrous.

"Rachel?" I nearly swallowed my heart. "What are you doing?" Oliver appeared from over my shoulder. It was four in the afternoon, and he must've just come from work because he wore a dark suit, white shirt, blue tie, and he held a laptop case in one hand and a few folders under his other arm.

"Oh, *hiiii*." Yes, I was aware that I sounded like a chipper psycho. "You *are* home."

His eyes went wide and a few of the folders he carried slid to the sidewalk. It might have been the demonically cheerful expression on my face, or maybe because I was dressed in inappropriate-for-daytime flannel pajama short-shorts and a men's ribbed white tank top. Either way, Oliver was staring.

"Are you…" He cleared his throat, treading over the pile of papers at his feet. "Are you okay?"

"Yeah." I nodded. "Oh, yeah, I wanted to see…see if you…" What? Wanted to buy some Girl Scout cookies?

"I just got home." His eyebrows bent as he studied me, his head tipped to one side. "Why don't you come inside?"

"Oh. Okay, thanks." Why hedge, since I was obviously standing outside his house. Or did he think I was there to visit his upstairs neighbor? Besides, I was starting to feel chilled, despite the seventy degrees of the April afternoon air. I wrapped my arms around myself, relieved that I'd had the presence of mind to keep my bra on, even though it was bright pink.

Oliver took a cautious step toward me and reached for my arm. When his hand encircled the curve of my elbow, I took in a sharp inhale, making no secret of how his touch caused a jolt to shoot through my body.

"Don't you want—" I glanced at his scattered folders on the sidewalk.

"I'll get them in a minute," he said, his hand still on my elbow. "I want you inside."

I think he was telling me about his commute or the weather as we climbed the fourteen steps to his front door. He unlocked it, nudged it open with his shoulder, and allowed me to enter first.

"Sit on the couch. There's a blanket."

I obeyed, shuffling across the creaky floorboards then tossing the blanket over my lap.

He went outside for a few seconds, then shut the front door, shrugged out of his coat, loosened his tie, and sat on the coffee table across from me. "You're not okay. You're shivering." He pulled the blanket so it covered my back. "Is it your family? Your brother?"

"It's me. I had a…" I pinched my eyes closed and just spit it out. "I had a dream."

When there was no reply to this revelation, I peeked. Oliver's brow was only slightly furrowed. "A dream."

I nodded, put both hands over my mouth, took in a jagged inhale through my nose, then let my breath out slowly.

"Your teeth again?"

"No, it—*no*!" He was seriously about to laugh, which made me furious. "Not that one. Another one. It's recurring."

"Ah. I have those sometimes. When I'm stressed. Want to tell me about it?"

"Stressed." I shook my head. So I did tell him—though not about how he was my dream co-star, but how I'd had the dream a week ago, and several times since. "I die," I said in a whisper. "Every time."

"Right. I got that." He nodded, but his expression remained blank.

"Each night, the details are more vivid and there's more of them." I stared into the middle distance. "I see my lifeless body, and I'm totally alone. There was pain before, but then there isn't. It's dark so I can't see where I am." I swallowed, a bit astonished that it was so easy to tell him. "It's not crystal clear how it'll happen, but it's not the *how*, it's the *when*. I know *exactly* when."

"Okay. When?"

"Two days." When I looked at him, he was smirking. "This isn't funny."

"A death dream?" He braced his hands behind him and sat back on the coffee table. "Come on, Rachel. Stop listening to Meghan. You've got Sarah freaked out because of your tooth."

"That's what I'm saying. That dream came true. And it's not the only one lately. It's like my brain is trying to send me subliminal messages."

"Like a warning."

"*Yes.*"

He held a fist over his chuckling mouth.

"Stop it." Though I laughed a bit myself. "This is embarrassing enough. I don't need you teasing me."

"Sorry, sorry." He cleared his throat.

"It's irrational, I know."

"If it's irrational, why are you here?" He leaned forward, clasping his hands between his knees. "Why did you come all this way? And why do you shake when I look at you?"

I wrapped the blanket tighter around me and pressed a hand to my forehead. "I'm just a little, you know, anxious."

"Terrified is a better description." His voice was softer, like he was talking to himself. "Because of a dream."

"This one dream could be defined as a nocturnal mini-series. I'm afraid to dream it again." I stared down at my lap. "I don't want to fall asleep. I don't want to be alone."

"You're not alone," he said. "And you won't be. Okay?"

I lifted my chin. Oliver was pulling at the knot of his tie, gazing past my shoulder into another room.

He was so unbelievably gorgeous. When I thought of him—of us—my attraction was stronger than I'd expected. More than when we were kids. More than a few months ago. It was a good question: Why did his glances make me tremble? Was it because of what we did in my dream? Or was it simply being here with him?

"Two days. You think you're going to die two days from now?"

If I wanted Oliver to be attracted to me, talking psychotic wasn't the way to do it. But that was not why I was there. "Yes," I said. I could only answer with the truth.

"Easy solution, then. We won't leave here for two days."

"N-no," I stammered. "I can't impose. I shouldn't have come."

"Rachel." He held a hand in the air. "Don't start with that. It's cool. See, from my perspective, it's simple. If you don't want to sleep, we'll sit up all night. If you *do* want to sleep…" He shrugged a shoulder. "This is a big place. You sleep, I'll keep guard. And if I think you're starting to lose it"—he paused as a grin touched his lips—"I'll distract you until it passes. Deal?"

"Thanks," I whispered, feeling prickles behind my eyes at his kindness. "Sorry about this. I got freaked out and didn't know what to do." This wasn't true, because when the real panic hit, I knew exactly where to go.

The smirk dropped when he sighed, his metallic eyes filling with compassion. "I won't pretend to understand what you're going through, but when I saw you standing on the street…" He looked away from me for a moment. "I've seen that expression on your face one other time. Something scared you enough to come here. Maybe it is because you think you're going to die on Saturday." He paused long enough for me to nod. "Well, I don't think you are. So you're staying with me so I can prove you wrong."

He stood, sliding the tie out from around his collar, then unbuttoning the top of his shirt while keeping his gaze on me. I swallowed hard, tried not to shiver, lost in that look in his eyes, in a memory of us together…forever ago.

"Play something"—he jerked his chin toward the guitar in the corner—"while I go change."

"Okay." I watched him walk down the hall, relieved that he hadn't mentioned calling the men in the white coats.

"Bang out something loud," he said, the joking back in his voice. "I want to be able to hear you the whole time so I'll know you haven't been abducted by aliens."

I laughed but it stuck in my throat. I wanted to be with Oliver, talk to him, explain how I felt, apologize for not trusting him with the truth six years ago, six days ago. But that was only the flicker of a thought now as I reached for his guitar. All I knew was he'd stopped his life to help me, and I wasn't even calm enough to wonder what that meant about his feelings for me.

Chapter Twenty-Seven

There were several well-worn books as well as a three-ring binder of loose sheet music. I flipped through it, curious to see what kind of music Oliver liked to play on his guitar. It was an eclectic collection, classic stuff from Dylan and John Denver, to songs I heard on the radio today. I decided on a song by Muse from a few years ago and settled into a dining room chair.

The way my fingers plucked the strings felt familiar and calming. I lost myself for a while.

"I always thought that should be played in the dark, surrounded by candelabras."

I stopped strumming. Oliver wore jeans and a blue V-neck tee, no shoes or socks. Sweet hell. "While ensconced in Liberace furs and diamonds?"

He laughed and leaned against the table. "Exactly."

"I'm sure that's just how Matthew Bellamy envisioned it." I plucked the E string.

"You've got a nice touch. Most pound this one out, thinking it's a rock anthem. You play by ear, too. I noticed that the other night when you were waiting for Nick."

"Oh," I said, not prepared for the suddenly broached subject of my ex-whatever.

Oliver ran his hand over the top of a chair. "Well anyway, since we're here for the long haul, we should cook something." He backed up toward the kitchen. As I followed, my heart felt heavy with too many unspoken regrets, but also light with gratitude.

The stew we cooked was Oliver's invention. Both chili and Tabasco sauces.

"Rach. Think fast." Drops of water hit me in the face. "You're staring at the wall."

"Thanks." It went on like that for a while. Oliver was serious when he'd promised to distract me if I showed any sign of meltdown. He'd flick water from his fingertips at me, or throw the occasional potato peel. After a while, he stopped asking if I was okay, he'd just yell my full name at the top of his lungs.

"*Rachel Anne Daughtry*!"

It always snapped me out of it, and sometimes I yelled back—"Oliver Fredrick Wentworth!"—making him laugh. And when he laughed, I laughed. Nothing like a yelling/laughing battle in an echoy Victorian house.

He turned on ESPN while we ate. During one of the time-outs of the double-header basketball game, Oliver excused himself, and I heard him on the phone. I took our dishes into the kitchen and moved to the couch, wrapping up in the blanket.

"Dial-a-Nurse?" I asked when he came back. "What

advice did she give you for dealing with a lunatic?"

He chuckled, checking something on his cell before tossing it on the coffee table. "Treat it like any other forty-eight-hour virus. Once the fever breaks, you're golden." He sat on the other end of the couch and flipped the channel from basketball to CNN. "Sarah's been calling. I told her you're here and that you're okay."

"Oh." I felt a blush spread across my cheeks. Wherever Sarah was, she was probably experiencing a meltdown on my behalf. "Crap!" I sat up straight. "I left Sydney at home alone. Rog's dog."

"I called Roger, too," Oliver said.

"You did?"

He nodded. "Sydney's taken care of."

My heart pushed against my ribs. I looked down, afraid I might cry. He was taking care of me again, and I hadn't even realized it. "Oliver," I whispered. "Thank you."

"You're welcome. And it wasn't Dial-a-Nurse. I had to confer with one of my work colleagues. Let him know I won't be in tomorrow." He cut me off before I could protest. "I could use a mental health day and obviously so can you." He massaged the back of his neck and gave a little groan, then pushed a hand through his hair, that wavy, gorgeous dark hair that I loved so much. Did it smell the same as it used to?

"Rachel."

"Hmm?"

He lifted his eyebrows. "You're staring at *me* now. Why are you looking at me like…like that?"

I didn't want to know how exactly I was looking at him. Was lust showing on my face?

He shot me one last sideways glance, then flipped back to the basketball game. "Lakers are up by ten, so *you* quit distracting *me*."

We didn't speak for a while. He flipped through a thick binder as we sat on far ends of the couch, the TV on low. I tried not to hear him breathe or see him move out of the corner of my eye.

After his third grunt of frustration, I asked, "What are you reading?"

"Some work things."

"It's probably your eyes. You stare at a computer screen all day, gets tedious."

He lowered his pencil. "Doesn't *your* day job shackle you to a computer? Writing up your little jingles or whatever?"

"Writing *jingles* isn't all I do. You have no idea—" His Cheshire cat grin made me stop. "Ahh, distracting me, huh?"

He snickered and went back to the binder on his lap. "I have an even better line of attack for when you really need it." He scratched out what he'd just written.

"You're about to wear that poor eraser down to a nub. Shouldn't you use a *computer* to work on computer programs?"

He shot a glance at me then back at his papers. "Um, this isn't for *work*-work." He rubbed his jaw and slowly lifted his gaze to me.

"Oh. It's for *your* company."

He nodded and looked away.

"Cool." My voice sounded unnaturally high.

He didn't reply.

Crap, I'd spooked him away from talking to me about opening his own business. For that, I sucked, and I deserved his incommunicado and distrust. Obviously, it was really important to him and I'd mocked it—because he hadn't had "a plan." I was thinking about straying from my ten-year plan, but that didn't stop me from being excited about the future, the unknown.

Oliver needed to know I totally got it. But this wasn't about me, so I pulled my feet up to sit cross-legged and scooted so I faced him. "Cool," I repeated. "Tell me about it."

"Nothing to tell."

"I heard you have an investor," I said, trying to remember what Ryan had told me at the color run. Though now that I thought about it, that might not be an extremely reliable source. Ryan had said Oliver never seemed satisfied with his job, when really he'd probably just misinterpreted Oliver's ambition as discontent.

"A few," he replied.

"Cool," I chirped enthusiastically. Ugh, that word.

Since I couldn't trust what I'd heard from Ryan, I had to think of something else. "So…have you submitted your SBA application?"

Oliver scribbled in his binder. "Last month." Finally, he looked up, warily. Or maybe he was daring me to make a crack.

"Oh, yeah?" I picked at my thumbnail, playing all-non-chalant, but over the moon that he hadn't told me to drop the subject. "Do you have clients?"

"Ten, so far."

"Yeah?" I'd been making small talk before, but this was interesting. "How do you go about that? Social media? Work fairs?"

"Networking, mostly. Roger was a big help at the beginning."

"Roger who?"

"Your brother." He moved the binder onto the coffee table. "We had lunch a few months back and—"

"Hold on." I lifted a hand, rewinding what he'd said. "I didn't realize you were hanging out."

"He travels to Japan on business a lot. So did I, last year. I'd been here a couple of weeks, and I ran into him at a party."

"When you met Meghan," I said without thinking. His mouth was still open, though he didn't confirm. "You called her when she left her jacket in your car. You were still Rad to me." I toyed with the hem of my shirt. "Did you know?"

"That you lived here?" He shook his head. "Not until that night."

I bit the inside of my lip. "Oh."

"Yeah, oh."

Why did he sound bitter when I was the one who'd had to live through watching my best friend fall in love with him? I glanced at the TV, though not watching it. Oliver frowned down at his phone, tapping violently at the keypad. Maybe it was my turn to distract him. It was a fair trade-off for all those potato peels and full-name shouting matches.

"Lakers are losing in overtime," I said conversationally. "But this game doesn't matter; they clinched their play-off seed last—"

"And that's another thing, Rachel." His sharp tone startled me. "I had no idea you followed sports. I had to drag you to that game we went to for your birthday."

My body flushed with heat at the sudden broach of subject—the past "us." I thought I was ready for it, but I wasn't.

He stared at me, waiting for an answer. "And when did

you learn guitar?"

"I've been playing my whole life."

"Except for eight months of your freshman year of college? You never mentioned it. Not once."

His accusatory tone made me flinch, flicked on my defensive stitch. "I thought it was nerdy so I didn't play for anyone. There was no way I was going to play in front of my *totally hot boyfriend,* and—wait, hold on." I exhaled in relief. Hopeful relief. "Is this you trying to distract me again? Because it's not funny."

"What?" He looked baffled. "No."

Okay. Now *I* was baffled.

"And now Sarah tells me you're moving back to Texas. Were you going to alert me to the fact or disappear again?"

My mouth fell open.

"Wow. You were, weren't you?" He sat back and crossed his arms. "You're with someone for eight months, you share everything with her, you think you *know* her—"

"*Oliver.*" I jumped to my feet. Confusion, defensiveness, and pent-up fury spun inside my brain like a blender. "That's not fair. This is the first meaningful conversation we've had since college. You can't claim you suddenly don't know me."

We'd never argued before. Not once. The way we were yelling now, though, it felt natural to me, necessary, like I had to get it out before I exploded.

"That's how I feel, like I don't know you." He was on his feet, pacing away. "Just because we haven't *talked* doesn't mean I haven't thought about—" He cut himself off. "You left that day with hardly an explanation."

"What day?"

"Seven years ago, Rachel. In twenty days it will be seven

years."

I inhaled a gasp like the wind was knocked out of me. All this time, he remembered just as vividly as I did. The realization should have been comforting, but I felt deflated.

"Oh," I said, dumbly. "Yeah."

"Yeah." His tone was sarcastic. "Did you assume I didn't remember? That I don't think about that day every time I look at you?"

The words hit like spraying bullets, weakening me even more. But I wasn't to blame for all of it, especially not these last seven months. "How am I supposed to know what you're thinking? Until now, we've barely talked. How do you think that made *me* feel when you moved here and totally blew me off?"

"I wasn't blowing you off, I was pissed at you for what you did back then. Then I thought I could forgive you and that pissed me off again." He raked his fingers through his hair. "But it happened so long ago, I didn't know what to say to you."

"So instead you paraded around with my best friend?"

His eyebrows pulled together. "If you're talking about Meghan, I went on exactly one date with her, and that was before I saw you. After that, I…"

My anger unclenched, just a tiny bit. "You what?"

"Nothing." He turned away, his hand kneading the back of his neck.

"No, let's hear it. You accused me of leaving you for no reason."

"I never said that."

"Whatever. This is stupid. After seven years, we're having our first fight—"

"Then let's make it *mean* something, Rachel. Tell me why we broke up. It wasn't because Roger forced you, was it?"

I should have seen the question coming, I should have welcomed it after all this time. But it felt like a punch in the stomach, deflating me all over again. I had to tell him the truth, though. No matter what happened to us after this conversation, Oliver needed to know.

"No," I began. "It wasn't because of Roger. We were teenagers; we didn't have a clue."

"That's bullshit. Did you get bored or just not love me?"

My stomach churned then hit the floor. "What?" I whispered, shock and grief gripping my throat like a noose. How? How could he say that?

"I've been thinking about it." He turned away, his hand massaging his neck again. "And that's the best explanation I came up with."

No, he was not going to ruin the memory of the most important relationship of my life. "Of course I loved you." I could barely speak around the lump in my throat as I walked toward his turned back. "It tore me apart to hurt you. You were my first love, Oliver, my first everything. But, my family."

He shook his head but was still facing the other way. "Stop it, Rachel," he muttered. "Do not blame your brother for this."

"I'm *not*." My chest shook with a sob—fortitude mixed with panic. "There were things I didn't tell you back then. But it wasn't you, it was me."

"No." He looked up at the ceiling, sounding exasperated. "Don't give me that line."

"It's not a line." I pulled in a breath. "It was you, but it was you because of me. I had this…this plan, these goals."

He shook his head. "What?"

"And because I was with you," I said to his back, "I couldn't keep up with them. But that was my fault, never yours. I wasn't honest with you when I should've been and I'm sorry. I got scared so I ran."

"Scared of what?"

"Of…of being with you, of the future. I was scared but I always loved you, always."

"You should've told me that." He whirled around and held me by the arms. "You could've told me, and we would've figured it out. You didn't have to run from me."

"Scared," I repeated through a shaky voice. "I'm sorry. We were kids and things got too intense."

"Intense? Like this?" His grip held me in place and he stared down into my face until I almost couldn't breathe, his eyes blazing. "We're not kids anymore, Rachel. Are you still scared?"

My breath shook as I nodded.

"Why?" His fingers pressed into my arms. "Why are you scared to be with me?"

"I'm sorry," I whispered, my mind and mouth at a loss for more.

"Stop saying you're sorry. *I'm* not sorry." Just as fast as he'd grabbed me, he let go and stepped back.

I stared at him, rubbing my hands over where he'd been holding, unable to process what had just happened.

"I didn't mean to hurt you." He turned away, his voice low and hoarse. "Or frighten you. I didn't mean for any of this."

My mouth was dry, my heart thudding hard and painfully. Part of me wanted to run away again, while another part was too stubborn to move.

"You should go to bed now." He still wouldn't face me. "But I told you I'd stay up." He shot one glance at me. "Go."

When I inhaled, my body shook with anger and adrenaline, from the memory of his hands on my arms. I marched away, not bothering to say a word. I entered the guest bedroom and stood in the dark. Oliver was banging stuff around in the other room. My temper flared.

Where did he get off? Yelling at me when I was trying to apologize. He was insane!

I kicked the door shut.

I had no idea what time it was. My purse and phone were out in the living room. The Lakers were playing on the East Coast, so the time difference made it probably close to midnight. Sleep was a long shot, but I stripped off my clothes and threw myself on the bed.

Chapter Twenty-Eight

I woke up gasping in a familiar cold sweat, my pulse keeping rhythm with the Budweiser Clydesdales. When I remembered where I was, I bit down on the duvet, trying to slow my heart.

It was a dream, Rachel, I repeated over and over, staring through the dark bedroom toward the window. But it was *that* dream…the one that had brought me to this house in the first place.

I swung my legs off the side of the bed, stood, and shivered. I wasn't wearing a stitch of clothing. Mine were in a heap on the floor somewhere. I felt for the closet door, opened it and touched what felt to be a row of dress shirts. I pulled one off a hanger and pushed my hands through the sleeves. It was huge like a mini dress, hitting me mid-thigh.

The hallway was pitch black. I hesitated for a second at my door, but the fear of what might be lurking in the dark shadows out there was nothing compared to the horrors I'd just faced in bed. No more sleep. I padded toward the kitchen. A light was left on over the stove, which guided me forward like a beacon.

I just wanted a snack or a glass of water—I was suddenly so incredibly thirsty and a little sick to my stomach, and my head hurt, too. All-over body ache. Maybe I could find my oils. Where was my purse?

As I was about to cross the threshold into the kitchen, the shutting of a drawer made me squeak. Oliver's back was to me as he crouched in front of the open cabinet below the sink. Hearing my squeak, his head jerked, looking as startled as I felt.

His gaze slid from my face and moved down my body. "Hoooly damn," he murmured.

That's about the time I remembered what I was wearing: one of his button-up shirts, though completely *un*buttoned and hanging wide open in the front. I yelped and pulled it around me like a double-breasted suit.

Oliver looked at my face and blinked. "I...you...*ow*!" He yanked his hand out of the drawer he'd just slammed shut and shook it in pain. With all his weight on the balls of his feet, he lost his balance and fell forward, one foot slipping out from under him. He caught himself by the other hand right before he would have face-planted on the tile. When he went to stand, he banged his head on a low-hanging cabinet door above the sink.

"Dammit," he muttered, rubbing the top of his head.

I giggled at the comedy of errors, but that shriveled in my throat when I noticed he was sporting a pair of black boxers. And nothing else. I was grateful there wasn't a cabinet door for me to bang into, because hoooly damn was right. I hadn't seen a more perfect nearly naked man since, well, him.

"Are you okay?" I approached him with a lifted hand,

touching the spot on his head where he was rubbing. "Ouch," I said in empathy when he flinched. He lowered his hand so only I was touching his head. I stroked it gingerly, feeling the swelling goose egg.

"You used to wear my clothes all the time."

"Hmm?" Though I'd heard him quite clearly. I withdrew my hand and turned to hastily button up my shirt.

"They always looked better on you than on me."

It was something about the dimness of the room or the lateness of the hour, but we were relaxed, like the fight had never happened.

"You're delirious. You need ice." I retreated to the freezer, pulled it open, and let the frigid air cool off my overheated body. "Sit down," I ordered over my shoulder. After gathering a handful of ice cubes, I grabbed a dish towel and sat in the kitchen chair next to him. "It's getting hot," I said, gently placing the ice over the lump on his head.

Oliver closed his eyes and leaned toward me. "Thank you for returning my Radiohead T-shirt."

I smiled at his closed eyes. "I knew it was your favorite." I repositioned the ice. "And since we're sharing stories, it was a horrible realization when I opened my closet and discovered that half the clothes in my possession were yours."

"You could've kept anything you wanted, instead of sending your roommate over with all my stuff crammed in two garbage bags." He opened one eye, only to narrow it at me.

"Sorry." I couldn't hide the smile in my voice.

He chuckled. "I'll bet."

"I *am*." I switched the icepack to my other hand. "I really am."

Another dry chuckle escaped his lips. "I know you are,

Rachel. So am I. For everything."

The dual apologies hung in the air between us, full of so much subtext—spoken and unspoken, six years of regret, and seven months of longing.

Almost involuntarily, my free hand touched the side of his face, his hard jaw and amazingly sexy stubble. I was touching Oliver Wentworth—really touching him—for the first time in nearly seven years. And nothing felt more natural.

He opened his eyes, looked at me and took the icepack, his hand lingering over mine. I was very aware that neither of us wore what could be considered proper clothing by any stretch of the imagination. I scooted back and stood. "I'll get you some aspirin. Where do you keep it?"

"Behind the mirror." He also rose to his feet.

I looked around. There were no mirrors in the kitchen.

"In the bathroom, Rachel." He was walking toward me. "You have to go through my bedroom first."

He stood before me while I tried unsuccessfully to not stare at his bare chest, the muscles leading to flat abs that would feel so amazing under my fingers. When I looked up, a slow smile stretched across his face, and I was no longer retreating from him. His hands landed softly on my shoulders, his thumbs skimmed the sides of my neck, making my legs feel like they were made of the rubberiest rubber.

"Want me to show you my room, or do you remember how to"—he paused as his eyes did a lightning-fast sweep down my body—"*get* there?"

"I haven't forgotten."

"Neither have I."

I closed my eyes, losing myself in the touch of our lips connecting. It was familiar and new and more mind-blowing than that first morning outside my dorm. His arms went behind my back, pulling me in so tightly I lost my breath for a beautiful, exciting moment. I let him hold me, take care of me, weak as a baby in his arms. When he finished with my mouth, he kissed along my jaw, a hot, sizzling trail to my ear.

"Oh, damn, Rach," he murmured against my skin.

"What?" My fingers dug into his sides.

"You're wearing that oil." His lips pressed to my neck, the notch of my throat, the other side of my neck. "Your body's like a treasure map. I can smell it all over you. Like nothing's changed."

"I missed you." This was so easy to admit while cradling his head in my arms, the familiar scent of his hair, of him, of us.

"You have no idea," he whispered in my ear. He pressed his mouth over mine again, his hands gliding down the front of my shirt. "You skipped a button." His fingers slid inside, touching my stomach, my hip bones, skin tingling against skin.

"Better take it off me then." I needed to get my hands on his skin, too. But my arms felt so heavy and weak that when I tried to wrap them around him, I couldn't, like they were paralyzed, drugged lifeless by too much desire, or like when you try to run in a dream, but it feels like your limbs are stuck in cement and you can't move them…you can't…move.

I sucked in a breath.

"Rach." His gray eyes were dark with passion. "What's wrong?"

I stared at the flawless apparition before me, realizing with horror what was really going on, why it felt like I couldn't move. Why all of this was too perfect to be real.

None of it was happening.

I was asleep!

Oliver wasn't standing with me half naked, all smoldery-eyed, kissing my neck, inviting me into his bedroom. I'd never woken up. I was still in the stupid guest bedroom, tangled around the stupid sheets, blissfully unaware that my subconscious was wreaking havoc on my hormones.

"Rachel?" His expression showed alarm, similar to when he'd found me on the street earlier today. Oh, bloody hell. Was *that* a dream, too? Had I dreamed it all? Was I actually at home alone?

The reoccurring dream of my death had mutated further. Would it now include the scene of Oliver inviting me in? Laughing with me? Forgiving me? Caressing his lips over mine until I couldn't breathe?

A sob broke from my throat. "I can't take it." I buried my face in his chest, finally able to fling my dream arms around him. "I can't relive this over and over if it's not true. I can't."

"It's okay." He rubbed my back. "What's going on?"

I sucked in another sob then crashed my mouth against his, hungry for him, thirsty and parched like I'd never been before. I gripped the back of his head and sucked his bottom lip, moaning, pressing the whole line of my body against his. What did it matter now if I was dreaming? I needed to peel off my shirt, pin him to the floor, and show him exactly how I felt before it was too late.

But I'd waited so long, and now it *was* too late.

It was a dream, and the further I let it go on, the more agonizing it would be when I had to replay it. I tried to wiggle out of his arms, but he held me against his chest.

"Let me…go," I whimpered weakly, my mind slipping from reality. "Why did I think I could come here? I'm *alone*."

"Baby." He rested a hand on my cheek. It felt so real, I

wanted to cry. "I'm here with you. You're not alone."

My heart pounded. Panic or dread or regret was burning a hole through my stomach like a torch, eating, bubbling upward. "This is part of it now. The dream, Oliver. Remember the blood?"

"There's no blood. You're perfect."

Past his shoulder, I caught sight of the green numbers on the oven displaying the time. A second jolt of panic made me thrash, pushing Oliver away. The momentum caused me to stumble back into the door jam. My head rattled and stung, white light burst behind my eyes.

"I can't catch my breath." I didn't want to die, but what could I do? For a week, I'd been forewarned. My legs gave out and I slid down the wall, landing bare-assed on the tile. Oliver was above me but I couldn't make out his words, because something new overpowered my attention.

Pain.

I grabbed my side and doubled over. The howl that echoed through the house came from me. Oliver was yelling, too. That seemed about right. He cupped the back of my head—a different pain shot through my body. He must've found the sore spot where I'd hit the door. But wasn't that in the dream? Despite my cries of pain, his fingers splayed across the back of my head, forcing it between my knees. He was telling me to take deep breaths, but nothing could stop what was coming…one day early. How unfair.

I felt something cold and flat against the side of my face. I was lying on my side now, dizzying pain making the room spin even though I was unmoving. Through the pounding behind my ears, I heard someone talking, but not to me. When I tried to pry my eyes open, I saw a face, then all went black.

Chapter Twenty-Nine

Wind swept off the bay and rushed across the front of my body. It was colder than it should've been, and smelled off, not nearly briny enough, or maybe I wasn't breathing right. Was I breathing at all? And what were those bright lights behind my lids? I didn't remember that from the dream, but so much of it was new this time.

Gravity changed. I was laying back.

"I don't know what happened." The voice above me sounded rushed and anxious. "One second she was fine, we were about to—well, and the next minute, she said she couldn't breathe, and then—" The voice broke off in a strangle. "She was screaming."

"What did she take?" Another voice asked. "What is she *on*?"

"Nothing. I was with her all night."

More lights flashed across my closed lids. Something cold and spongy covered my mouth, forcing stale air down my throat. It felt good, so I sucked in a deep breath.

"Rach, baby." From the same direction as the voice, a hand touched my arm, squeezing it gently. "What's wrong with her?"

"We don't know."

A wave of white pain hit. The thing over my mouth muffled my scream. Those same hands were on my forehead, combing through my hair. The voice was at my ear, soft but strained. "Baby, it's okay."

This part couldn't be real, because I recognized the voice. Just to be sure, I forced my eyes open. Oliver's face hovered above me, breaking my already-broken heart. I batted at the breathing tube over my mouth.

"Rach, shhhh." The look in my eyes must've conveyed my confusion. "You're at the hospital." His hands were on my cheeks. "Do you remember what happened?"

I tried to speak.

"She's conscious and she's breathing just fine now," he said to someone across from him who I couldn't see. "Does she have to keep this damn thing on?"

A different pair of hands pulled the breathing tube off my face. I coughed, adjusting to breathing on my own.

"Ms. Daughtry." A bearded man in blue scrubs appeared to my right. "We're going to run some tests, but all indications point to—"

"*No.*" I tucked my chin, straining to find him, to see him again, but the new pain was blinding, forcing me back to a laying position. "Oliver, Oliver." I whimpered the name like a prayer.

I was stunned to see him at my side again. "I'm here. I called Roger, and your parents are on the way."

"I told you this would happen." My right side burned

like I was being split in half. I screamed and rolled away, squeezing my eyes shut.

"Rach, Rach, Shhh, listen to me. I have to tell you something. Look at me. Look at my face, Rachel."

I obeyed. Would Oliver's beautiful, steely eyes be the last thing I would ever see? When I managed to focus on him, he was smiling.

"You're going to be fine, sweet pea. Okay? Keep looking at me. Good, that's good." He ran a hand through my hair. "I've been such a jackass and we wasted so much time but when you're better, I'm taking you away—no more waste. We'll get married and have ten kids and…" He scrubbed the heel of his hand over his eyes. "I love you, and I'm going to love you every day of your life, Rachel Daughtry. Keep looking at me. Rach?"

I wanted to tell him I loved him, too. I want to scream it. I tried. So hard. Before I could even tell him good-bye, a tall white-coat elbowed him aside. Oliver's protesting voice faded away as I was wheeled around a corner.

I counted six florescence light panels on the ceiling as I passed under them. Then I closed my eyes and was gone.

• • •

The smell was a big clue. The annoying, repetitive beeping was the final giveaway. I was in a hospital room, but that was about all I knew. I'd been laying there for a while, wiggling my toes and fingers—ten and ten—counting the heart monitor beeps, and wondering when I would hear something new. The first thing I saw when I opened my eyes was my mother.

"Honey." She scooted her chair to the side of my bed.

"How do you feel?"

"Okay." My voice sounded weak and hoarse. "Thirsty."
Screaming-thirsty, actually.

Mom held a pink plastic cup with a built-in bendy straw up to my mouth. I took a few sips.

"What happened?"

"You don't remember?"

"Not really." I concentrated, thinking back to the last thing I could recall. "I was at his house. We made dinner and he…took my knapsack with the rusty cup."

"What, honey?"

I rubbed my eyes. "It's hazy."

"Rachel, honey." Mom placed a hand over mine. There was a tube attached to it. "Do you know where you are?"

"Disneyland?" Mom looked alarmed. "Hospital, I know."

"You're in the post-anesthesia care unit." She glanced at the beeping machine over my head. "Once your vitals stabilize, they'll move you to a regular post-op room." She scooted closer and her voice dropped. "You had acute appendicitis, honey. When the appendix becomes inflamed, it has to be removed before it ruptures. A few hours ago, you had an emergency appendectomy." She was purposely dumbing down the medical-talk in the explanation. She knew I wasn't stupid; she must've been worried. "The surgery went well, but it took you a few extra hours to wake up from the anesthesia. You would start to come around but fade out again."

"I don't remember any of that."

She smiled. "You'd been moved to recovery by the time we arrived. We flew here as quickly as we could."

"Dad's here? Where's Rog?"

"Roger wanted to fly home, too, but we told him not to."

"When can I go home?"

"Your father is outside talking to the doctor. I'll let them know you're awake." She opened the door to my room. As she was about to step into the hall, she stopped. "Your friend Sarah's been asking about you." Mom extended an arm, beckoning, and Sarah appeared in the doorway.

"Hey, you. Can I come in?"

"Sure." My attempt to wave her forward made me nauseous. "I would sit up, but I think it might kill me."

Sarah's smile turned into an empathetic cringe as she tiptoed toward the chair Mom vacated. "How do you feel? I mean, I know you've been cut in half, but are you okay?"

"She's so badass, Rach. She totally yelled at the nurses."

"Why?"

She scooted her chair closer. "Before your parents got here, Ollie wanted to see you, but he's not family so they wouldn't let him in, but he kept going on and on about it, so they threatened to kick him out of the hospital."

While speaking, she'd been applying lip balm. The strong strawberry scent made me queasier. I swallowed, both parched and liquefied at the same time. As I reached for the cup of water, my side felt like it had a chunk bit out of it.

"That's when your parents showed up and yelled at everyone. The nurses were pissed, but at least they didn't kick him out."

After a few sips of water, I gingerly laid back down. "Who got kicked out?"

"No, no, I said Ollie *didn't* get kicked out. He hasn't left since he brought you in. He's being a royal pain and ticking everyone off. Rachel? Are you all right?"

I hadn't meant to make that weird noise, but when my head started feeling fuzzy and the lights were too bright, I slammed my eyes shut, massaging the bridge of my nose with a knuckle. "Sarah," I murmured. "Was I at his house?"

"Yeah. He was with you when you got sick." She squeezed my tube-free arm. "I got all your voicemails yesterday. I was in a four-hour lab. I'm sorry. I called when class got out, but you didn't answer, so I called my brother. He said you were with him but he wouldn't let me talk to you. Said you were under security lock-down."

When I chuckled, the pain in my side returned. "Wait, I've been here all day and all night? It's Sunday?" Sarah nodded. "So it *didn't* happen."

"What didn't happen, sweetie? Want me to get a doctor?"

There was a tap on the door. I expected to see a surgeon to check my vitals or inspect my stitches, but it was Oliver.

"The nurses are letting you in here?" Sarah asked.

"If it's okay." He nodded at someone down the hall I couldn't see. "But since I was…disruptive, they're only giving me one minute." He looked at Sarah. "Leave us?"

"I'll go get a Coke." She disappeared without another word.

Oliver leaned against the closed door, about a mile away from me. "How do you feel?"

I groaned.

"What?" He rushed to the side of my bed. "Pain?"

"No. I've been awake for ten minutes, and I'm already sick of that question."

He smiled and sat down. He was unshaven and his hair was mussed. The long sleeved black T-shirt he wore was wrinkled and untucked. He looked better than a dream. Then I *did* feel pain.

"S-sorry about this." I tried to sit up but collapsed again. "Sorry you got dragged into it."

"You could've died, you…" He exhaled slowly, pushing up his sleeves one at a time. "If you'd been home alone — it came on so fast — you could've passed out. We were lucky."

"Lucky," I repeated dryly. So I actually had been at his house. That part wasn't a dream. But had we gone for a hike? I remembered that, too. Had I worn his shirt? Had he kissed me blind?

"It's all a blur," I said aloud, not meaning to.

"You don't remember?"

Only glimpses of memories were coming back. Dreams and truth were tangled — like the swirls of Sarah's painting. I couldn't trust myself to distinguish what was real and what wasn't.

"I don't know," I admitted. When I looked at Oliver, at his bent expression, he was the one who looked in pain. He stood and walked to the door. "You're going?"

"Nurse Ratchett will ban me if I break her rules. But I'm glad you're okay. I'll leave you now." With one hand on the knob, he looked at me in a way that reminded me of something else, another crumb of a memory: I saw his face, heard his voice; he called me sweet pea, said he loved me. If that had been real, why was he leaving? I bit my lip, my insides trembling and aching, reaching out for him.

Oliver pulled open the door, but then looked back at me. "Unless. Rach…"

Just then, a white coat entered and my father came rushing in after. Oliver was gone.

Chapter Thirty

Once I was out of recovery, I slept for a full day, waking only for food and to be poked at by cold metal objects. On release day, I didn't even get to go to my apartment, but was wheeled to the hospital curb and loaded into the back seat of an airport shuttle next to my mother.

During the sixty-five-minute flight to Santa Barbara, I nodded off and on, doing my best to listen to Mom's doctorly instructions for achieving full recovery. It seemed I was to be their prisoner for at least a week—in the bedroom where I grew up.

Krikit was there when we arrived, relishing—a little too enthusiastically—that *I* was finally the one who needed help.

"Justin Timberlake is gay," was the first thing I said.

She gaped at me. "For that, I'll be removing your other vital organs while you sleep."

A few days later, Meghan came over. We went for a painfully slow stroll up the block. She held up most of the conversation with talk of Ryan and wedding plans.

"Gio's designing my dress." Megs bared her teeth in a fake smile. "She's insisting."

"Oy." I cringed in sympathy. "That'll be, um, fun."

It wasn't until we stopped at the subdivision's playground that she turned the subject to what had happened. "They totally cut you open, babe." She helped me into a swing.

"My stomach looks like Scarface."

She sat on the swing next to me. "No more two-piece bathing suits."

"Yeah, *that'll* be my excuse this summer."

Meghan swung for a while, pumping her legs, wind blowing through her hair the higher she got. When she slowed down, she said, "So, you were with Rad when it happened."

Hearing his old nickname reminded me that, not so long ago, my best friend had a major Jones for Oliver. I began cautiously, ignorant of how much she knew. "It's not what you think."

"I'm not upset about it. I'm with Ryan. I love him." She looked down, smiling sweetly at the grass. "*Damn*, do I love him." She took a long swig from a tall water bottle. I grinned, silently thanking Ryan and his good influence. We all needed Megs healthy and around for a very long time. "Anyway, things with Rad never took off. Were you interested in him the whole time?"

I bit my lip, not sure how to answer that honestly. "No."—which was the truth—"but it's a long story."

She tipped her chin to face the sun. "I plan on hanging out right here to work on my tan. I could use a long story."

I lifted my feet, allowing the light wind to blow my swing around.

I'd only seen him alone that one time, right after I woke up from surgery. Sarah stopped by my room the next day. Some girls from work sent flowers. Giovanna was a pretty permanent fixture. But every time Oliver came, there were always other people around.

Clear-headed now, I still had a difficult time piecing together exactly what had led up to being rushed to the ER. Pain and stress can mess with the memory, I knew that too well. In addition to the appendicitis, I'd bashed my head pretty good. There was still a lump. I was in no position to completely trust my memories of that night.

"Do you remember when I told you Oliver and I knew each other our first year of college?"

"Yeah."

"That wasn't the whole truth." I stared down at the patch of dirt between my feet. "We dated back then." I let the sentence sit.

"Dated," Meghan repeated. "As in…"

"As in, he was my boyfriend for eight months."

"So, you really did have a secret lover back then? Wait— you didn't tell me? And then he moved back here and you *still* didn't tell me?"

I nodded, waiting for the explosion.

After a beat, Megs exhaled a laugh out her nose, then she laughed out loud. "Well, that *explains* it. Half the time I thought you wanted him and the other half I thought you hated him."

"Uh, no." I swallowed, my throat raw and dry—side effects from surgery. "I broke up with him. It ended badly." *Ha ha. Understatement of the century.* "Very badly. I wanted to forget it so I never told anyone. Then seeing him again was…weird."

"Babe." She gave me a disapproving eye. "You could've told me."

I lifted my chin and laughed. "Ha!"

"What?"

"Seriously? You were so into him. There was no way I'd do that to you."

"Rachel." She lifted her feet off the ground so her shoulder bumped against mine. "You're my very best friend."

"And you're mine."

Which was all that needed to be said.

"If you're not dating now, how did it happen you were at his house that night?" This seemed like a logical question, so I told her about my dream and about being afraid to be alone. Saying it out loud should've made me feel like a mental case, but I knew Megs understood.

"Any new dreams lately?"

"Not a one. Which is so weird. Pain meds must be blocking my chi."

She agreed with this assessment and started swinging. "So, to recap, you were having reoccurring nocturnal death premonitions, and decided to go to Rad's—"

"Meg. Please don't call him that. He hates it and so do I."

"Well, now." She pressed her lips together in a smile. "So. You thought the fourth Horseman of the Apocalypse was after you and you wanted to die with Oliver. Is that the gist?"

I groaned and looked away.

"I'm not judging. I just want to get it right." She swung for a few minutes then continued. "What happened right before the appendix thing?"

"I'd been asleep, but I had a nightmare so I got out of bed. Oliver was up, too, in the kitchen."

"Does he sleep in the nude?"

I could have answered this accurately—based on information from seven years ago—but refrained. "Irrelevant," I said. "I don't think he'd been to bed yet, anyway."

"Okay, so it's the middle of the night and you're in the kitchen. Then…?"

"We argued."

"What about?"

I bit my lip. "I think it had to do with basketball."

Meghan frowned. "You're not giving me anything."

"No, wait." I touched my head. "That was before I went to bed. Out of nowhere, he started yelling at me about never going to games with him in college. He brought up stuff from years ago, totally went off on me. He wanted to rehash why we broke up."

"Huh. Go on."

"After that, I went to bed."

"Got it. So you were arguing then you stomped off."

"I didn't stomp. I stormed."

"Uh huh. What next?"

This was where it got fuzzy, so I spoke with caution. "Oliver hit his head, so I got him some ice. He was talking about how I used to wear his clothes."

"Why?"

I remembered this part clearly. "Because I…I hadn't worn anything to bed that night, so I was kind of borrowing one of his shirts."

"I see." Meghan scratched her chin. "So you were tenderly pressing ice against the man's head while naked under his favorite shirt. I'm sure *that* wasn't a blinding turn-on for him or anything."

"You're making it sound more calculating than it was."

"What was he wearing?"

I didn't have to think hard about that detail, either. "Boxers."

"Rachel Daughtry." Meghan pressed a finger to my shoulder and made a sizzling sound. "You were seducing him."

"I wasn't. This is coming out wrong."

"Did you kiss?"

The question made my heart thrum, I could feel my pulse in my stitches. "I think so. I'm pretty sure." Some memories of that night were too vivid to not be true, like when I'd touched his face and he looked up at me, and he'd ran his mouth across my neck, caught me when I'd crumpled to the floor of the kitchen.

"Babe." Megs knocked my shoulder. "I can tell by your expression that we have a lot of catching up to do."

That we did. As we walked back to my parents' house, Meghan gave me an earful of psychobabble, how my fear of losing Oliver again manifested itself by causing me to dream about dying at his hand. This didn't make sense to me, but Meghan was the expert here, so I listened and nodded and counted the steps until I could take another pain pill.

Her words echoed in my head as I drifted off to sleep that night. Blissfully dreamless.

Chapter Thirty-One

My parents and I returned to San Francisco a week later. With Roger overseas for another few days, they didn't want to leave me alone in the apartment. Even Sydney was still at doggy sleep-away daycare. Mom was literally clinging to the front door while Dad loaded their bags in the cab. If they missed their flight back to Switzerland, I might have another medical emergency. I loved my parents to death, but Mom had never gotten over her hovering. Luckily, Sarah showed up before Mom decided to change her plane ticket.

I gave my mother one final hug before I yanked Sarah inside and shut the door.

"She cares; it's sweet."

"Yeah." I laughed. "What are you doing on this side of town in the middle of the day?"

"I was over at the community college. They had a one-day painting seminar that USF doesn't offer. Pre-Raphaelites." She stepped over my purse and the duffel bag I'd borrowed from Krikit. "Please say you're coming back to work tomorrow. Moron Bruce is on a rampage. You could do his job so much better than him."

"You copied me on all the emails you sent to him. You could do it better, too."

"He's a moron," we said together.

"So, seriously. How are you doing? Is everything"—she waved her hands in the general vicinity of my stomach—"healing?"

"I had a doctor's appointment yesterday and another in a couple of days. So far so good."

"You look great."

I laughed and reached for my stack of mail. "Yeah, right. I look like death."

"*Rachel.* Don't joke about...*that.* We were so worried; you have no idea."

"Sorry." I lowered the pile of magazines still wrapped in plastic. "I sometimes forget I was catatonic for an entire day."

Sarah shook her head. "It's just nice to see you back home."

"What else went on last week? Besides Bruce the moron being a moron?"

She flopped down on the couch. I did the same, just not as much flopping. "I painted a lot, trying to beef up my portfolio for finals." She told me about having two lunch dates with two different guys and then skipping out on Tim's party Friday night.

"Why didn't you go? Not that any sane person needs a reason to avoid such an event."

"I drove Ollie to the airport that morning then crashed

at his place all weekend. So damn good to get away from campus drama."

"Yeah, nice break," I said with a breezy smile, but that wasn't the part of her explanation that interested me. "So…" I played with the cuff of my sleeve. "Your brother took a trip?"

"He's in Vancouver again. It was supposed to be for two days, but there's some problem and he'll be gone all week. They just had a snowstorm up there. In April!"

"Huh." I felt a combination of disappointment that he wasn't here and impatience for Sarah to talk about him some more. But I didn't know what to say, so I stuck with the weather. "We're, uh, lucky we live in a temperate zone."

"Did he call you?" Yeah. Sarah was much better than me at getting right to the point. "I asked him last week if he'd talked to you, and he said he didn't have your number. Whatever. So I programed it into his cell. I asked him again the next day, and he said no."

"Oh. Uh, no." I stood up and returned to that unsorted mound of mail on the kitchen table, trying not to feel too shattered. "I haven't talked to him at all." I sifted through envelopes and magazines, stacking them into random piles.

Sarah muttered a very impressive compound swear word. She must've been taking lessons from Bruce in my absence. "He's such an *idiot*, Rach."

"Bruce?"

She gawked at me, her mouth hanging open. "No. My idiot brother who's in love with you."

"Oh." I lowered myself into a chair, feeling lightheaded. "Him."

"I'm *sorry*, Rach." She didn't sound sorry at all; she sounded ticked. "But it's all so *stupid*. He camped outside your hospital room for two days, and everyone on your floor heard you crying his name before you went into surgery. The nurses told me about it when I got there."

"I did what?"

"Nobody told you?"

"Oh, no." I covered my face with my hands, trying to remember. Trying not to remember.

"He's my brother and you're one of my best friends, and it's just *stupid*. What are you going to do?"

I lowered my hands and shrugged.

"Right," she snapped, then scoffed sarcastically. "That's exactly what *Ollie* did when I asked him. He *shrugged*." She lifted her shoulders extra high in a mocking gesture. "What the hell does that even mean?"

I almost shrugged again, but was afraid she'd clock me.

"So what if he's in Canada?" She stood up and started pacing. "Do cell phones not work across the border? Then I was thinking, maybe he's super busy 'cause of his new client or whatever and then I'm like, well, so what? He should call you, Rach, and—"

"Sarah. Not helping." Though her thoughts were pretty much right along the same track as mine.

Her bottom lip started to tremble, then her expression completely broke as she burst into tears. Why *she* was the one who needed comfort, I had no idea. But I walked to her with outstretched arms and let her sob into my shirt.

"I'm sorry." She sniveled. "I didn't mean to yell at you. It's just, I love him and I love you and…"

"Shhh, I know."

She jerked away and eyed me in concern. "Did I hurt you?" She gestured toward my missing appendix region.

"I'm fine." Though I did have to blink back a few tears of my own. "Whoa. Remind me to never get on your bad side." I went to get a box of Kleenex when I saw a letter on the corner of the table. The envelope was thick and glossy. The raised logo where the return address should be made my heart stop.

I grabbed it and tore it open, nervous butterflies in my stomach. I had to read the first few lines twice. My heart sputtered, lightened.

"Rach?" Sarah sniffed. "What's wrong?"

"It's from *Redbook*." I displayed the letter trembling in my hand. "I sent them a short story months ago. They offered to buy it for publication, and an editor wants to talk about signing me to a series contract."

"*Redbook*?" Sarah repeated. "The magazine?"

I nodded, feeling an expression of total disbelief on my face. Then joy.

"Oh, Rach." She broke into a huge grin, and her eyes watered up again. "That's amazing!"

"I'm supposed to email the editor's assistant and set up a time."

"You're going to write for *Redbook*, one of the most uber-glam magazines in the world! You'll be famous." She gasped and covered her mouth. "OMG. Rach." She lowered her hands. "You're just like Carrie Bradshaw."

I laughed, about to explain how the real world worked, but then I thought, aw screw it, and I let out my own high-pitched squeal, embracing the joy. "Totally fabulous, right? Manhattan cocktails and Manolo Blahnik strappy sandals for everyone!"

Now if only I could track down that Mr. Big of mine.

The second Sarah left, I sat on my bed and reread the letter from *Redbook*. After numerous rewrites, I shot an email to Julia Charleston, Vivian O'Neil's assistant.

After that, I knew I was in for a long wait, which didn't stop me from making a pot of tea and glaring impatiently at my empty inbox screen. I assumed it would take much longer, since they'd had my stories for months, but I received a return email from Julia before I'd finished my third cup. Vivian would be telephoning me in two days, one o'clock my time.

The joy hit again. I'd really done something. I was in the middle of changing my entire life, with absolutely no plan. A few nervous doubts tried to push past my excitement, but I wouldn't let them in.

Besides dodging Bruce, the first thing I did when I returned to work the next day was schedule a three-hour block on my work calendar: one hour before the call, one hour for the call, and one hour after. I was nothing if not thorough.

The rest of the day, I did my best to unbury my desk from the two weeks I'd missed work.

That night, I had a dream. The first since I'd been at Oliver's.

Chapter Thirty-Two

"Where's the new Vondome copy?"

"You'll get it, Bruce."

"It's due to the clients by five."

I slammed a fist on my desk and glared up from my computer. "I said you'll get it. Lay the hell off."

He flinched back, opened his mouth, then closed it. "Okay. Just don't be late, Ray-Ray."

"Have *I* ever been late with an assignment?" The dude wasn't worth losing my temper over, but enough was enough. "And do not call me Ray-Ray."

"Fine. Rachel. " He rolled his eyes, but he'd also gone a little pale. Finally, my message had gotten through. Huh. I liked the appendix-free Rachel. She had balls.

Being Bruce, however, he swore under his breath then left my cube.

Moron.

Sixty seconds after he left, I went to the small conference

room I'd reserved on the shared calendar, closed the door, and locked it. My phone interview was in five minutes. I'd meant to take the call in my car, but the morning had gotten away from me. Yeah, thanks, Bruce. I put on some lip gloss, turned to a clean page in my notebook, double-checked that my cell was fully charged, and waited.

Forty-five minutes later, it was over.

I glanced down at the notebook page that was now covered with questions, answers, names, arrows, asterisks, and at the very bottom…a dollar amount. I circled it twice. And grinned.

Just as I was about to pull out the candy bar I kept in my purse for emergencies or celebrations, there was a knock on the conference room door.

Seriously, couldn't the moron stay out of my grill for one hour? I growled, pushed back from the table and yanked the door open. "Bruce, stop being such—*Oliver*."

Seeing him at my office was so completely out of context, I almost asked if he was lost.

"Hi," he said.

"Hi," I said back. The happy flutter that hit my stomach was instantaneous.

"The receptionist tried buzzing you."

"Oh. I was on another call." I gestured over my shoulder toward the conference table. "I had my desk phone on hold."

Oliver nodded. "I told her I'm Sarah's brother so she let me up."

The flutter, my lovely, happy flutter flew away. "Oh. You're here to see Sarah." I scooped up my notebook and phone and walked toward my cube, not wanting Oliver to see my tragic expression before I had time to fix it. By the time I reached my desk, I was certain I looked more present-able. "She doesn't intern on Tuesdays. Not this semester." I pushed papers around my desk at random. "You didn't know that? She'll be in tomorrow afternoon and—"

"I know she's not here. I came to see you."

"Oh." I hated how often I was using that word. But I was trying to limit the number of times I said "cool." Appar-ently "oh" was my filler. "Have a seat." Much too formally, I pointed at the one empty chair in my cube.

I sat but Oliver remained standing. He wore a dark blue suit, one I'd seen before. But the jacket was off, the tie was loose, and the top two buttons of his white shirt were undone. His dark hair lacked a certain, I don't know, evidence of being combed? His whole picture of rumpled sexiness made me hot under the camisole.

"I thought you were in Canada."

"I took a break from my meetings but have to be back tomorrow. I caught a flight out of Vancouver early this morning. It got grounded in Reno."

"Grounded? Why?"

He looked at me kind of funny: half pity, half…some-thing else. "Because…" I followed his finger pointing at the wall of windows behind me. I hadn't noticed how dark it had gotten. Not just dark; the sky had an eerie green-gray tint. And when had it started raining?

"Storm?"

"Major." We both stared toward the windows. "The North Bay's already flooding. It's coming from inland over the mountains and pressure from the bay is holding it in. One of those 'perfect storm' conditions."

I strained to look east. The sky appeared much more

ominous in that direction. "It's a mess out there," I said. When I glanced at Oliver, I noticed the top of his head was wet, and so were his shoulders. "You said your flight was grounded."

"In Reno. I rented a car and drove."

"Through a line of storms?"

He nodded.

"Oliver Wentworth. That's dangerous!" I jabbed a finger toward the window. "Why did you do that?"

He dropped his gaze from me and started re-tucking his shirt. "I told you, I came to see you."

I felt an "oh" forming on my lips, the lamest thing in the world to say. "Oh." I said it anyway. And strangely enough, it was exactly what needed to be said. Oliver lifted his silvery eyes to mine, and our gazes locked. "Ohhh," I repeated, smiling this time.

I couldn't help envisioning how he looked that night at his house when we were alone in the kitchen, the lights out and his shirt off and our bodies pressed together.

We both jumped when my desk phone rang.

"Want to get that?" His voice was thick and hoarse, and I wondered if he'd been picturing how I looked that night, too, naked under his shirt.

"No." My voice came out just as hoarse. "I sure don't want to get that."

Oliver's lips quirked with a smile, and a fiery ball of heat pounded where my heart should've been. He took a step toward me right as a loud group from the creative team paraded past my cube.

"Rocky, let's go," one of them said. "Emergency staff meeting." She waved her hand, beckoning me to follow.

"Can you wait here?" I said to Oliver, hoping my quick-but-steady gaze would convey everything I was thinking and feeling and dying to tell him. "I don't know how long I'll be but—"

"Grab all your files on Shreveport," my impatient colleague said. "I forgot a pen. Can I borrow one? It has to be black. And bring extra paper. Come on."

I sighed. "I'll be right there, hold on." I gathered up the necessary materials and was literally being muscled down the hall when Oliver caught my wrist.

"I just sent you a text." He glanced at my cell balanced on top of the folders in my arms. "Check it when you can." He dropped my hand as I was pulled away.

Fiery heart still pounding, the second I got settled in the conference room I discreetly pulled out my phone.

I need to see you, his text read. *Can you meet tonight?*

Well, what did I expect it to say? *Rachel. You pierce my soul. I love you more than the new version of Adobe Illustrator.*

This was a real man. Not a Jane Austen novel.

I thumbed my reply of *Yes, I'll let you know when I'm through with work*, silenced my phone, and slid it in my pocket.

My mind spun all afternoon. The staff meeting was way too long, way too boring, way too moronic, and I obviously couldn't pay attention to anything Claire or Bruce said because, A) the offer from *Redbook*. Huge. And, B) a wet-shirted Oliver appearing at my office. Double huge.

After the meeting, I headed to my cube, prepared to blissfully daydream for the rest of the workday. Before I sat, I remembered I'd silenced my cell. When I pulled it out, its

Someday
MAYBE

face glowed with a new text message. It had been sent ten minutes ago.

Don't drive all the way home in this weather. Come to my house. When?

I bit my lip and grinned, grateful that I'd shaved my legs this morning—both legs. Screw daydreaming when I could have the real thing!

As I shut down my computer, I glanced out the window. It was raining buckets now. In the meeting, no one had mentioned the bad weather. I supposed they expected us to stay inside the office until it cleared. Not a freaking chance.

I'm on my way, I texted, then grabbed my coat.

Chapter Thirty-Three

Even though it was pouring, the second I parked, he met me at my car down the street from his house and hurried me up the fourteen stairs, dumping his umbrella at the corner of the stoop.

"Whoa. Think the drought's officially over?" I said, wiping drops of rain off the front of my skirt.

"Get in here." He shut the door and brushed rain off his shoulders. "If you need dry clothes, you know where I keep my shirts."

I easily caught the flirtatious tone in his voice. "I think I'm okay." And my happy flutter was back. "So," I said conversationally.

"So," he repeated. "Thanks for coming." I followed him into the living room. "Do you want a drink or something? Are you hungry?"

No appetite at the moment, I wanted to say. "I'm fine."

We sat on the coach. Me on one end, Oliver on the other.

I didn't exactly love that seating arrangement.

"Well, you look a lot better than last time I saw you—no, I don't mean at your office earlier, I meant at the hospital." He dropped his chin and chuckled. "You looked good today. Really good. You look good now."

"Thanks."

He exhaled another chuckle and messed with the collar of his shirt. So cute. My heart and stomach flamed all over again to see he was nervous. I was, too. After so much time, and after being as close as two people could be, we were starting from scratch. Nervous flutters and all.

He'd changed his clothes since he'd been at my office. He was in jeans and a gray shirt. The color set off his eyes, and his freshly shaved chin looked so smooth it was all I could do to not to crawl across the couch and stroke it.

Starting from scratch.

"So, you wanted to talk?"

"Yeah." He was all fidgety, touching the center of his throat to straighten an invisible tie. "To be honest, though, the timing is pretty rotten."

"Um." I glanced at him then out the big picture window. Was he talking about the storm or my surgery or what? "I'm not sure…"

He slapped his hands on his thighs, not the squirmy romantic hero, anymore. "I can't tiptoe around this, Rachel."

"Okay."

"My sister told me about your job offer."

That was strange. Sarah was there when I'd read the letter from *Redbook*, but I hadn't had a chance to tell anyone about the contract. I'd barely ended my phone call when Oliver had shown up.

"Is it official?"

"Pretty much," I said. The sudden look of pain that crossed his face confused me even more. I never wanted to see him in pain again. Ever.

"Okay, okay." He ran both hands over his face. "You're moving back to Texas."

"I am?" I was totally lost now. "I assumed you meant New York."

He dropped his hands. "What?"

I thought for a second, then couldn't help laughing at the mistake. "They want me to write for them. I got the news today, but I don't have to move anywhere. Why would Sarah think—"

"Wait a minute." Oliver lifted a hand. "You're not moving?"

"Sarah knew my old boss at *Dallas Morning News* wanted to rehire me."

"But you're not—"

"Then I got the offer from *Redbook*. It's not full-time, though, but I couldn't have done it without you, I mean I probably wouldn't have had the guts if I didn't know what you were doing, ya know, with your company. So thank you, Oliver, thank you for showing me—"

"*Rachel*." He threw both hands in the air. "You're not moving?"

"Oh." Had I forgotten to answer that? "Um, no."

His eyebrows slowly inched up, hesitantly. "You're staying in San Francisco?"

I pressed a hand over my fiery heart, beating only for him. I had a lot more to thank him for, but that could wait. "Yes," I said.

Then it was quiet.

There was so much space between us. Like, literal space between where I sat and where he sat, and suddenly, I was the one getting fidgety. "You know what." I cleared my throat. "I think I could use a drink after all."

He stood and looked down at me. "Anything else?" His eyes displayed that "I'm picturing you in my clothes" expression again, and I could smell him—all freshly shaved and showered—as he walked past me into the kitchen.

I peeled off my jacket and draped it over the back of a dining room chair, which I should've done when I'd first arrived, since it was a little rain-damp, and his couch was leather. Luckily, the black camisole I was wearing underneath hadn't gotten wet. Despite being briefly caught in the downpour and wind, my hair was hopefully salvaged, as I'd twisted it into a bun thing during my meeting. But then I caught my reflection in the glass of one of Sarah's paintings.

No, this wouldn't do. What had Meghan said before about me trying to seduce Oliver the other night? It hadn't been the case then, but there was no time like the present.

I pulled the pencil from the makeshift knot, and my hair tumbled to my shoulders in big, heavy waves. I did a quick finger-tease at the roots to give it that perfect windswept-chic look, then I kicked off my peep-toe sling backs.

Let the seduction begin.

"Need any help?" I asked, positioning myself on one side of the kitchen's doorframe, doing my best Lauren Bacall. Oliver was bent over the sink with an ice tray. "Contemplating hitting your head again? We should have the ER on speed dial."

He chuckled, but when he caught sight of me leaning on

the doorway, all film noir femme fetale, the laugh dropped off.

"Rach."

"No!" But I was too late.

Somehow....again...Oliver whacked his head on the low-hanging cabinet above the sink. Those Victorian kitchens really weren't built for people over five-foot-five, much less a mountain of a man like Oliver.

"*Seriously*?" He hissed and clutched his head.

I rushed to him. "Does it hurt?" He turned his head and eyed me. "Sorry," I said over his grumbles of pain. With one hand on his arm, I scooped up some ice in a towel and led him to a chair. This was becoming a habit. "Sit," I commanded, then I knelt on the floor beside him. "Oh, it's not nearly as bad as last time. Just keep the ice on it for a while."

"This is your fault," he muttered.

I laughed. "Stop moving. You might have a concussion."

"You said that last time."

"Hold this here." I took his hand and made him hold the ice pack in place. "You need aspirin."

As I made a move to go, he caught my hand. "Wait." He looked into my eyes, the towel of ice slipping from both our grasps. He took my other hand and stood, pulling me up with him, then leading me to the middle of the kitchen. With a playful squint of his eyes, he glanced to the right and the left then repositioned us a few inches to the side. "This looks safe."

"For what?"

Silently, he took my face in his hands. The pressure of his lips was gentle at first, as if he really was afraid one of us was going to smack into something if we tried this again. Then his fingers slid into my hair and my neck bent back. I fisted the front of his shirt and hung on.

Bright, multicolored bubbles popped behind my eyelids, and when I wrapped my arms around him and squeezed, he exhaled the sweetest moan, sending tingles wherever he touched.

With a break of our kiss, Oliver glanced over my shoulder then began backing me up. "Hold onto me," he said in a whisper. A moment later, my back hit the wall. "Still conscious?"

"Yeah."

"Got all your teeth and vital organs?"

I grinned. "Only the ones I'll need."

He swept the hair off my shoulder, moving his mouth to my neck, concentrating on the sensitive spot behind my ear that he knew I loved. I was grateful to be against the wall so I didn't have to worry about falling…falling…falling…

Seven years ago, Oliver had not been my first kiss, but he'd been the best, like no boy existed before him. Now, as my body, mind, and soul took time to be reacquainted with his, it truly felt as though there was no other man in the world but him.

Oliver Wentworth was who I was meant to kiss forever.

"I'm not dreaming, am I?" he whispered, his mouth at my ear.

"Not unless I am, too." I moved to his neck, inhaling the smell I'd been craving for years.

"Do we do *this* in your dreams?" He pinned me gently to the wall, one solid thigh sliding between my legs.

"No," I whispered, heart racing, as he rested his forehead to mine. "My dreams are never this good."

"Sweet pea."

"Did you call me that at the ER?"

"You don't know?"

"I was really out of it. I figured half of what I thought happened was delusional."

He took my face between his hands, so tenderly. "What do you remember?"

"You were there with the ER doctor."

He nodded and brushed his thumbs across my cheeks. "What else?"

"I had a breathing tube and you yelled at the doctor to take it off."

He laughed softly and kissed a corner of my mouth. "That's true, too." After kissing the other corner, he drew back to gaze at me with those beautiful eyes. "I love you, Rachel."

It was the most natural thing to hear him say to me, and my whole body lit from within, pooled with a soothing, familiar warmth. "You said that at the hospital, too. Actually, you yelled it."

"Oh, *that* you remember?"

"A while ago, a lot of things started coming back." I combed my fingers into his hair and brushed the tip of my nose over his. "I love you, too." It was the most natural thing for me to say to him.

"I know. I wasn't the only one yelling bloody murder in the hospital that night." There was a grin in his voice that I felt in my toes. "They must've thought we were crazy."

"Here's your crazy." My new appendix-free moxie kicked in, and I pushed myself off the wall, grabbed him tight and spun us in a one-eighty. "Your turn to hold onto me." I crashed my mouth over his, backing *him* into the wall this time.

Until I heard a thud. "Ow." He grunted over my mouth. "Damn, woman."

When I pulled back, he was rubbing his head. "No. I can't believe we did it again."

"It's fine." His mouth launched at my neck, but my hands were in his hair, and he winced the second I bushed against the goose egg.

"Okay." I pressed my hands to his chest and pushed him back. "Seriously now: ice and aspirin. You" — I took him by the hand — "sit on the couch. I'll be right there." But he just stared at my neck, breathing hard, not finished. The hungry look on his face was beyond relishing. "Oliver — couch."

"Fine." He blew out a long breath. "Will you at least wear a nurse's uniform?"

"Go." I gave him a shove toward the living room.

After locating a proper icepack from the freezer, I passed it off to him then hurried to his bathroom in search of aspirin. I found it behind the mirror, alongside a tiny bottle of essential oil, the cinnamon I thought I'd smelled here before. I couldn't help smiling. So much had changed between us, grew. Yet so much was the same.

When I returned to the living room, he was stretched across the couch, icepack on the floor, eyes closed.

"Oliver, sit up."

He mumbled something defiant.

I marched to his feet at one end of the couch. "You have a head injury so you can't fall asleep." All he did was slightly rearrange his body.

I planted my hands on my hips, ready to dump the ice-pack over his head if I had to. But I thought of a better plan. With one hand on either side of the couch, starting above his feet, I crawled up his body.

His eyes flew open. "What are you doing?"

"You obviously need something to keep you awake. Might this do the trick?" When my face got to his chest, I lowered onto my elbows and stretched out across him, arranging my body so I fit into every curve of his. "Here." I lifted his head and placed the ice behind it. "Now don't move."

But neither of us could obey this prescription. His arms went around my back and I inched up so my face was over his.

"How do you feel now?"

"My head hurts in two places and there's a woman on top of me."

"Mmm." I rested my lips on the side of his neck. "She's trying to help. Is it working?"

His arms tightened. "I'm beginning to feel...so much better."

"Good." I moved to the other side of his neck. Oliver's hands splayed across my back, moving in a slow circle until they hooked around my sides, his fingers sliding under my shirt. I bit my lip and moaned in heavenly anticipation.

"No—sorry," he whispered in a rush. "Umm, here?" He moved his hand off my still-healing wound. But I felt no pain at that spot, only cold when he was gone.

"Gentle." I placed my hand over his. "Stitches."

"It's okay if we...?"

"Mmm-hmm. I'm beginning to feel so much better, too." I leaned down to plant a kiss on his mouth, but he turned away.

"Rach." His eyebrows bent. "I wanted to come see you after the hospital. I almost followed you to Santa Barbara."

"Why didn't you?"

I felt him shrug. "You were busy healing."

"Oliver." I rested a hand against his cheek. "I am in love with you. I would've healed faster with you there." I ran my fingers into his hair and pushed the melting icepack to the floor. "Promise you'll always be around to help me feel better."

"I promise." He took my hand, kissed the palm then linked our fingers. "I thought about you a lot over the years. When Meghan said your name on the phone that day, I was tempted to call her back and ask if you were single. A few days later, Sarah filled me in on some of the gaps." He ran a finger across my cheek then circled my lips. "I've wanted to do this since the first moment I saw you again."

"Oh, geez." I blushed. "Not that day on the running trail."

"Rach." A soft groan rumbled in his chest. "*Definitely* that day."

I leaned down, my hair spilling around his face.

"Mostly though, I've been dying to do *this*." Deftly, he pushed the cushions off the back of the couch and rolled us over. His warm, heavy weight pinned me in place. I squealed his name once, then there were no more words.

"When did the power go out?" I asked, noticing that the room was pitch black and the overhead fan had stopped spinning. Had the earth stopped rotating, too?

Oliver lifted his chin to glance over the back of the couch. "Huh. No idea." He lay back down. "Listen to the rain," he whispered, trailing a lazy finger up my spine. I buried my nose in his neck, then pressed a cheek against his chest. *I'd rather listen to your heart.*

"Do you have to go back to Vancouver tomorrow?"

"Hell, no." He nuzzled into my neck. "They know they have to start getting along without me." He held back my hair to look at me. "I gave notice. I know that scares you, but it's not like before, Rach. You don't have to be afraid of a future with me."

"I'm not." I smiled, so touched by his concern. "I understand now what taking a leap of faith means. I want to do that with you, and I was serious when I thanked you before. You probably don't realize the effect you've had on me—on the decisions I've been making lately about my job." I placed my hand over his. "I might be quitting, too. Sooner than later."

"Really?" He squeezed my hand, almost like he was afraid I might bolt. But he had no idea how my decision only made me feel closer to him. After a moment, his grip relaxed. "You mentioned *Redbook* earlier."

"They offered me a pretty good freelance contract for a newbie. I never thought I'd even consider leaving the security of corporate America for the great unknown."

He kissed my temple. "We'll take that leap together."

"Thank you." I hovered over his mouth for a second, then kissed him. Hard.

"You're welcome," he said, sucking in an inhale when I allowed him to breathe again. "Though I'm not sure what I did."

"You were just being you."

He ran a hand down my back, curling it around my hip. "What time are you going into work tomorrow?"

Someday
MAYBE

"Hmm." I wrapped a leg around his. "I think I'm feeling another round of appendicitis coming on. Better stay home."

"Finally some good timing for us." He pulled me onto his chest, kissed me, told me he'd missed me and that he loved me. While locked in his arm, it was like something had been returned to me, a missing piece from my soul I didn't know was gone. Suddenly, I remembered how it felt to be one half of two.

A while later, Oliver nodded off. When I rolled off the couch, he jerked awake and grabbed my hand. "Where are you going?"

I knelt down and leaned over his sleepy face. "Shhh." I ran a hand through the front of his hair. "I need my phone. I want to leave my boss a voicemail about tomorrow."

He yawned and rubbed his nose, eyes closed. "Tell Moron Bruce you won't be in 'til next week." He ran his hand down my arm, resting it on my hipbone. "I had a scary dream, so you can't leave me."

It was my turn to watch him sleep. And later, waking up. My favorite part, too.

I kissed his eyelids. "Never."

The power was still out and the room felt stuffy, so I cranked opened one of the huge picture windows. Fresh air and sounds of the city drifted in. I inhaled and leaned against the ledge, staring out at the San Francisco skyline, only partially lit.

I placed that call to Bruce, and Oliver and I didn't leave his house for three days, living quite contently on pancakes and Chinese delivery and each other. I sent Sarah one text: the "thumbs-up" emoticon. I sent Oliver one text from bed: the heart with an arrow.

. . .

Six months after I'd left NRG Interactive, I reminded him of something else I remembered from that night at the hospital. "You promised we'd get married and have ten kids, Oliver. *And* you said you would take me away."

He stood from the couch, walked over to where I sat at the dining room table, and closed my laptop with the new manuscript I was preparing for *Redbook*. "Such impatience, Rach." He smiled. "Four days from now isn't soon enough?"

I glanced past his shoulder at the long garment bag hanging outside the closet. It was unzipped, showing the top of my new white dress, the one Oliver hadn't seen yet.

I bit my lip and looked up at him. "Why didn't we elope?"

"Because our sisters would kill us." He pulled me off my chair and into his arms. After a quick squeeze, he took my left hand, kissed the spot next to my diamond ring, then moved my hand to the top of his right shoulder. "And because I wouldn't miss this for the world." We did a slow box step around the dining room, while he hummed our "first dance" song in my ear.

I smiled so big my cheeks hurt, while I clung to Oliver… the man of my dreams, my partner and coach in taking scary leaps, the nineteen-year-old boy who brought me *Dawson's Creek* and took care of me every day.

"After this technicality is out of our way"—he spun me under his arm then bent to kiss my neck—"we'll get started on those ten kids. Twenty, even."

"Keep dreaming," I whispered.

BONUS CONTENT

Read on for a bonus scene from Someday Maybe*!*

The night before, we'd moved from the couch to Oliver's room and his much more accommodating king-sized bed. Other than a few trips to the kitchen, neither of us left until Oliver suggested I join him as he tested his new showerhead. I was more than willing to try it out. After we diminished the entire supply of hot water, I scurried back to bed, pruney-skinned but glowing, snuggled under the covers, and waited for my man.

"Rach," Oliver said, coming out of the bathroom, steam trailing behind him. His hair was wet and he wore a damp white towel around his waist; the sight bringing all kinds of sexy things to mind that I'd like to test out on him. "Would you check an email for me?" He pointed at his cell on the nightstand. "It should be in my drafts folder. Unsent."

"Sure. Is it for work or something?"

He rubbed his chin. "Not exactly. It's dated the third of this month. Do you see it?"

I scrolled through his email folders. "Found it." As I was about to pass him the phone, I caught sight of the name. "Wait. It's addressed to me."

He nodded.

"You wrote this on the third?" I did some quick calendar math. "That's the night we…in your kitchen…when you took me to the hospital."

He nodded again. Something playful and secretive flashed in his gray eyes.

"Want me to read it aloud?" I asked.

Oliver laughed under his breath. "Please don't."

Eager for him to return to bed, but curious to see what he'd written to me the night after we first kissed again, after seven years, I temporarily tucked away my hormones, and my eyes devoured the following words:

I can't just sit here, helpless, ten feet from the door where they wheeled you away from me. Helpless. Not when I can still feel perfectly how you kissed me just moments ago, still hear your breath, see the look in your eyes when I knew you were as relieved as I. But you kissed me, then you were gone, like seven years ago. Though my heart isn't broken this time. Instead, my heart has never felt such hope. It burns with hope—which is almost as painful. When I kissed you, the words weren't said that needed to be spoken. I didn't say then what I needed you to hear, even if you already knew, have known all along. So much of my life has led to tonight, to be with you again and show you everything I feel. These last eight months have been agony, not being able to touch you the way I wanted to, the way you deserved. To be loved by me. I can see the door to your room—forbidden to me—and all I want is to burst through and take you in my arms. I heard you crying out for me. Your voice was broken in pain, causing my heart to break over and over, because I couldn't help you. But the words you said...the words you called to me...still now, I can hardly believe to be true. If they are... Could you still... after all this time... Rachel, do you really still love me? No, I can't bear to think that way, though nothing in this world would make me happier. Nothing. But until I see you again, until I look into your beautiful face, the face that has haunted my dreams for seven years. Until then, I can only hope. Telling you I love you was the easiest thing to say to you, even as the doctors took you away from me. I never stopped saying it in my heart. I never will. Please wake up soon. Please let me tell you I love you. Today. Tomorrow. Forever.

Overpowering happiness. That was what Oliver Wentworth brought to my life. Heart pounding, I blinked back the tears that hadn't already rolled down my cheeks at his exquisite, perfect words. A stream-of-consciousness love letter meant only for me.

When I looked to where he'd been standing moments ago, he was gone. Instead, he stood beside the bed, beside me. Then he was sinking down to my eye level, like the first day we'd met in the campus cafeteria. The first day I loved him.

"Oliver..." I spoke around the burning lump in my throat.

"I love you," he said, his voice breaking in the manliest way, even though the words had already been said. Drops of shower water clung to his lashes.

"And I love you." I touched his cheek while he brushed away the last of my joyful tears. "This is the most beautiful... Why didn't you send it to me?"

"I almost did, many times. But I decided to tell you in person." He leaned in and kissed me, slowly, our breaths and souls mingling, blending into one. "Now scoot over so I can show you."

Acknowledgments

Thank you to my tireless Entangled Publishing team for making another book dream of mine come true. Thank you to unbelievably patient and amazing friends who helped me by reading drafts, listening to me rant, meeting for lunches, and being on IM whenever I was super needy—which has been pretty often lately. Hugs and kisses and sexy guys in suits to you all!

About the Author

USA Today bestselling author Ophelia London was born and raised among the redwood trees in beautiful northern California. Once she was fully educated, she decided to settle in Florida, but her car broke down in Texas and she's lived in Dallas ever since. A cupcake and treadmill aficionado (obviously those things are connected), she spends her time watching arthouse movies and impossibly trashy TV, while living vicariously through the characters in the books she writes. Ophelia is the author of SOMEDAY MAYBE; DEFINITELY, MAYBE IN LOVE; ABBY ROAD; the Perfect Kisses series including: FALLING FOR HER SOLDIER, PLAYING AT LOVE, SPEAKING OF LOVE, and MAKING WAVES; and the upcoming Sugar City series for Entangled's Bliss line. Visit her at ophelialondon.com. But don't call when The Vampire Diaries is on.

Also by Ophelia London...

DEFINITELY, MAYBE IN LOVE

Spring Honeycutt will do whatever it takes to get her sustainable living thesis published. "Whatever it takes," however, means forming a partnership with the very hot, very privileged, very conceited Henry Knightly. As they work on her thesis, Spring finds there's more to Henry than his old money and argyle sweaters...but can she drop the loud-and-proud act long enough to let him in?

ABBY ROAD

LOVE BITES: A SUGAR CITY NOVELLA

THE *PERFECT KISSES* SERIES

PLAYING AT LOVE
SPEAKING OF LOVE
FALLING FOR HER SOLDIER
MAKING WAVES: A PERFECT KISSES NOVELLA

Made in the USA
Middletown, DE
19 April 2015